The
CURSE
of the
MOLDAVIAN
TANGO

Michael Dunn

◆ FriesenPress

Suite 300 - 990 Fort St
Victoria, BC, V8V 3K2
Canada

www.friesenpress.com

Copyright © 2018 by Michael Dunn
First Edition — 2018

Illustrated by Edward R. Turner

ISBN
978-1-5255-1915-4 (Hardcover)
978-1-5255-1916-1 (Paperback)
978-1-5255-1917-8 (eBook)

1. FICTION, MYSTERY & DETECTIVE, HISTORICAL

Distributed to the trade by The Ingram Book Company

Acknowledgments

My sincere thanks to Sarah-Kate Skinner and Maggie Parker for their sharp eyed advice. Special thanks to Eleanore Dunn, my wife who is my greatest fan and critic for keeping me on the straight and narrow. And a very special thanks to my old friend, Ted Turner for bringing the book to visual life.

The early morning phone call just about floored Dizzy. He had no idea one of his lifelong dreams, always flickering just out of view, was about to come true. Joe Ramirez, his agent in New York City, had just called to let him know that he had just landed a contract for a European tour for his jazz band. This would be an eighteen-date tour through a half-dozen countries with his seven piece band. Hardly believing Ramirez's words, he was sure the agent was putting him on.

"It's the real thing, Dizzy. Ya gotta be ready to board ship from New York in exactly six weeks. The money is good too... very good. Round up everyone. There is a lot of preparation work to do. I have started already on tickets and accommodations—you know, the usual stuff. But you have to put together the best show you can come up with."

"Don't worry about that, Joe. I imagine it's why you were able to land such a gig in the first place. Our great shows."

"You got it. I'll mail the details shortly. Take care."

After fixing himself his first coffee, Dizzy picked up the phone.

He delighted in phoning everybody in the band so early in the morning. They would still be asleep and probably curse him, which would be followed by forgiveness once he told them the news. There were six calls to make.

"Jesus, Dizzy, do you know what time it is?" Or, "This had better be good!" Or just plain, "What the ##!* is going on?"

The curses did an abrupt turn to gratitude when the news was announced. Dizzy laughed to himself. There's nothing like the words "European tour" to catch a musician's undivided attention, no matter what time of day.

Joe Ramirez never could get the time zone business figured out. He was always calling Dizzy at some ungodly hour. Dizzy had gotten used to it some time ago.

"Yeah, yeah boss, I know, but I just had to call you with the good news."

It was 1938 and the band was based in San Francisco. They gigged sometimes six nights a week and spent most of their time on and around the West Coast. Dizzy's band had gained a great reputation up and down the coast and they had also played in the big cities in the East. None of the musicians had ever been out of the country before. Enormous planning would be needed for the collective trip, including acquiring passports, figuring out their best and most interesting pieces to play on the tour. They needed best set list for concerts at different venues in cities they had only heard about in geography class or in the newspapers. None of them spoke anything other than English, so while they were in Europe, they would have a tour manager who would take care of things like reservations and transportation. The whole tour was being arranged by Ramirez in New York in collaboration with an agent in Paris. Dizzy couldn't help wondering if Ramirez had ever woken up his French counterpart at some ridiculous hour like he was used to doing with Dizzy.

This all came about six weeks after the death of Dizzy's mother, Daciana. His father had died a few years previous. Dizzy was in the process of dealing with his mom's estate, which didn't amount to much except for the modest family home. The house and everything in it had long been willed to him.

Thinking he would keep the house, he set about going through the whole place to see what his mother had left behind in closets and the attic. He took a couple of days, having decided it was time to go through the attic from stem to stern. There were the usual boxes, old lamps, and family memorabilia. Everything was covered in dust and cobwebs. He was never fond of spiders and was mildly uncomfortable amidst massive examples of their silky art hanging from everywhere he looked.

An hour into the task, he found a few letters in an old box. The ink was faded on decaying paper. He carefully looked at one of them and it was in a foreign language. There was no envelope with an address or any indication of a date. He brought the old correspondence down to his kitchen table. A number of questions occurred to him all at once. Who wrote these letters, when, and from where? They might contain clues as to his family background, perhaps even the information he had always sought from his parents. He made up his mind to find someone who could translate them.

When Dizzy had finished going through his mother's belongings, he threw out a pile of stuff or junk or whatever you would like to call it. He kept the letters, of course, and the following day their presence triggered a memory he had from childhood. He must have been ten or eleven years old and was asking his mom to tell him about the "Old country" as his parents always referred to their country of origin. His mother reluctantly began to say something but after a few halting sentences, Dizzy's father jumped up and began giving her hell and warned her never to speak on such matters again. Dizzy got the gist of all of this from the sound of the language and not the words, for his dad was suddenly shouting at his mother in his native tongue. He had never heard such an outburst before and had never heard more than a few words of Romanian around the house. And yet here he was listening to an angry tirade. He didn't have to understand the words to grasp what was happening. It was a Romanian way of saying: "Shut up and do not speak of this again."

A month before leaving for New York, Dizzy did managed to locate a person who might be able to translate the ancient letters of which there were five. Each one was two or three pages long. They appeared to have been authored by two different people from the looks of the handwriting. But that was all he could ascertain. There were no dates or addresses anywhere in any of them and the handwriting was, at least to Dizzy, hardly barely decipherable at all. He had placed a want ad in the paper asking for a translator and a Mr. Anatolie Zanfir phoned Dizzy a few days later. Mr. Zanfir would need a day and charge Dizzy a flat rate of $20, which was fine with Dizzy.

Anatolie Zanfir returned Dizzy's letters along with the translations two days after meeting with Dizzy. Zanfir explained that the translations were incomplete because of an unfamiliar dialect and that, combined with the atrocious handwriting, made the task impossible. He typed what he could figure out and offered Dizzy a partial refund for his failure to complete the job. But Dizzy refused his offer and told Zanfir that he was sure he had tried his best and it wasn't really his fault if it was impossible. A deal was a deal and Dizzy was grateful for his efforts.

About two weeks before departure date, Dizzy received a large envelope containing the tickets which that would take them by train to New York and the steamer tickets for France. The train trip was pleasant, if a little long, across the States. A lot of time was consumed by playing cards in the bar car and enjoying multiple libations till until closing time. They were all happy to reach Grand Central Station, where they were met by Ramirez, who had made all of the necessary arrangements for accommodations and getting them to the ship at boarding time. A complicating factor in the accommodation department was that the two Negros in the band had to be lodged in another hotel separate from the white boys—as they jokingly referred to themselves. Nothing new for Ramirez. It was business as usual.

Dizzy's group had been among the first to integrate white and black musicians. This situation wasn't always welcome in certain areas of the States, but Dizzy had the fortitude to hold firm on this policy.

He felt he had seven of the best musicians in the whole country with him and he wasn't about to let some bigoted idiot tell him he couldn't integrate his band. He lost an occasional gig over this, but he gained a tremendous amount of respect from people across the social spectrum. This helped to make his band much sought after.

There was much excitement among the seven band members at the prospect of playing in Europe. Though they had all toured throughout the United States, this felt like the major league had come calling. The anticipation was tinged with some nervousness at the novelty and scale of the project, but they knew they were at the top of their profession. Each musician had the confidence gained from experience and hard work. This band was a well-oiled swing machine who would get any crowd up and dancing right off the downbeat.

The band would board a passenger liner and spend a week or more at sea. Again, none of them had ever been aboard a ship. They looked forward to the adventure of crossing the Atlantic. All they really knew was that the ship would land in Le Havre on the northwest coast of France. Ramirez had arranged everything down to the last detail as usual, so the musicians didn't give things a second thought. They were off to play music in faraway places and that's all that mattered. Everyone was thrilled at the prospect of playing in Europe. Several of the band members had fantasied about such a scenario, but none had thought it would ever happen. Things like that happened to the "old pros." Now, they realized; "Hey this is us. It's our turn."

Once in New York, a place where they had played frequently, they relaxed for the three days before sailing. Several of the boys went up to Harlem to catch some live music in the evenings, sometimes meeting old musician friends in the process. Reactions to the impending European tour ranged from congratulatory to a little jealousy from fellow musicians. That seemed understandable.

At the appointed hour, ten o'clock at night, they were all down at a dock in Brooklyn. A convoy of three Yellow Cabs laden with musicians, instruments, and baggage pulled up beside a great white ship. They were all awestruck at the size of the vessel. None of them had ever been this close to an ocean liner before, much less aboard one.

An attendant guided them up the gangplank, showed them to their rooms, and welcomed them aboard. The ship, "Josephine," was operated by a French company and racial segregation didn't exist on board.

The two Negro members of the band were housed in the same area as their white counterparts. The band had been all around the USA, but this was all something new to them all.

The musicians all had some expectation of what was going to happen, and their enthusiasm for the oncoming voyage knew no bounds. They were full of questions about the ship.

"Man, how fast does this thing go? What in Hell is a nautical mile, anyway? How do they know where they are in the middle of the ocean? Does only one guy drive this thing?"

What started out as a fun trip turned a little sour a few days out when a storm hit and sea sickness gripped practically everyone aboard. Impromptu jam sessions in the lounge became out of the question when the only thing the musicians could do was groan from stomach cramps and throw up.

There went the romance of sailing the ocean blue to Europe. Their arrival at Le Havre came not a moment too soon, although the storm and the gut wrenching illness had subsided by then. They hadn't been amused by the whole adventure so far.

The French agent, a Monsieur Painchaud, was waiting at the docks and greeted them as they disembarked. He immediately impressed the musicians as typical of his country, although it couldn't be ascertained that any of them had ever come face to face with a bona fide Frenchman. He was a short, balding, and nattily dressed individual in a three piece pinstriped suit, and said "Bonjour" to everyone individually as he shook hands. He then addressed the band in a thick accent.

"Welcome to zee France, mes amis Americains. We will put your valises in zee bus and we go to Paris immédiatement. We arrive to your hotel in maybe trois heures."

Then he smiled. "If we are fortunate."

The band had a lot of touring under their belt and their routine was to line up every piece of luggage and instruments and do a count. For this trip, that total count was twenty-three objects. Unless they reached this total, nobody went anywhere. Painchaud was having trouble figuring out why the musicians didn't let anything be placed aboard the bus until the rows of suitcases and instruments were counted twice. Then, with everyone agreeing that the correct number had been reached, everything was loaded up.

With everyone on board, the driver slowly pulled out of the dock area with a godawful noise coming from a growling transmission. It would not be a quiet trip, but it wouldn't last long and at least no one would get sick again.

Dizzy sat with Painchaud up front and tried to get as much information from him as he could regarding the itinerary and venues. Beyond the French dates, Painchaud didn't seem to know much. He said, "All zee renseignments are at zee office in Paris."

"Where do we play in Paris tomorrow night?"

"Ah Monsieur Dizzy, you play at zee Salle Pleyel."

"What is the Salle Pleyel?"

Painchaud looked incredulous for a second.

"Mon Dieu, mon ami, zee Salle Pleyel is a very famous place, like your Salle Carnegie in New York!"

It was Dizzy's turn to look incredulous.

"Are you serious?"

"Mais oui, mon ami. You start your tour... how you Americains say, wiz a bang." He was smiling.

Dizzy stood and turned to face the rest of the band seated behind them.

"Gentlemen, listen to this: our first gig tomorrow is at someplace called the Salle Pleyel. Monsieur Painchaud tells me it is the Parisian equivalent of our Carnegie Hall."

The band let out a collective gasp.

For whatever reason, they all thought they might be playing at some small theatre somewhere, but they were walking right into the lion's den on the first night. They wouldn't have minded except that they hadn't been able to practice on the ship and in thirty-six hours, they would be on one of the country's great stages.

Dizzy calmed them down a bit.

"Listen, guys, we are all pros here. We know the tunes backwards and we'll be playing to an audience that is just nuts about American jazz. We are the real McCoy. A couple of good rehearsals and we'll be fine. I know we couldn't play aboard the boat without barfing into our horns but we haven't forgotten how to play. Gentlemen, it's just another gig. We will have to be on the money, but we do that very well."

Spike, the tenor player and homespun philosopher in the band, could always be counted to come up with the right remark for any situation. "Man, we gonna show them Parlez Vous jus' how it's supposed to be done."

Samuel "Spike" Washington was a barrel chested man with ebony skin and stood over six feet tall, but was a gentle and mild mannered man with a great sense of humour. His background, however, had a rough tinge to it. The great grandson of slaves, he grew up in the slums of Chicago among the roughest of the rough and had a scar or two to back it up. If a fight broke out in a bar, you would certainly want to be on his side.

His uncle died when he was sixteen and left him an old saxophone. He had never really considered playing an instrument, but became curious about it. He started to try to play it, and before long, he was making it work. There was hardly enough money in the family to put food on the table, but Spike scrimped here and there and was occasionally able to get a lesson from various teachers. Like Dizzy, he was a complete natural and before long, he started to play a few gigs.

He once saw Dizzy's band performing in Chicago and was so impressed by their sound that he wanted to be part of it. He approached Dizzy after the gig. "Mr. Dizzy, I've been looking for your sound for years. I would sure like to sit in sometime, just for the fun of it."

Whether it was the flattery or sincerity from Spike, Dizzy decided on instinct to try him out. He liked Spike right away and a date was set up so he could audition with the band. Dizzy had been considering a tenor player to compliment Lenny, who played alto.

Spike played with a voice and phrasing that made him sound as if he had been part of the band forever. Three songs into the audition, Dizzy had made up his mind: Spike would stay. They became fast friends and Spike's creativity became an inspiration to everyone.

The grandeur of the nineteenth century Salle Pleyel produced an incredible and overwhelming atmosphere, especially for the wide-eyed travelers. With 2400 seats, the Salle had three tiers. No one in the band had ever been in such a cavernous space. Used to small, crowded stages, they found themselves in the middle of a stage the size of a parking lot. They rehearsed the afternoon of the gig. The acoustics were like nothing they had ever experienced. The sound enveloped them as if they were in a cathedral. Their nerves were calmed by the rich sound and by concert time, they felt ready.

Sometimes a break from things allows a player to come back musically refreshed. This is exactly what happened in the Salle Pleyel. Fresh after their oceanic break and with a good rehearsal, they exceeded all expectations from the audience and critics, surprising even themselves in the process. With three encores, they gained a great boost of confidence and were ready to tackle the remainder of the tour.

The band members were having the time of their lives, with sold out concerts and a growing reputation that ensured royal treatment in every city they played. The experience they shared was unlike anything stateside. Sometimes in America, it felt as if musicians were considered the hired help. Now, they were all eating in the same restaurants and staying in the same hotels. Integration was new to all of them and Dizzy privately wondered how the reaction to American style segregation would affect them after returning to the USA. In Europe, the visiting artists were being accorded every courtesy imaginable, and treated with a respect they had never known before. This was a real eye opener for all of them. Arrival at a venue always found a crew of people at their service to help them with anything they needed. Their instruments were carried for them, people took them for lunch, bought them drinks, and paid the tab. They found it a little unnerving at first, but only for a little while. Getting used to courtesy and respect can happen pretty quickly.

The first six gigs were played in France, then on to Italy, where they played in Rome. Then it was off to Berlin with several stops in between. Traveling for the most part was by train. Trains there were very different from the New York Central or Union Pacific, with comfortable compartments and wonderful food and wine.

Jazz was relatively new in Europe and although it was not to everyone's liking, it was gaining popularity. Jazz aficionados everywhere were usually cut from the same cloth, so as word spread about this hot American band, it was one successful concert after another.

The musicians were giddy with their artistic and critical successes. They played hard and had a little fun sightseeing. More than once, one of them could be seen having breakfast with a mademoiselle, a fraulein, or a signorina. This strange place called Europe was indeed exotic and fun. It was all so different from what they had known in America. All of the musicians were educated in music but world geography had never been their strong suit.

Dizzy hadn't had time to deal with the letters and Mr. Zanfir's translation before leaving for New York, so he carefully put everything in a manila envelope and packed them in his suitcase, intending to look at them in a spare moment on the road. Events took over for him and the musicians, and it was only later that he remembered them. He opened the envelope one night alone in his hotel room and began to try to make sense of what was before him. Zanfir had carefully made notes as to what letters he could translate and attempted to put things in some order. It didn't seem orderly to Dizzy. However, he read several sentences that had references to a castle, a few times the month of November was brought up, and they mentioned something called Saltatio Mortis, which Zanfir translated as a death dance.

Some referenced people dying in connection with it, and the words for sorrow and penitence were mentioned. There wasn't enough continuous information to allow any sense to be made of anything. From what Dizzy could make of it, it was all dark and foreboding. Zanfir, however, offered the opinion that these were not correspondence, per se, but possibly writings like a diary, as there were no salutations, nor were they dated or signed like letters.

Before their trip, they all knew Europe was 'over there,' but had never given it much thought. Now, they were traveling and working in sophisticated cultures that seemed to change every time they landed in a new country—a new language, new money, new food, and not a hamburger to be found. This caused a little grumbling at first, but the food was so good that they could all wait for their return to have a hamburger with all the fixings.

Spike liked to laugh at them. "Man, you can eat burgers until they come out of your ears when you get back home. I had a hamburger here yesterday and it tasted like a baseball glove! They don't know nothin' about burgers here. Jus' enjoy what you got. I'll bet you miss this food when we get back."

Lennie replied; You won't believe this but a bunch of our fans took me for lunch yesterday and this one guy had a plate of frog's legs put down in front of him. I ain't never seen anything like that in my life and they all insisted that I try one. I bit into this thing and it tasted kinda fishy...like a frog, I suppose. Then this other guy has what looks like a raw hamburger on his plate. Turns out, that's exactly what it is. No bun, no fixin's, just the raw meat. Baseball glove or not, at least Spike's burger had hit the stove. The tour was having one of its silly moments.

They each had different perceptions about where they were. For Dizzy, the trip was his first introduction to what he always heard referred to as the old country. His parents never really spoke about their background except in vague references. He realized for the first time that the old country was in fact a collection of places, each very different from the others. These differences fascinated him and he made as many mental notes as he could and jotted stuff down in a small notebook for later contemplation.

Dizzy's grandfather immigrated to America in the latter part of the nineteenth century. He had come from the country of Moldova. Dizzy didn't know anything about this distant country, as no one in the family ever really spoke about the place other than an occasional reference. He never really knew where it was until geography class in high school. There, he discovered it was a tiny country sandwiched between eastern Romania and western Ukraine. He had no idea what the place was like or how people lived there. His parents weren't of much help. Any questions he had for them about Moldova were met with vague responses. They described the tiny country as being quite poor but very beautiful, but that was basically it. He could not get any more information. They showed little enthusiasm or desire to talk about their background. No one had ever spoken more than a few words in their native language in his family. It was all part of the past and was obviously going to stay that way. Dizzy had accepted this but had always kept a curiosity inside him about his ancestral land.

Like countless immigrant families coming from a myriad of old countries and landing at Ellis Island, his grandfather's family name was changed. He walked through the door of the immigration building as Josef Polozenzki and walked out into his new country as Josef Pollen. It was the first step taken into the great American cultural melting pot. Removal of characters like Z, X, W, and sometimes K helped to make the name fit with others in the country. When the immigration officer could read and pronounce the name, that was settled right there. The family names of millions of Americans lost letters at Ellis island.

Josef eventually settled in San Francisco and worked out his days as a tailor. He had two sons, Joseph and Andrei. Andrei became Dizzy's father in 1902. He called his new son Josef. No one remembers how or why, but at a young age, Josef acquired the nickname Dizzy. He might have objected to this as soon as he learned the meaning of the word. Kids do not always like their nicknames, but in this case, there was a great baseball player at the time called Dizzy Dean, so the name wasn't all that bad. It stuck until his dying day. He was an only child.

Dizzy grew up in an ordinary American way, playing baseball in the street with other kids and taking his girlfriend to the movies on Saturday night. His dad loved jazz and had a collection of seventy-eights of the time. Dizzy grew up hearing Louis and Bix, among others. The trumpet fascinated him and he took it up in high school as soon as he could. He discovered he was a natural musician and became good very fast. He soon started to play in some local bands and by graduation from high school, he was an accomplished musician.

The engineering profession also attracted him, but that would have to wait a while, as that level of education would cost money—of which the Pollen family had little. His work life took him through several uninteresting jobs but he always played music on the weekends. He became the go to trumpet player for bands needing a good sub and did the occasional recording date. The music business was kind to him. He worked hard at it and became a top rate jazz trumpeter. Playing steady for a few years eventually pushed the prospect of becoming an engineer further and further into the background, until it vanished.

CHAPTER 2

In the course of the concert tour, Dizzy kept making observations about the things he saw and the people he met. Of course, in his youth, he had met a number of people with European backgrounds. The family next door were of Italian heritage, the Chiarellis, and across the street lived the Schmidt family from Germany. They had been in the USA for a generation or longer, and apart from their names and the food they sometimes ate, they were very Americanized. Mr. Chiarelli went to baseball games and occasionally took Dizzy along with him. He ate hot dogs with too much ketchup and spoke flawless English. Hans Schmidt had a slight accent, played a respectable game of golf, had a fascination about Model A Fords, and was always tinkering with them in his driveway on Saturdays. He owned three of them. There were other people of European background but they all seemed quite ordinary.

Now Dizzy was inside these old countries, meeting people, and it wasn't long before the enormous differences between German, Italian, and French people became clear. They were all nice people, he thought, but all different. He would get up early in the morning before anyone else in the band and go for a long walk through the strange streets, looking at everything and wondering about what he saw. A careful observer, he would stop somewhere for a coffee and a pastry or sandwich for breakfast. He loved sitting at outdoor cafes people watching as he sipped on coffee with a kick to it. None of that Chase and Sandborn percolated stuff here; this was real heart starter. He stared at buildings, noting architectural details and the unusually small automobiles putting along the early morning streets. Dizzy's favourite time of day had always been early mornings, and observing a city or town waking up provided endless fascination. The strange surroundings populated by early morning street goers made him feel alive and inspired.

He was so fascinated by what he was experiencing that for the first time in his life that he began to seriously wonder about his own ancestry. If things were this different in Western Europe, what did his ancestral country look and feel like? Who were these Moldovans he descended from? What did his ancestors do? Why did they leave and immigrate to America? Were there members of his family still there? How did the writings he was carrying around relate to any of this?

He had never really pondered these questions before. He just accepted that he came from some small country in Eastern Europe that no one talked about (especially his family), and practically no one knew anything at all as to its location or history. Admittedly, he never paid much attention to this forgotten land until now. His personal old country began to insert itself into his thoughts. It was time to find out more. The band played in a venue that was close to a library, and Dizzy found himself staring at an atlas showing the countries of Eastern Europe. He found the place, but noticed something that really surprised him. The last date on the tour was in Bucharest, Romania— another place he had only heard about but certainly knew nothing of. It was one thing to play jazz concerts in places like Rome or Paris, but did they have a following in Romania? This was certainly getting off the beaten track. What really caught his eye was that Bucharest looked like it was about 100 miles from the border of Moldova. He would be as close to his family's place of origin as he was ever going to get. He made up his mind that he would at least try to set foot on Moldovan soil.

All kinds of questions swept over him all at once. How could he cover the last hundred miles to Moldova? He really would need a car. How to get hold of a car was foremost in his mind. Could he find someone to drive him there?

What kind of a place was this? Would anyone speak enough English to help him find family members?

He became angry at not having pressed his own family for answers over the years. It always seemed like they were never going to talk about it, so he had always let the matter drop. His father's vehement rant at his mother had showed Dizzy that silence about the old country was the law in their house.

Here he was in Europe, and within ten days, he would be practically on his ancestral doorstep. He sensed an excitement that he had not experienced before. This was a chance to see where his family came from. The possibility of meeting a Polozenzki somewhere captured him and he began to think about this as the tour progressed.

The trip to the last concert in Romania seemed interminable. It was a long way to Bucharest and they were glad when the bus finally stopped at an old grand dame of a hotel in the middle of the city. It wasn't lost on anyone in the band that they had reached the edge of the world as they knew it. Paris was one thing, but this place was something else.

The architecture was very different, and some of the buildings were fancy and ornate. People dressed differently from France or Italy too. It was quite a majestic city at first glance. They were met by a Mr. Deacon from the American consulate within minutes of their arrival. He told Dizzy that there would be a reception at the consulate for the band. Theirs was the first American jazz band ever to show up in Bucharest and the consul was a big jazz fan. As Dizzy would find out the next day, the consul had pulled a few strings with the State Department and got the band all the way to Bucharest.

The consul, Mr. Henry Washburn, was always anxious to show off American culture in any way he could. A somewhat flamboyant individual, he had decided to make a splash about the whole event with this reception. He had asked, through Mr. Deacon, if Dizzy and the band would play a few tunes Dizzy said he would be honoured to do so.

The concert was to take place on Saturday night in a small theatre not far from the consulate. It was not a big venue like they had played in France and Germany, but an ornate nineteenth century hall.

However, Dizzy's mind wasn't on the concert. By now, the show was polished to the hilt and they were on a roll. He found himself trying to figure out how to get himself to his newfound destination. He had already made up his mind to attempt the trip and was going to inform the band after the gig that he would not be returning to the States with them.

Later that night, the band settled into their hotel, which was full of beautiful old world rooms with tall ceilings and fancy bureaus and beds. The boys were happy campers after the gruelling bus ride. A few of them went to the bar while the others indulged in some badly needed shuteye.

There was a knock at Dizzy's door and the bellhop handed him a note. It read: "Dear Mr. Pollen,

If you are not too fatigued from your journey, I would be honoured if you would join me for a drink at the bar."

It was signed by Washburn, the consul.

Dizzy was delighted at the invitation. He was already thinking of ways to broach the subject of getting to Moldova and if anyone could be of help, it would probably be Washburn. He wandered into the bar, where a gentleman got up from a plush chair walked over to Dizzy, his hand outstretched.

"Mr. Pollen, welcome to Bucharest. I'm Henry Washburn, the American consul."

"An honour to meet you, Mr. Washburn."

"Sit over here, please. What's your pleasure?"

They both sat down. "First of all, please call me Dizzy, and I could use a scotch straight up."

"Good, and please call me Henry."

At the consul's signal, a waiter appeared and Washburn said, "Doua pahare de scotch pe plac. Fara gheata."

"Well, at least you know enough of the language to be able to order the good stuff."

"Actually, I am fluent in the language. I studied languages in university. I was fascinated with the Romance languages. I studied French, Spanish, Latin, and Italian. I am fascinated by Romanian, as it is on the outer fringes of the Romance family. Languages have always held a special place in me and I jumped at the chance to work in Romania when the job came up. There's enough Latin-based vocabulary to enable me to make sense out of Romanian and I did study some when I first got here."

"I only speak English and music."

"I wish I could play music, but even though I have a good ear for language, it has always eluded me. I took the obligatory piano lessons as a kid, but too many raps on the knuckles from Sister Cecilia's ruler soon convinced me to find a better way to waste my time. I am, however, a great lover of music. I am enamoured with and listen to all kinds, but I must confess my love of jazz surpasses the rest. I am pleasantly baffled at improvisation. Theoretically, I know how it must be done, but the act of making up a song as you go along seems like some kind of black magic to me."

"We all have black magic in us. Believe me, I would find learning several languages to be real black magic. You were born with yours, and I mine. We have both discovered our respective black magics. That makes us lucky. Some people never discover theirs, but I think everyone has something they would be real good at."

Henry raised his glass. "To black magic. May it always be with us."

"To black magic."

They clinked glasses and Henry ordered two more.

"Where were you born, Dizzy?"

"San Francisco. My grandfather immigrated to the States from somewhere in Moldova. I have no real idea where the family lived."

Dizzy went on to explain to Henry how his family was almost completely silent on the matter of family history and how any queries were rebuffed.

"The thing is," said Dizzy, "I have become curious about the country of my family's origin. I never really gave it much thought after my family was mum on the matter all of my life. It is only since I landed in Europe that my curiosity has jumped into the forefront of my thoughts. I always knew my family came from the great collective European old country, but until now, that seemed some distant entity in a geography book.

I realize that I am now close to my own old country and am quite sure I will never get this close to it again. The chances of that happening more than once in my lifetime, I figure, are slim." He paused to take a drink of his scotch. "This is our last concert and I am considering making arrangements not to return with the rest of the band. We don't have any work lined up anyway, so I won't be missed for a short while. I am determined to get to Moldova and at last see where my ancestors sprang from. I am not going to worry about finding anyone, because like I said, all I know is that my family came from there. Beyond that, I know nothing."

"Fascinating."

"Do you have any advice? Any assistance I could solicit from you would be greatly appreciated. Have you been to the place?"

"So far no, but I keep wanting to visit. Unfortunately, my work here pretty well keeps me in Bucharest. Maybe you will get to go and return with some good stories."

"If I do, I'll be sure to give you a full report upon my return."

"Thank you, Dizzy."

"Listen, my friend, I have to get back to my office to make sure the wheels are turning smoothly for the concert and reception. We'll talk more about this tomorrow. I just may be able to help you."

They shook hands and Washburn left the bar, settling the bill on the way out. This left Dizzy more hopeful than ever that he would reach his new goal, but he decided not to get too worked up about it in case it proved impossible. He did think that Washburn was sincere in his offer to help. The consul impressed him as a straight shooter, a no nonsense fellow. He polished off his glass and went back to his room.

The fatigue brought on by the bus ride from Hell and the two scotches caused Dizzy to crash on his bed. He fell asleep fully dressed, not waking until 8 a.m. Groggy and still half asleep, he decided on a shower. Feeling refreshed, he wandered out on to the street, as had become his habit since he got to Europe. He loved the early morning street activity, or lack thereof. He noticed that people here were dressed a little differently and the cars were fewer in number. For the most part, they looked like older models. There were a few horse drawn wagons about. The metal capped wheels on these wagons accompanied by the rhythm on horseshoes made quite a racket on the cobblestones. He felt that he had stepped back in time and he mused to himself as to whether his music would be completely strange to this city. He found a small cafe, pointed to a bun or pastry, and had no idea what he was about to bite into, and knew nothing about the value of the strange new coins in his pocket. It was all great fun just pointing at things he wanted to try and holding out his hand full of coins, letting the server take what was needed.

Most of the other band members kept musician's hours and unless there was a bus or a train to catch, getting up before 11 a.m. seemed out of the question. Dizzy was okay with that. He was happy to be on his own to wander around, explore, and collect his thoughts. He wanted to try to observe all that he could, and he kept thinking how lucky he was to have this great opportunity to play his music in Europe for all kinds of people, many of them having never heard American jazz before. He wanted to keep these memories alive as long as possible. These morning meanderings were his meditation, or at least that is how he thought of them. By the time he would play the gig at night, he had built an impression of where he was he felt a little more connected to his audience having walked the streets among them.

It was a Saturday and he had time to find a library. He knew he couldn't read much of anything that was in there but he did find an old European geography book in English. It was dated from the early 1900s.

He thumbed his way through musty pages and found the section that talked a little about Moldova. There wasn't much, but he learned that it was under domination by the Romans in antiquity. Then it became part of the Byzantine Empire. Throughout the dark and middle ages, it was invaded by Huns, Goths, Avars, Magyars, Bulgarians, Mongols, and Tartars.

Dizzy didn't know who most of these peoples were but it looked to him that Moldova must have been in a geographically strategic area, as it seemed that everyone went through the place with an army at one time or another. He wondered if he might be a descendant of a Hun or a Goth. He dismissed the thought, thinking that was too far back to ever figure out.

Returning to the hotel, he picked up his horn and went to the theatre for rehearsal. Everyone arrived by 4:30 and they played for an hour. They were good and ready. The concert was to begin at 7:30, and the reception would be at the consul's home an hour after the concert. Transportation was arranged, the invitations had been sent, and everyone had sent back their RSVP. There would be fifty-five people at the soiree. Dizzy had agreed to play a few numbers at the reception and this was a great draw, as the guests would get to hobnob with real American jazz musicians. In times like a reception or party, everyone in the band was amused at how the people looked at the American musicians as exotic. Stateside, they were regular Joes in a band, but here in Europe, they were from a faraway land playing new and exciting music.

The theatre had about 450 seats and there wasn't an empty one in the house. In fact, the demand was so great for tickets that it looked like a second show would be arranged. About two hundred people had been turned away from the first show.

Before the gig, Washburn met Dizzy backstage.

"Dizzy, is it possible to do a repeat show tomorrow afternoon?"

"I don't see why not. We are here anyway and delaying the bus by one day shouldn't make a difference. We have a free few days in Paris before going back to the States."

"I know its short notice, but by the time you finish tonight, I can have it all arranged and you'll be back on this stage at 2:00 Sunday afternoon. I'm sure we will fill the theatre once again. We have at least a few hundred people clamouring for tickets and by tomorrow, we will sell another two hundred just from the word of tonight's gig."

"Sounds good," said Dizzy."

Washburn continued. "We'll talk after all this is over. Let's see if we can get you going on your trip to your old country, as you call it. I have a few ideas I've been thinking about, but that will be for tomorrow. Good luck tonight."

"Thanks. I hope we can knock 'em dead"

"I have no doubt."

It was 7:20 and everyone was assembled backstage. All were happy and confident. Dizzy chose the moment to inform them that a second show would happen on Sunday afternoon due to the demand for tickets. No one said much. It meant leaving a day later but an afternoon gig would allow them to get a good night's rest before boarding the bus. It would be a long trip back and no one was really looking forward to it. Postponing the trip for any reason seemed like a good idea when they thought about it.

Dizzy snuck a peek from the edge of the curtain at the audience. Full house. They were getting used to this. They had played all of their concerts to full houses and each of them would never forget the experience of their tour in Europe. Soon they would be returning to the States, where work was sometimes scarce. At least they were returning with a wad of cash in their pockets. With all of the sold out concerts, the boys were flusher than they had been in many years.

At 7:30, a hush came over the house. The theatre manager came onstage and said a few words in Romanian, which no one in the band understood, of course. Dizzy was waiting to hear his name, which was the cue to go on stage.

After about a minute of incomprehensible chatter, the manager said, "Si acum, am onoarea de a prezenta Dizzy Pollen si orchestra lui de jazz."

He walked on stage, followed by the members of his band. The audience erupted in a loud applause with about half them on their feet already. *They are ready*, Dizzy thought. He decided not to say anything first like he usually did. Normally he would give a few words of welcome and thanks, but tonight he decided to just launch into their first tune, "Rosetta." They were right on the money and things only got better from there. The concert ended two hours later, non-stop with three encores. The audience was ready for more, but the band had run out of steam and that was it. There was still the business of the late night reception, at which they had agreed to play a few tunes.

CHAPTER 3

They were chauffeured back to the consul's home about fifteen minutes away. It was an old, swanky place with wrought iron gates opening onto a long driveway up to the house. Dizzy had previously read "Gone With the Wind" and the consul's home reminded him of Tara. People were arriving already and when his car stopped, the people near him broke into applause. *A guy could get used to things like this*, he thought. *I should enjoy it while I can. It won't happen back home.*

Dizzy and the band members who rode with him entered the main hall. It was lavish to their eyes with a giant chandelier overhead. Fine scotch, brandy, and some local Romanian liquor that really seemed to pack a wallop were being served at the bar. The musicians made a beeline to the bar for a well-deserved picker upper after expending so much energy at the gig. Dizzy helped himself to a scotch, turned around to find Washburn walking towards him.

"That was incredible, just incredible this evening. Congratulations. What a fine band you have put together. Everyone is a master of his instrument. Tell me, are the arrangements all yours?"

"Yes, generally, but as you can imagine, I have had some expert help along the way from the guys. We spend a lot of time working these things out and a lot of the ideas spring out of the collective. That's one of the reasons I have been blessed with these great musicians. I seek their creative input all the time. Everyone contributes something or other toward the music besides the actual playing. They all are quite musically educated and not to make full use of their talents would be such a waste. I do not have an ego that tells me that I have to be the top dog and everything comes down from me. We are all equally important. Once we are all working together, the music flows freely. It's a matter of trust between the musicians. I'll swear that some of these guys are incapable of playing a wrong note, and if anyone did, they would turn it around to be part of a phrase and it would make perfect sense. It's the black magic we talked about yesterday. All of these guys have it in spades."

"Yes, I can certainly see that. Now, let me introduce you to a few people who are most anxious to meet you. A visit by American jazz musicians to this part of the world, as you can imagine, is practically unheard of. There is a mystique about you gentlemen gracing us with your music and presence at this time. You are the exotic flavor of the day. Enjoy it while it lasts. I'm sure it doesn't happen much in the States."

"You got that right."

Dizzy was presented to a variety of people at the reception, including a few politicians, some artists, and a few local musicians. All were curious as to his life as a jazz musician and some asked some interesting questions. At least the ones who could speak English who seemed to be roughly half the people there. Washburn made himself available to translate questions and answers when the language barrier presented itself.

A woman across the room caught Dizzy's eye. She was a petite woman with dark hair and a great smile. She was talking to several people in an animated fashion with many gesticulations. He heard her talking in Romanian but occasionally he thought he heard an English word. Curious, he picked up another scotch, sought Washburn out, and asked him if he knew who the woman was.

"She works as a translator in a government bureau not far from my office. Her name is Ekaterina Vancea. She speaks English. A bit of a character. Very vivacious and charming. Would you like to meet her?"

"Actually, yes."

Washburn led Dizzy over to where Ekaterina and two couples were talking.

"Hello everyone. I would like to introduce you to our special guest of honour. This is Dizzy Pollen. Dizzy, may I present Mr. and Mrs. Chescu, and Mr. And Mrs. Valente, and this is Miss Ekaterina Vancea." The usual polite handshakes and salutations were exchanged. The Chescus spoke English well, the Valentes less so. Much to Dizzy's delight, the lovely Ekaterina spoke perfect English.

"Very happy to meet you. You and your band are truly great. I have never heard anything like it."

"Thank you very much. It was such a pleasure and honour to be able to bring our music so far away from its home."

After a few pleasantries, the Chescus and Valentes resumed their conversation in Romanian, leaving Dizzy and Ekaterina to chat. Dizzy offered her a drink and when she accepted, and they both stepped up to the bar. She ordered the Romanian firewater and he stuck with his scotch.

They clinked glasses. "What do you think of our city? Have you seen much of it?"

"I walked around for a few hours yesterday," he replied. "There are certainly some beautiful plazas and buildings. I must confess that I know little about your country and city. We just got off the bus and when you have been on busses for the last month like we have, coming into one city begins to look just like every other city we have been to. We are dropped off at our hotel and sometimes we don't really to have a chance to do anything but play the concert and we are off the following morning."

"So you and your band are going back to America right after your last concert tomorrow?"

Dizzy caught a slight sense of disappointment in Ekaterina's voice and at the same time, he became aware of another reason for not wanting to return to America right away. He found himself quite attracted to her. In a short period, this unusual woman had stirred his imagination and he wanted to get to know her better. To his eyes, she possessed an unusual beauty, a kind of exotic aura, and it had been a long time since he had glanced across a room and seen someone who had caught his attention like that. He also had a moment of caution and didn't want to play his hand completely right now.

"I will be here a short time after that."

"I am glad to hear that, and I hope you don't think that I am being too forward, but I would be happy to show you around the city if you have the time."

Dizzy's thoughts were racing and he flashed onto scenes where he and Ekaterina would be in an art gallery or a sidewalk cafe wandering through the city. He was trying to be cool about this and not show that he was crazy about the idea. He wanted to display the perfect balance of matter-of-factness and enthusiasm.

"If you have the time, I certainly do, and it would be nice to be shown this interesting place by someone who knows it and speaks English. I will be happy to accept your offer."

He wondered if he said that right.

"I look forward to showing you the place. You know, they call Bucharest the Paris of Eastern Europe. There are many beautiful and interesting things to see, and it will be fun to show them to you."

Dizzy was bubbling with anticipation. He had not counted on this and briefly wondered whether all this was happening according to some karmic plan. It had been an improbable stroke of luck, and now here he was at the end of the tour with the word from Washburn that he would help him in his quest to get to his old country. Conversing with Ekaterina made it seem like it was all supposed to happen that way. Somehow, she seemed to slide in as one more piece of a puzzle. He knew some kind of picture was going to emerge eventually, but he had no idea how any of this would play out.

"I have promised Mr. Washburn that the band would play a few songs here tonight, so I should gather everyone up before too much scotch flows. Will you stay around for a while?"

Ekaterina was standing close to him. "I would not miss this for anything." She was smiling and it was then that Dizzy, looking straight into her eyes, noticed something quite unusual. She had beautiful, dark brown eyes made up with makeup expertly applied, but that wasn't what Dizzy noticed. Not wanting to stare (well, that was all he wanted to do), he just backed away. "I'll just play for a few minutes. We'll do three songs then that's it."

He gulped down his scotch and made his way to round up the band. It took ten minutes and they were all ready to go. They had parked themselves in a corner of the room to capture maximum sound projection. The piano was there, so all was good to go.

He turned to the band and said, "Ideas? I want to play something we didn't do at the gig."

"Stardust," said Jimmy the piano player.

"Good. Let's start with that and think of something for the second and third pieces. I want to end on a kicker."

They were all a little tired and had consumed a few drinks, but they played a great rendition of Stardust, followed by Hot Lips and Stompin' at the Savoy. The assembled crowd loved it, as they were standing so close to the musicians. A few couples danced up a storm around the room as if they had been waiting for this opportunity all evening.

Now it was time to quit for good. All they had to do was get themselves to a 2 o'clock gig tomorrow and that would be the end of the tour. Dizzy hadn't told the band of his plans not to return to the States yet, but that would come tomorrow when the time felt right.

Ekaterina was talking in a group of people after the band had finished, and everyone was putting the instruments in their cases. Dizzy walked over but was stopped several times by enthusiastic fans who showered him with compliments. Some wanted his autograph. He was gracious as usual but his mind wasn't on them. He finally reached Ekaterina. "That was wonderful," she said. "I am very taken by this music. You must tell me about it sometime."

"I would love the opportunity."

Then Dizzy decided to tell her that he wasn't returning to America with the rest of the band members.

"I am going to tell you something but you must promise to keep it a secret for a short while."

Ekaterina looked at him and half whispered, "I can keep a secret. I work for government officials. I have all kinds of secrets."

Dizzy laughed. "That sounds like you are a spy."

"Maybe I am, but one doesn't have to be a spy in order to keep secrets."

She was smiling and Dizzy saw it in her eyes again: some great mysterious secret resided there and he would have to figure it out on his own. He wanted to compliment her on her beautiful eyes but decided against it. He would let the mystery be for now.

"I am not returning to America with the rest of the band after the last concert. I have business that I want to take care of and I will be here for a while. I haven't told the band yet. I want them to hear it from me. I will let them know tomorrow."

"Your secret is safe with me.

Again, at the risk of seeming forward, I'm glad you are staying."

"It's not forward. I'm glad to be staying also. And so, at the risk of me seeming forward, would you have dinner with me tomorrow night?"

"Two forward people having dinner together. It will make for some interesting conversation. I will certainly come to the concert tomorrow. Will you play that first song again? It was called Star something."

"Stardust. Written by an American composer called Hoagy Carmichael."

"The people who brought me here are leaving and I will go with them. It looks like your band wants to leave also. They must be tired after all that. We will meet at the concert tomorrow. I will find us a nice place to eat and it will be your first stop on my guided tour of the city. And as a spy, I know all the secret places."

He went to shake her hand but it wasn't the standard handshake. She clasped his hand in both of hers. She held on for longer than the usual polite handshake, with a slight extra squeeze just before letting go. She looked at him and laughed. "Goodnight, Mr. Dizzy. I had a great time."

Dizzy might as well have been zapped by a hundred volts coming off her hand.

"Goodnight, Spy Girl Miss Ekaterina."

Catching the mystery in her eyes again, he watched her melt into the exiting crowd. The song "Them There Eyes" popped into his head, causing him to laugh to himself. He joined the rest of the band as they shuffled out and rode back to the hotel.

"Man, you done been lookin' real soft at that young lady. You gonna be lassoed if you ain't careful," Spike said.

I should be so lucky, he thought.

The best time to inform the band of his plans would be after the concert. That way, there would be no distraction during the gig. Dizzy hadn't ever spoken to the band about his family's origins. He was simply from San Francisco and no one had ever asked about his background. His reasons for not returning to the States with them would be revealed tomorrow. They would understand.

CHAPTER 4

Sunday afternoon at 1:00, the band started to warm up in a rehearsal room. They played for about fifteen minutes and that was it. Another concert coming up in forty-five minutes and they were all ready. It was the third daytime concert in the whole tour. They had done one in Berlin, where they sold out a large concert hall on Saturday night and Sunday afternoon.

Fifteen minutes before show time, Washburn appeared backstage. He walked over to Dizzy.

"Another sold out house. The last ticket sold at eleven this morning. The theatre manager said he'd never seen anything like the run on the ticket office today."

"That's amazing. I wish we had that fan base in the States. These people all over Europe have shown support that I have never really known before. They have really gone crazy about jazz. We do the occasional sold out show but that is usually in clubs that may hold 175 people, maximum."

"Well my friend, there are another 450 people out there ready to crown you the King of Romania."

"Yes, I can see it now: King Dizzy the First of Romania."

Washburn laughed. "Come by my office tomorrow any time after 10 a.m. We'll work on your other problem."

"Thank you very much. I'll be there, and by the way, the musicians wanted me to convey their thanks for the party last night. They all enjoyed themselves."

"Thank you. It's not every night that we have seven guests of honour. I will catch the concert from a balcony seat. See you tomorrow."

Come show time, the band launched into "Them There Eyes." Dizzy hadn't been able to get it out of his head since last night. He thought he would play it just to get the tune to stop playing over and over in his head.

Throughout the first few numbers, Dizzy scanned the audience to see if he could spot Ekaterina. Even the first rows were some distance from the band. He never played with his glasses on so unless she was seated no farther than row three or four, spotting her was out of the question. The stage light glare prevented anyone from seeing any further back than that. Not wanting to distract himself from the music, he stopped looking and the show went on tune after tune for about forty-five minutes. At one point, he turned to say something to one of the musicians and saw Ekaterina watching the show from backstage. She somehow got there after the band had gone on stage.

She was smiling at Dizzy, momentarily distracting him. He was elated. She was right there about twenty feet away wearing a black dress making her quite camouflaged among the black stage curtains. With no lights back stage and her black hair, all he could see was her face and hands. She made a gesture with both hands outlining the shape of a star and then pointed skyward and looked up. Dizzy suddenly remembered that he would play Stardust for her.

Now, he was distracted in the best way possible. He turned to the piano player and called for Stardust. The piano started the verse, cueing the band. Everyone fell into place and Dizzy played his solo like he had composed the song himself. *Pure black magic,* Dizzy thought as the last strains faded out. He would remember this one forever.

The remainder of the gig went as hoped with everyone at their best, perhaps with the collective realization that this was the last gig and nothing like this might ever happen again. They were thousands of miles from home playing at their best and being appreciated like never before. Each savoured every moment of it down to the third encore. Then the spell was broken and it was packing up time. They all shook hands and hugged each other. They had enjoyed such a great time with everyone knowing that each member was at the top of their game. The moment was now and no one dared think about the future. Tomorrow, the Ministry of Reality would call, they would board the bus from Hell, and begin the long journey home.

Dizzy decided that now was the time to reveal his plans. They would all have one last breakfast in the morning together. He told them to gather around for a minute.

"First of all, words cannot express the gratitude and honour it has been to play with you gentlemen. What a blessing this has been for all of us. It would be wonderful if this ever happened again, but if it doesn't, what a hell of a ride this has been. We will spend our dotages boring our grandchildren with stories about this trip. They can never take this away from us."

"Man, they ain't ever goin' to shut me up about this one, that's for sure," said Spike. Everyone nodded.

"Now, what I have to tell you is that I am going to stay here for a while. I will not be on the bus with you tomorrow."

"What?" they asked.

"I'll make a long story short. My grandfather emigrated from the neighbouring country of Moldova. The border is around a hundred miles from here. I have no idea where my ancestors lived but I am so close that I have to see the place I originated from. I know nothing about it, but I have been drawn to visiting since we arrived in Europe. I'll never get this close again. I will be back stateside a little after you and we'll be playing again in no time. This is just something I have to do right now."

"Wow! That's really cool," one of the guys said. "Good luck. That should be quite a trip."

Dizzy gave his horn to Spike to take back to the hotel.

"I'll pick it up later."

Spike took the horn. "Oh yeah, you's pickin' up everything tonight." He winked at Dizzy.

"Get outta here."

The musicians parted company, leaving Dizzy backstage. Ekaterina was standing on the stage where he had stood playing. He looked at her for a second but didn't move. He just wanted to take the moment in and make it last. Something had clicked in him and he instinctively sensed that his life had just taken an abrupt turn. She was looking out over the where the audience sat, watching the last few people disappear through the exits. Wondering what she was thinking, he was hesitant to interrupt the moment. He knew absolutely nothing about her so far.

The beautiful Ekaterina had ambushed his thoughts for the last twenty-four hours. He was anxious to get to know her better but at the same time, he just as captivated by her unspoken mystery. Making time stand still a few seconds longer, he walked out to her. She turned toward the stage entrance.

"Good afternoon, Miss Ekaterina."

"Has everyone gone?"

"Except for us. It's our turn."

"That's good. The concert was wonderful, but I suppose you know that already."

"I know that we played well and that the audience was enthusiastic about our music. We played well because it was our last gig and everyone was feeling a little sad that it was all over. We were inspired to do something special to remember the night. Years down the road, we will always remember the last night best of all. It was our finale." He smiled.

"Now, Miss Ekaterina, I seem to remember we have a dinner date as my first stop on your guided tour of the city."

"We do and we can go right away. I found us a nice place."

They walked slowly out of the theatre. Dizzy was a little surprised that it was still light outside. They almost never played daytime gigs. They walked in silence for a short distance. Dizzy savoured the moment walking beside her until they reached a wide intersection. Ekaterina, as if to make sure he would not stray off in the wrong direction, looked up at him. "I'm going to be forward again." She smiled and took his hand.

"The drivers here are insane. You may not be used to this."

"Oh, I am more used to it than you think, but you are the guide and having you hold my hand is an unexpected pleasant perk."

"What is a 'perk'?"

"A little extra added pleasure, in this case."

They walked in silence for another two minutes, arriving at the door of a restaurant that went down several steps below the sidewalk. Dizzy had not found the silence awkward. The short walk had been intoxicating with her proximity, her perfume, and the feel of her hand. They entered and the maître d' showed them to a small table by a corner window. They sat down facing each other and Dizzy felt nervous for the first time in her presence. It was an unexpected reaction. Not one to be stuck for words normally, here he was facing this beautiful, unusual woman and wasn't at all sure how to start the conversation. He decided he should just dive in.

"So this is where a spy takes her suspects for interrogation." The minute he said it, he thought it was a dumb opener.

Ekaterina broke into laughter. She hadn't expected that. "Yes, and you are in for the interrogation of your life. But I never conduct an interrogation without wine. Shall I order some red?"

"By all means. This will give me some time to think up some answers."

Dizzy had lost some of his nervousness now. Nothing like a little laughter.

"In the meantime, I will interrogate you first. Tell me, are you from this city?"

"I was born here and have lived here all of my life."

"So besides being a spy, do you do anything like write, play music, act, drive trucks, or run races? Anything like that?"

"I have done some acting. As a matter of fact, I have acted on the same stage as your concert this afternoon. I am trying to write a play but I am finding it easier to recite other people's words than to write my own. I don't drive trucks and have no intention of ever running a race."

"Your English is perfect. Where did you learn?"

"My father taught English at a university and made sure that I learned it. I got good enough to act as an interpreter and translator. I work for various government departments. Whoever needs me at the time.

I get to translate meetings and such. Most of it is dry and boring, but the pay is not bad."

The waiter arrived and Ekaterina ordered a bottle.

"The menu is in Romanian so lucky for you, I can provide expert translation."

" I don't need to know. Order something and surprise me."

"Really?"

"As long as it isn't the deep innards of some animal, I don't mind being surprised."

Dizzy looked around and took in the old restaurant. It was dark and subdued, and very quiet. People were eating and talking in low voices. Ekaterina ordered the food and they began a conversation that was to last over three hours. He learned of her background, her family, interests, and her likes and dislikes.

She asked about life in America. She wanted to know about racial segregation, of which she certainly knew something. She asked about the two Negro musicians in Dizzy's band. He told her that since they were in Europe, it was the first time in their lives that the band could all stay in the same hotel and all walk in the same entrances. This was not permitted at the time in the States. They had only quite recently been able to play together on the same stage, and not everywhere at that.

"It must be quite wonderful for them to be treated as a real person at last."

"Yes, and they are wonderful musicians, really talented, and the band wouldn't be the same without them. Practically the whole *raison d'etre* for just about all of the music we play can be attributed to them. Not the two individuals in particular, but jazz was invented by and large by the Negros. If it wasn't for their musical creativity and abilities, our American music would be much poorer for it."

About halfway through their conversation, the door opened and two musicians walked in. Their attire was quite different from the rest of the patrons. Both were dressed in bright, gaudy outfits. The taller of the two had a chartreuse green silk shirt with a red scarf. He was carrying a violin and bow without a case. His complexion was quite dark. The second musician was dressed in a white shirt with red baggy pantaloons with black leather boots. He wore a beret type hat and was dark all right, but not so much from his complexion as his several days' worth of a black, unshaven beard. Dizzy had never seen the instrument he was carrying before. It looked a little like a guitar but with extra strings attached to a long arm growing out of one side of the instrument.

"Those are interesting looking people. Who are they?"

"I'll tell you later. Right now just listen to them play. I think you may have never heard music like this. I'll tell you what I can afterwards."

The two musicians stood in the centre of the room. The violinist brought his instrument up to his chin and his partner had his strapped on like a guitar.

What happened next completely astounded Dizzy. They began to play a song at breakneck speed. The song was like nothing he had ever heard before. The scales and chords were quite unfamiliar to him. He heard passages that led into other passages through chordal riffs that didn't make sense to him but it all worked. The passion that these musicians played with was ferocious. The song lasted about five minutes and changed time signatures three times, then ended with an impossible flourish. The patrons in the restaurant applauded mildly. Dizzy's applause was much more enthusiastic and he was a little taken aback by the apparent lack of enjoyment from the other diners.

The duo then played a second number. This was much slower in tempo and had passages in which the intonation was strange to Dizzy, but again, it all seemed to fit and work. The violinist left his partner and began to stroll from table to table. The sounds from his violin were more haunting than anything he had ever heard. Several of the patrons broke into tears when the violinist played at their tables.

When he approached their table, they were holding hands and the enchanting music had Ekaterina in tears in no time. Dizzy looked at her and tears welled up in his eyes too. They were both overcome with an uncontrollable melancholy, which lingered after the player moved on. The song ended when the last table was played to. The guitarist then removed his hat and went around each table saying something and several patrons put some money in it.

Dizzy reached into his pocket and pulled out a banknote worth around about five dollars (or so he thought). He put it into the hat as it passed their table and the man looked momentarily surprised but smiled. "Va multumin, Dumnezeu sa va benecuvanteze," he said. Then he moved on. The musicians then left the restaurant as quietly as they had entered.

"What did he say?" Dizzy asked.

"He said, 'Thank you and God bless you.'"

Dizzy and Ekaterina looked at each other as he quickly pulled out the handkerchief from his suit jacket and wiped her tears away. He then brushed his own eyes. "I have never heard nor could I have even imagined what I have just heard."

"What kind of music is that? Who are those people?" Dizzy's head was spinning with curiosity and emotion. He wasn't able to collect his thoughts in any logical way. The last ten minutes of his were like nothing he had ever experienced. It had all been so unexpected. He had shared some common emotion with Ekaterina that had brought them both to tears. He had spent a lifetime spent in music only to discover some completely sophisticated other-worldly music played by virtuosos.

He took her hand. "Now, it is my turn to interrogate. Tell me everything about what just happened here." He would have to settle with talking about it for now, but he really just wanted to hold Ekaterina close to him while he collected himself. Not a man who generally shed tears in a restaurant with a woman on a first date, Dizzy was quite shaken by the whole experience.

"The people who played that wonderful music are called Tiganni. They also call themselves Roma. In your language, they are sometimes called Gypsies. They are nomadic people who populate the whole of Europe as kind of separate society. They are famous for their music and as you have just heard, some of it is very sophisticated music. None of it is written down. These people continue to teach each other from early childhood. The man playing the violin in all probability is unable to read or write but as you have heard, he is a master of his instrument. He is well known around here. His name is Spatzo and they say he started to play the violin at three years old. I don't know anything about the other man. I have not seen him before."

"I wonder what the instrument was that he played. He is a master accompanist."

"I think it is called in my language a harpa chitara. That would translate as a harp guitar."

"That makes sense, given all the extra strings on it.

There are no words for what I am feeling right now. I have played music all of my adult life having worked hard to be good only to hear something which has made me feel like I know very little."

"I wouldn't think that way. I can tell you that if Spatzo had come to your concert, he would have been as impressed by you and your group as you were by him tonight. Remember, he is a master musician and he would easily recognize another master, even though he would find a song like Rosetta or Stardust as strange to his ears as his music sounded to you. But he would see and hear the virtuosity."

Dizzy hadn't thought of that. He found that remark interesting. His thoughts were still racing. "What I wouldn't give to have my band hear those two musicians, but I suppose they have walked out of our lives by now."

"Are you serious?"

"Absolutely," said Dizzy.

"I'm sure they are at a restaurant nearby. They play from place to place most nights. It's still early and I'm sure your guys are probably sitting in the hotel, probably in the bar.

If you can gather them, I'm sure I can get the Roma musicians to play for them. We will have to pay them a little money, but if each of your boys puts in a few dollars, they will play for as long as you want. It's not much, not like the money you get for your concerts. If they have the equivalent of about ten dollars, they will be very happy. That's probably more than they will make in five restaurants."

"What a wonderful, crazy idea," said Dizzy. "How can we make that happen?"

"There might be a problem though. Gypsies are not allowed in the hotel, so we may have to listen to them outside on the street. They are discriminated against in a similar way to your Negros. However, it is Sunday and there may be a way to get them into the hotel without anyone finding out. We will, how do you say? Sneak them into one of your rooms."

"How can you do that?"

"Leave that to me. It's probably better if you don't know. What is your room number?"

"Four thirty-six."

"Get everyone into your room and wait for us."

The bill was quickly paid and Ekaterina walked to the next restaurant. They could faintly hear the music emanating from the place. Dizzy made his way back to the hotel where most of the guys were in the bar.

"Listen, guys, it will take me a while to explain this, but I want everyone in my room in fifteen minutes."

"What are you talking about?" said Spike.

"I have an amazing surprise for..."

"God, man, don't tell me you have already bedded the young lady you were with a few hours ago."

"Of course not, but it does involve her. I promise you something completely interesting and you will thank me for it afterwards. Just allow me to surprise you. You can all come back here afterwards and it will be something new to talk about. We'll go up in fifteen minutes."

Ekaterina opened the door of the restaurant. She walked in and waited by the door. The waiter came up to her and asked her where she wanted to sit. She told him she was waiting for the musicians. This was really unusual, but he let her stay. Five minutes later, they had finished their song, which had reduced a number of the diners to tears. She had not looked at it in this way before but she suddenly realized this was their forte. They could make anyone cry with the melancholy and drama of their music. They went around making people cry with their passionate music and got paid for it.

Ekaterina spoke to them partly in their own dialect.

"I have a group of American musicians visiting here and I was with one of them earlier in the last restaurant where you played. They are a seven-piece band but none of them has ever heard anything like the music you play. We will pay you well to come and play a few songs for them. I want to show off our Romanian music and you can do this perfectly. Will you come and play for them? It's not far away."

"We would be happy and honoured to do so. My name is Spatzo Weiss."

"Yes, I know who you are. I'm Ekaterina Vancea. Now, we will have to sneak into the back door of the Hotel Metropol. I know how to get you in and we will have to be careful and get up to the fourth floor without being seen. I'm sure you understand. They have to leave tomorrow and this is the only chance for them to hear your music.

I will go up there right now and in five minutes, come to the back service door. I will be waiting to let you in. Do not be late; I can't stay back there forever. Here's an advance."

She slipped him the equivalent of five dollars, promising more when they had finished playing. That was as much as they made in the restaurant and there was more to come. Ekaterina made her way to the hotel and knocked on the back lane door, which was the service entrance. It led into the janitor's room and fortunately, one of the janitors answered. She explained that she was going to bring some musicians in for a private party and it was to be a surprise. She passed him a banknote for the same amount as she had given Spatzo, which was two day's salary in his world.

"Don't worry, if anything goes wrong, I will take complete blame and not let you get into trouble. I know the manager. I need you to guide me to room 436 without being seen."

"I can do that."

About seven minutes later, there was a soft knock at the door and much to Ekaterina's relief, Spatzo and his partner stood outside. She explained to him about having to sneak up to room 436 and the janitor would guide everyone without being discovered.

The janitor led them down a corridor and into another, which led to a set of service stairs. They came out on the fourth floor a few feet from the room. They waited in the shadows while Ekaterina went and knocked on the door. Again to her relief, Dizzy answered and she waived the Tiganni into the room.

The entire band was there and they looked surprised. A beautiful girl had just entered the room with two unusual men carrying instruments. Dizzy closed the door and announced, "Gentlemen, this is Ekaterina Vancea. I don't know these two gentlemen, but I will let Ekaterina tell you about them. We heard them play in a restaurant tonight and I have never heard anything like this in my life. They play music that obviously has different rules than our own, and I had to have you hear them. They are virtuosos on their instruments. The tall guy plays a violin. The other plays a funny guitar-like instrument which Ekaterina says is a harp-guitar."

"These gentlemen are Roma, or Gypsies," Ekaterina said. "It is Gypsy music that you will hear.

They are not supposed to be here. We had to sneak in and if they are caught in here, they will be thrown out quickly. I promised that we would pay them. It will cost everyone about two drinks' worth and they will be very happy with that. We have to be ready with the money in case the manager bursts in and kicks them out. I apologize for the liberties I have taken here, but Dizzy told me that you absolutely had to hear this."

"That's cool," said Spike.

"I can't wait," said Jimmy.

Ekaterina asked Spatzo if he would play the two songs he had played in the restaurant. Everyone sat down in chairs, on the bed, and on the floor.

Spatzo put his violin in place and the music started. It was every bit as fast and furious as it had been in the restaurant—probably better, as Spatzo was now showing off his musical culture to visiting foreigners. He was flying with the violin with the solid accompaniment of his friend. Dizzy looked around the room and was delighted to see the reaction of the musicians. They were wide-eyed and astonished as he had been in the restaurant. They had an instinctive knowledge of what was happening but had no idea about the rules and theory behind this music.

When the piece was over, Dizzy jumped up and prevented them from clapping so as to prolong the moment. If they carried on long enough, there would surely be a knock on the door from the manager and maybe even the police.

Ekaterina asked Spatzo to play the slow piece that he had played in the restaurant.

This time, Spatzo really poured on the drama and passion. He was playing to people he had never seen but was aware that they were visiting musicians. His tone and articulation was even better than she had heard in the restaurant. He moved around the room and played to everyone individually. The intensity rose with every passage and when he had finished with his flourish of false harmonics, most of Dizzy's band was in tears. The room fell silent. No one spoke until Dizzy said to Ekaterina, "Please thank them for us while I collect something for the guys. Tell them that none of us have ever heard anything like that in our lives and we are very grateful for them coming here to play for us."

"Yes, I will, but hurry with the collection. I'm sure the inevitable knock at the door will happen soon and the three of us will be escorted out of here. I will meet you back at the restaurant a little later."

Sure enough, there was a loud knock at the door. Dizzy opened it as he collected the last of the money the boys had dug out of their pockets. It amounted to about twenty-five dollars worth—as much as the Gypsies could expect to make in a week's worth of playing the restaurants.

A dour-faced house detective who didn't speak any English sternly motioned to Ekaterina and the Gypsies to get out.

"Lesi afara acum! Lesi afara acum!"

One did not have to know Romanian to understand what he was saying. Ekaterina left with the two musicians in tow, closing the door behind her.

"Well, gentlemen, whaddya think of that?" The band was practically in shock. There was a momentary silence broken, then someone said, "What the hell did we just hear?"

Dizzy did his best to explain who they were but there were many unanswered questions. All he could really tell them is that he would have to try to get some more information on the Gypsies and their music.

"Man, those cats could really play. Imagine trying to keep up the tempo on the first piece."

"I ain't never heard no violin played like that before," said Spike.

"You jus' don't see cats dressed like that anywhere."

The musicians chatted about what they just heard and Dizzy slipped out of the room. He went downstairs through the lobby, getting a nasty look from the house detective on the way. Dizzy smiled back at him and carried on down the street towards the restaurant, where he found Ekaterina waiting for him. Relieved, he hugged her on an impulse. She felt soft and yielding, her hair brushing his cheek. *My God, that feels nice*, he thought. They slowly, slightly backed away from each other.

"That was really cool organizing that little concert for the boys. Are you in any kind of trouble for sneaking them in?"

"Probably a little," she replied, "but the hotel manager is a friend of the family and I think I'll just get a bit of a warning not to do that again. The real sin in all of this is that I brought Gypsies with me. I am not supposed to spend time bringing Gypsies into hotels. It's all part of the general discrimination towards the Roma people. I was happy to get away with what happened. Your musicians got to hear probably the best Roma musician in the country up close. As musicians, they were impressed, I'm sure. When I explain why I did this, I'm sure he will understand. I'll still get a talking to but it will be just a little less severe."

"Can we have a drink somewhere?" asked Dizzy

"There's a little place just down the street."

Dizzy reached for her hand and took it in his as they walked slowly to the bar. "Boy, this has been quite a day so far."

What he was really thinking was that he was holding Ekaterina's hand and enjoying it so much that he hoped the bar would have been farther away, but they were there in about three minutes. They hadn't spoken. Each was thinking of the day's events and how special it had become for both of them.

They both sat at a table in a dark corner. Dimly lit by a candle, Dizzy couldn't take his eyes off Ekaterina's face.

"I think I could use some of that Romanian firewater they had at the reception. I didn't try it there because I had to play, but I'm ready for some."

"It's an acquired taste but you might as well start now."

The waiter brought a couple of shot glasses of the stuff along with some water.

Dizzy just about gagged on the first sip, bringing a giggle from Ekaterina. It left a strong but pleasant aftertaste. After the second sip, he realized that he could develop a fondness for the stuff.

They talked for the next two hours until closing time. Life stories mostly. Dizzy asked Ekaterina about her flawless command of English.

"My father, who is highly educated, made sure that I would be equally so. He encouraged me to read just about all of the books in his library and I became obsessed with learning all kinds of subject matter. He is a liberal thinker and wanted me to have as complete education as possible. He didn't want me to be married off, never to use my knowledge, and spend my life raising children. This, as you may know, is not conventional thinking in my father's social class. He wanted me to have mastery over at least one language beside my own. I chose English."

He laughed. "Good thing. Otherwise I might have been trying to communicate with you in Russian or Greek."

As they were getting ready to leave, she said, "You haven't told me why you want to go to Moldova."

"It's a long story and I will tell you next time I see you."

They left the place and started walking toward Ekaterina's flat. The night air was crisp and Dizzy put his jacket over her shoulders. She took his hand this time and they walked through some dark and deserted streets. They were large streets with little lighting and no traffic except for the occasional taxi. Dizzy was surprised to see a horse-drawn wagon clattering along. They said little, having both talked a blue streak since dinner in the afternoon. They were digesting what the other had said in the course of the evening.

Ekaterina stopped. "This is my place." She pointed to a second floor window of an old apartment building. A large wrought iron gate looked like it needed a large old fashion key to open it.

They were facing each other and finally Dizzy was hoping to do what he had wanted to do all evening. Throughout all the conversation his mind kept drifting to one thing.

And that's exactly what transpired next: a long gentle kiss. When they parted, Ekaterina said, "Goodnight Dizzy. I had a wonderful time."

"Me too. When can I see you again?"

"I am working for Mr. Washburn all of next week. You can find me at his office and we will think of something to do." She laughed and pulled a large key out of her purse that looked like it came from a jailer's key ring, and opened the creaky gate.

"Do you know the way back to your hotel?"

"Yes, I will find my way back okay. Goodnight, Ekaterina"

With that, the giant gate clanked shut, Ekaterina disappeared behind her door, and Dizzy walked back to the hotel, completely forgetting that he had left his jacket on her shoulders. He thought that it had been a long time since he was so gaga over a beautiful woman that he would forget his jacket like that. He was genuinely happy and looked forward to a good night's sleep.

As for Ekaterina, she didn't notice the jacket until she was halfway up the stairs. She too laughed and wondered how she was going to return the jacket to Dizzy. After all, a woman returning a gentleman's clothes does come with certain implications, if someone witnesses the act. She would need a private moment with him to accomplish this. But that would be for tomorrow.

CHAPTER 5

"Good morning, Henry."

"Good morning, Dizzy. I understand you had an interesting evening last night."

"It certainly was. It's only 10:00. News spreads quickly around here."

"Ekaterina is working here in my office this week and I got the story from her. Says she organized a little concert for your band with a couple of Gypsies in your hotel. I don't want to know how she pulled that one off, but she does have her ways."

"It was certainly interesting and I'm so glad the boys had the opportunity to hear something like that.

They were astounded as was I. None of us had ever heard anything remotely like it. The concert, as you put it, lasted exactly two songs before some dour looking house detective banged on the door and escorted Ekaterina and the two Gypsies out. I hope she is not in trouble for it."

"Probably not, given the circumstances. You guys are heroes today and certain allowances will be made. Ekaterina wouldn't have done that unless she knew that you and your band would be impressed with the Gypsy musicians, and your status in this town is right up there. There will be no serious repercussions. Even the hotel manager was at the concert yesterday afternoon, so he will understand the situation. He will probably wag a symbolic finger at Ekaterina and warn her not to do that again, but only because that is what is expected from him."

"Impressed is putting it mildly, but those impressions will last a long time. Those two guys reduced the whole room into a valley of tears. I have never seen anything like that in all my life in music. I certainly hope to hear some more of that music before I leave here."

"Wonderful. Now, we have to see about getting you to Moldova. It looks like I can get you a car for your trip. It's an old one but it is in good condition and not in imminent danger of breaking down. It actually belongs to the consulate but we have a newer one we use on official business. The other one hasn't been driven in months and I can't see where we'll need it anytime soon. If you pay to have the oil changed in it and have it greased, then it's yours. I'll show where to take it for this."

"That's very generous of you. Thank you. I will gladly pay to have the work done on it."

"I will give you a kind of visa, which I am permitted to do, indicating that you are on official business. It's not diplomatic but it does carry some weight. It should help at the border, which can be unpredictable. Just saying you are on official business and showing the visa should be enough to work away problems. I'm not supposed to do this, but we are so far from any kind of officialdom here that I can get away with it. No one ever checks up on these things around here. This is truly a forgotten corner of the world in many respects."

"Again, that is most generous of you. Thanks."

"It's one little thing that I can do, as you have certainly made my day. As you can imagine, hearing live jazz is not something that happens every day. The last time for me was in London three years ago. I have been starving to hear some good music, American style, and I got to hear two concerts in two days." He smiled.

"I'll arrange to have you get the car tomorrow in the morning, then you can take it to the garage. Ekaterina can write you a note in Rumanian to give to the mechanic. By the way, she wanted me to let her know when you arrived.

She wanted a word with you. She is down the hall to the right in her own little office. You can just go and knock on her door."

"Thanks, I will. And thank you for arranging a car for me. I had no idea that I would be able to drive to Moldova on my own."

"Come in."

"So this is where spies work in the daytime."

"I wish the work was more spy-like and interesting. I'm translating the boring minutes of a bureaucratic meeting concerning trade imbalance with Bulgaria."

"How long did it take you to remember you were still wearing my jacket?"

"Probably about the same amount of time it took you to realize they you had forgotten it. Not long."

"Do I get to spend some time with you after you have finished clacking away at that typewriter?"

"I've got to finish this today, then I'm free. Another two hours, I think. Why don't we meet in the restaurant at 4:00? You'll recognize me: I'll be the only woman wearing a man's jacket."

They both laughed. Dizzy leaned over and whispered, "That was fun last night. I had a great time."

"Me too." She smiled. "I'll see you later."

Meeting Ekaterina had thrown a curve ball into Dizzy's plans. He was going to go to Moldova all right, but by now his head was becoming filled with thoughts of her and they were crowding and cluttering plans. As far as he could remember, he hadn't really told her of his plans, only that he was going to stick around for a while with a short trip to Moldova.

He thought to himself that he would do this today and let her know the real reason he didn't return to America with the band, although he also thought that Washburn may have mentioned it in passing. At any rate, he'd better let her know so she wouldn't think he was trying to hide things. Besides, maybe she had been there and knew something about the place. His own information was so sketchy he was beginning to realize his almost complete ignorance about the place. There was a sense of reticence about the trip and at the same time, a real excitement about venturing into the complete unknown on his own.

He walked to the restaurant at four and sure enough, found the only woman in a man's jacket perched at the bar.

"You weren't hard to spot. For a spy you stand out way too much."

"Sometimes a spy can hide in plain sight so no one will suspect she is hiding."

He did like the way they carried on this game. To him, she looked exotic and mysterious—not to mention drop dead beautiful. She was not only wearing his jacket, she had on an odd-looking fedora and a tie with slacks, looking not at all like she did at the concert in her black dress.

They sat at a corner by the window. He was, as usual, happy to see her. They ordered some wine, toasted each other, and he decided this was the time.

"You wanted to know why I want to go to Moldova, so here goes. Although I am known to myself and the rest of the world as Dizzy Pollen, my real name is Josef. My ancestors immigrated to America in the nineteenth century. The name Pollen is a contraction of Polozenski. Our ancestral name was changed to Pollen when my grandfather landed in New York. I never really gave any of this much thought until I realized that I was going to be near Moldova at the end of the tour. I then became curious about my ancestral land, of which my parents would never talk. No amount of prying could extract any information about what they called the old country.

I know next to nothing about the place and I just wanted to go there out of curiosity, as I'm fairly certain I will never be this way again. This is a long way from home."

"Yes, I can see that you would want to take advantage of the opportunity. I have never been there, despite its proximity. I do know a little about the place, but not much, I'm afraid."

"In some ways, I'm happy to not know a lot. I don't have a great interest in the place except that somewhere in it lie my origins. I don't really expect to find any family there. I cannot speak the language and would have absolutely nothing in common with anyone there. I am an American, born and raised. I'm just a little curious and opportunistic given my present circumstances."

"My impression is that it hasn't left the nineteenth century yet. It's very backward and poor, and there are always rumours of strange goings on."

"What kind of strange things?"

"Oh, bizarre religious sects, witchcraft, cults, strange rituals. Things like that. I have never had the desire to go there. I don't think there is a high degree of literacy or education. It is mostly an agricultural country and very poor overall. It has been overrun by every army that came through the place. Its geographical position put it squarely in the path of armies who warred in the dark ages and middle ages."

"I did gather that from the little I have read. I suppose I should have been better prepared with a little knowledge about the place but I never really thought in my wildest that I would ever get this close."

"Maybe that's all right. Now you have no real expectations. Every part of the trip will be a surprise and an adventure. You can tell me all about it when you get back. I will be interested to hear your impressions. And rest assured, I will interrogate you until you tell all." She smiled and winked.

They ordered a meal and talked some more until they realized it was almost 9:00. It suddenly felt as if they had been there forever.

"I'm getting tired. We've been talking for just about five hours," said Ekaterina.

"So am I. I guess we should go."

Dizzy settled the bill. Savouring every moment, he put his arm around Ekaterina's shoulder and they walked slowly towards her place. They hardly spoke. It felt to both of them like a slow dance, the music ending at the imposing iron gate in front of the apartment.

They held each other and kissed. It was more passionate than their first tentative kiss the night before.

"I know what we are both thinking, but it is too soon," she said.

"I'm okay with you thinking that way. You are probably right—but only probably."

She laughed. The tension was broken and they shared one last short kiss. Ekaterina pulled out her jailer's key, clanked open the lock, and said, "Good night Dizzy," squeezing his hand. "You know where to find me in my little spy office." She had that mysterious expression on her face that would just about knock Dizzy over every time she used it.

"Good night, Ekaterina. I don't think I have mentioned this, but you have a great name. Who would ever think to put an 'E' before Katerina?"

"We spies have our ways," she said as the gate clicked shut. She winked at him and started upstairs.

The next day, Dizzy had farewell breakfast with the band in the hotel dining room. It was cheery and sad at the same time. It was great to eat together but they would not be playing together for some time. Each musician could find temporary work with other bands but as a unit, it was anybody's guess as to when they would enjoy working again. The bus departed with everyone wishing Dizzy good luck with his trip. They all were confident that they would back "soon" whatever that meant.

Dizzy then walked over to Washburn's office in hopes of getting his car situation settled. He didn't have to wait long. Washburn turned up with a car key in his hand.

"Here's the key to our car. You can use it as long as you want. I have made a short list of things to have done on it and gave it to Ekaterina for the mechanic. She also has the address of the garage. She is probably awaiting your presence in her dungeon down the hall. She will take you to where the car is kept."

"Henry, I can't thank you enough for all of this. You have been more than generous with your time and attention."

"I am happy to be able to assist you. Your music has re-charged my batteries and made me slightly homesick—temporarily, I hope. We are both a long way from home, as you know. I have been here for three years and although I really like it, I sometimes miss the accoutrements offered in the States. Odd things like listening to a baseball game on the radio, some American music, and a good old fashioned hot dog overflowing with all the fixin's. It's the little everyday things you begin to miss after a while. All those mundane and ordinary trappings of the life and culture we grew up with. You know, I rarely even eat a bloody hot dog, even when I attend a baseball game, but here, I find myself craving one. Oh, they have great sausages and the like here, but somehow the vision of a ball park frank seems like a meal fit for a prince. I know that absence is supposed to make the heart grow fonder, but I had no idea that would extend to a doggone hot dog. Imagine that!"

"I've only been gone a little over a month but I think I know what you mean. But I am on the adventure of a lifetime and have not had time to think of what I am missing. Everyday has opened up new doors and I have jumped at every opportunity to enter and look around. I am trying to be as absorbed and captivated as possible and try to remember everything that I have seen and experienced so far. After all has been said and done, I will only have these memories, and I have a feeling they will become more precious as time goes on. Through coincidence and a few strokes of dumb luck I'm here at a perfect time when I could have been back playing the same old tunes to a sometimes largely disinterested audience. You cannot know what the recognition we have received on this tour has done for us. We are all re-charged and sitting on top of the world. People have listened intently to what we have had to say here. What a welcome situation that is. We are flabbergasted by the whole experience."

"That's great. In some ways, I envy you. I'm sure it hasn't always been this good, so I am really happy for you and my being able to provide you with a car is an honour for me. Anyway, you should get going. I have stuff to do."

"Thanks again, Henry."

Dizzy went down the hall knocking on Ekaterina's door.

"Abandon hope all ye who enter here," she said through the door.

Dizzy was slowly finding out that Ekaterina's sense of humour was unpredictable. He was never quite sure what she would say next.

"I have an important message from Agent IXE-13."

"Come in."

Dizzy opened the door to find Ekaterina standing facing him, her feet slightly apart, her hands on her hips, defiantly looking him straight in the eyes.

"This better be good," she said sternly.

Dizzy was startled for a second. He then crossed the small room towards her, placing his arms through the space between her arms and waist. He pulled her to him and kissed her. She hadn't expected that at all. She put her arms around him and kissed back passionately for a few seconds. She pulled back slightly and they both broke out in laughter.

"Agent IXE-13. Where did you get that?"

"Frankly, I have no idea."

"It's so good to see you."

"Same here, Dizzy. I have the paper from Henry about the car for the mechanic. If you want to wait an hour, I'll be through here for the day and we can go together. I will have finished my work on Bulgarian trade imbalance."

"That sounds good. I'll walk around awhile and will come back in one hour."

He touched her hair and kissed her on the cheek. "Careful to get those numbers right. You don't want to annoy the Bulgarians. I've heard they can be pretty mean."

"I'm not afraid of them. I've taken on a half-dozen of them in a bar fight and walked out unscathed."

Dizzy walked around for an hour lost in thought. His mind wandered all over the place, but mostly he thought about Ekaterina. He was trying to sort out his feelings toward her. Should he ask if she wants to come to Moldova with him? If so, what then? If not, what happens afterwards? He eventually had to return to the States. Would she come with him? Could he prolong his stay here? He had enough money to last quite a while. He had nothing lined up gig wise at home. Did Ekaterina feel the same way towards him? What would happen when they finally expressed their emotions towards each other?

They obviously had a severe crush on one another. His rambling thoughts went on and on.

On the way back, he decided to play everything by ear and take one thing at a time. He didn't want to jump to any conclusions, and he certainly didn't want to scare off Ekaterina. Anything to prevent that.

The only thing that made any sense was to open up to her and have her do the same. The uncertainties had to be dealt with and that would at least clear the air. Better to admit uncertainness than to try to hide it. He knew covering up uncertainty usually backfires, and the last thing he wanted was anything to go wrong.

Arriving back at Washburn's office, Dizzy knocked on Ekaterina's office door.

"Don't tell me its Agent IXE-13 again!"

"I have orders not to let you out of my sight."

"Oh well, I might as well make it easy for you to follow your orders. Enter."

"Have you finished dealing with the Bulgarian trade imbalance?"

"Just now. Perfect timing. Come over and give me a kiss, and we'll go find the car."

"No argument here."

He walked over and kissed her. It was tentative at first, then they stayed that way for what seemed the longest time, with the kiss becoming as passionate as either of them could have hoped. Dizzy was beside himself with excitement. He could hardly breathe or see straight. Ekaterina was melting in his arms.

"We better go find that car," she breathed.

"I guess so."

They walked out of the office and when they were on the street, she took his hand. They walked for five minutes until they came to a double door, for which Ekaterina produced another large medieval looking key. With a satisfying clank, the lock sprang open. Dizzy pulled the doors open to reveal a ridiculously small automobile. It was like opening the door of your house and finding a small puppy sitting there.

"My God, Washburn has given me a toy car!"

"I guess our small cars look like toys to Americans, but let me assure you, it's real and reliable. I have only seen two American cars and they look like houses on wheels. I haven't driven this car, so you can start it up and drive us to the mechanic. I know where he lives."

Dizzy got in the driver's seat and when Ekaterina sat down beside him, she gave him the key.

He was a little uncertain as to how everything worked. He fiddled around with the gearshift to get the feel of it, then noticed the name Fiat on the steering hub. Ekaterina told him it was called a Fiat 500, made in Italy.

"They call it a Topolino," she said. "I think it means little mouse."

"Certainly well named."

Dizzy put it in neutral, turned on the ignition, and pressed the starter button. The starter motor whirred for about thirty seconds, then the engine sputtered a little and died. He tried again, only this time the engine coughed into life after about five seconds. Ekaterina got out to close the garage door behind them.

Dizzy lurched ahead, not being used to the precise feel of the tiny car. He crossed the doorway and with the doors closed behind him and Ekaterina back in the passenger seat, they were off to the mechanic's house. By the time he got there, he really liked the car. It was like nothing he had ever driven, and certainly not like the four door Plymouth he had back home.

"Mr. Washburn told me that the car wouldn't take much time to fix, so we can probably have it back at the end of the day," Ekaterina said.

"That's good. Can you get some time off so we could go have a picnic somewhere tomorrow?"

"Yes, I can manage the afternoon off, I'm sure. I will make us something to bring and have everything ready. We can pick it up at my place and I know a nice place by a riverbank about forty kilometres from here."

They delivered the car to Astor the mechanic. She gave him the note listing what should be done to the car. They conversed in Romanian for a minute, then she turned to Dizzy.

"We can go. He'll have the car ready in two hours. We will come back for it then. In the meantime, we can go and eat something. I will buy us something for our picnic."

They ate in an outdoor place down the street. Dizzy's mind was full of the same thoughts that were plaguing him earlier, but he held off talking about any of it. He thought the picnic would present the best opportunity for what was going to be a serious and intimate conversation.

That evening they went to a classical music concert. This is something that Ekaterina did quite regularly; Dizzy, less so. It wasn't that he didn't enjoy concerts, but his profession usually kept him busy in the evening. Musicians usually all work at the same time and don't often get to hear each other's gigs. They sat holding hands, listening to Mozart for an evening. Dizzy enjoyed the whole experience of sitting in a gracious old theatre beside the lovely Ekaterina, with whom he was rapidly falling in love. He thought that it couldn't get much better than that. On one level, he felt total bliss; on another level, what the hell was he going to do about all of this?

They drove to her place afterwards. Dizzy parked in front of the iron gate. They sat in the car for a few minutes talking quietly. "I know we have to talk about us," she said. "It's obvious that we both feel the same way, and if I am not mistaken, we are both a little afraid of what tomorrow will bring for us. You are a long way from home and just passing through. Sooner or later, you will have to leave, and I am afraid. I have been thinking about this all day."

"I can't tell you not to be afraid when I share your fear, and yes, I have also been thinking about this, especially today. You have suddenly become a kind of monkey wrench in my life."

"Monkey wrench—what on earth does that mean?"

"Sorry, it's an American expression meaning that someone has dropped a wrench into a smooth running machine and suddenly everything breaks down and nothing is the same after that. I didn't count on you walking into that reception and meeting you after the concert. I have stopped thinking about anything else since that moment. Everything has been re-arranged and to be quite honest, I really don't know how to handle all of this. My life was on a normal path, all of the pieces were in a predictable position, and suddenly I am presented with a new piece that is supposed to fit somewhere but I don't know where. The thing is that the piece seems to belong to the picture and I have to find out how to make it fit properly. Does that make any sense at all?"

"Interesting way to look at it, but I can see what you mean. It may be a little different for me, but a new piece has been put in front of me also. I see a place for it, but I'm afraid it might be a mistake. I guess that is why I am afraid."

"As a musician, I am used to improvising and playing music, making it up as I go along. I have been doing that for so long that it has become normal for me to approach things in small sections and deal with each one after the other. That way, anything I have just played will set up the next part. I'm not good at a long range plan with no deviations. I am always ready to make changes to keep something going in the proper direction. It has spilled over into the part of life that doesn't play music."

"That makes sense," Ekaterina said. She leaned closer to Dizzy and with the look that would floor him every time, she whispered in a conspiratorial voice, "And just how are you going to play the spy girl by ear?"

Dizzy kissed her for what seemed like an eternity, then buried his face in her hair and whispered, "How am I doing so far?"

Ekaterina, with a very sensuous look in her eyes, answered, "Almost too good."

She reached into her purse and pulled out her giant key. "Would you like to see what lies beyond the forbidden gate?"

"I have been wondering about that for days now. I have been trying to imagine, but I think it is beyond comprehension."

"I certainly hope so. Come with me."

CHAPTER 6

Dizzy woke up just as the dawn was breaking. The first grey light slipped through the window. He was careful not to move, as he just wanted to have this moment last for as long as possible. After a few minutes, he inched his way up on the pillow so he could look at Ekaterina as she slept. Looking at her in semi-darkness, sleeping with her hair over the side of her face, he listened to her shallow, rhythmic breathing. It was fascinating and mesmerizing at the same time. She was barely visible. Everything about her was mysterious and surreal in the faint light. It was the beginning of not only a new day, but one with a piece of the puzzle that was beginning to fit in a place that Dizzy never knew existed.

He stared at her until sleep overcame him and as he drifted away, she moved a little. Her head was closer now and he could smell her hair as consciousness faded. He woke up hours later to find Ekaterina looking down at him. It was much lighter in the room now. She sleepily whispered, "Good morning."

For a second, he just stared at her face, so close to his, before the full memory of the last eight hours hit him.

"My God, it's the spy girl. She's taken me to her lair."

"Yes, and it took a lot to get you to talk."

"Did I tell all?"

"No, which is why I have to keep you captured."

"That is the best thing anyone has said to me all day."

They kissed again and didn't get up for another few hours. They then had coffee and Dizzy left for his hotel for a change of clothes while Ekaterina prepared the picnic meal. She had given him the large key to let himself back through the forbidden gate. He was beside himself with a giddiness that can be so rare in life. No matter how good things could get, there was always something about a first time for anything. It marks a road or a change of life like a starting line. Everything on the backside of it becomes a 'was' and everything else is a 'will be.'

They drove for about an hour and with Ekaterina's directions, they wound up in a small, flat clearing at the end of a gravel road beside a fast, small river. It was the perfect place for the occasion. They were in a small clearing with long soft grass nor far from an old Romanian maple tree. They spread the blanket and cracked open the wine. They kissed, ate, drank, and talked. This is when Dizzy was planning to have his serious talk with her. It was still going to be serious; however, having spent the night together was certainly going to modify the situation a little. He hadn't counted on that when he planned the day.

They lay side by side on their backs, watching clouds going by and listening to the running water.

"This is where I had planned to talk about us, but you brought the subject up in the car last night. I certainly was not expecting what happened between us."

"Yes, I know what you mean. Somehow it changes things a little. Well, probably a lot."

Dizzy thought as carefully as he could with his spinning head. He was head over heels in love with her and he knew this with enough certainty, that he decided to let her know right now. He turned over and raised himself partially on top of her, his hands on her shoulders. "Ekaterina, you may suspect this, but I have to confess that I have fallen in love with you. I think I fell for you the night of the reception. I know this may seem fast, but it's how I feel. So now you at least know that much."

"I feel the same way. I am in love with you also and I know it has happened fast, but there it is. I guess we have to figure out our road from this point."

"I have to tell you that all of this is so sudden that I really don't know how to react to it, but I feel the way I feel and there is no looking back. We need to think carefully about this. In a few days, I was going to go to Moldova and then go on my merry way back to the States, but that seems to be far more complicated now that you have entered my life. You remember our conversation about a new piece of the puzzle presenting itself? Well, today that piece seems a lot closer to fitting into the picture than it did yesterday."

"I know what you mean. We have time to talk and think things out. I was thinking of being forward and asking you to take me on your trip, but I think you will need that time on your own, and I need a little time too. I never had much desire to see that place anyway, but I just wanted to be with you. I can wait for you though. You have been thinking about this for a long time and you have to do it on your own, like you planned it."

She then pushed him off her onto his back and rolled herself on top of his chest. "Just don't you dare fall for some Moldavian cutie who makes eyes at you. I will make you confess. You know I have my ways."

Then she laughed and kissed him. She put her head on his shoulder and they stayed that way for quite a while until Dizzy sensed that she had fallen asleep. He was careful not to move so as not to wake her. He got drowsy then and dozed off himself. A loud thunderclap woke them with a start. A few seconds later, the sky opened up with a sudden ferocious downpour. Grabbing everything as quickly as possible and stuffing it into the car, they were both doused by the time Dizzy started the motor and they putt-putted their way back to Ekaterina's place. They were a little cold and shivery when they got there. Ekaterina poured them a drink of the Romanian fire water, they hung their clothes to dry, climbed into bed, and stayed there until morning.

Over breakfast, she showed him a map of the region, which included Moldova.

"You can take this map. The roads aren't very good and they have everything from big trucks to horse drawn wagons on them. The drivers are all crazy. Be really careful. Do not pass a gas station without stopping to fill up, even if your tank is still half full. You never know where the next station is. Not all the towns have them. The easiest way to leave here is to go down past my place for three blocks. You will see a large white church with a gold dome on top. Turn right there and you are on the road to Moldova."

"Sounds easy enough."

"When you get to the border here," she pointed to the map, "having an American passport will almost certainly cause the border people to demand some kind of a bribe. They are not very nice people, and they all carry machine guns and they may be drunk. Those jobs usually seem to go to people who have gotten out of line somehow and as punishment, they get transferred to some lonely border outpost. Here's a carton of American cigarettes. I got them from Mr. Washburn. I explained the situation to him. Keep half of them hidden under your seat, and put the rest of them where you can give them away. Pack them in the top layer of your suitcase. When they open it, you can give them the cigarettes. That will make them your friend for life." She laughed.

"Washburn also gave me a visa that says I am on some kind of official business."

"That's good, but you have to realize that in all probability, these guys can't read, and showing them something they can't read might embarrass them. No, cigarettes will be much easier to deal with. Even the stupidest border guard knows what a package of Lucky Strikes looks like."

"I thought you said you had never been there."

"I haven't, but I have been to Bulgaria many times and stupid, underpaid border guards in this end of the world are all the same. It doesn't really matter what country around here you visit. It's always the same. American cigarettes are the best passport."

"Live and learn," he said.

"I should leave tomorrow. I shouldn't be away for more than three or four days. Probably less time than I would have, but then, I didn't have you to come back to. I will be back soon. It will be an interesting trip. I don't know why or how, it's just a premonition."

Ekaterina put her arms around him. "Please be careful, Dizzy. I have heard strange things about the place and I can't say that I like the idea of you travelling there alone. Maybe your family escaped to America for something other than to better themselves financially. They never talked to you about it, and maybe that was for a reason. They may have been involved in things that caused them to have to get out fast and never come back."

The letters! Dizzy thought. *My God, I have those letters and an expert trans-lator right here!*

"Listen, Ekaterina. I have been so blinded by recent events and my feelings for you, I forgot that I have something I want to show you. Just before leaving the States, I found some old letters among my mother's possessions. I am sure that they give a clue or two about my Moldavian ancestry. Someone looked at them before I left but couldn't properly translate them because he said they were in an unknown dialect. I'd like you to look at them and tell me anything you can about their meaning."

Dizzy retrieved the letters from the bottom of his suitcase and gave the envelope to Ekaterina. She sat at the table, open the envelope, and spread the letters along with the notes from Zanfir out in front of her. She studied the papers for a good five minutes without saying anything. She finally said, "Dizzy, this is about as crazy as it gets. Your friend was right. Some of this is in a dialect that probably vanished some time ago. Two different people wrote these papers. I don't think they are letters, but they are accounts about something referred to as the Saltatio Mortis. This means 'Dance of Death.' It seems to happen once every seven years. I think the writers were old people, from their handwriting, and they didn't know how to write very well. They mention something about killing people in a castle and other people being chased out of the country. There are no names anywhere, nor any location. Most of it doesn't make any sense at all. I'm afraid I am of no more help than the other translator." She looked worried.

"Dizzy, now I am more frightened about your trip than ever. What if your ancestors were the people killed or run out of the country?"

"My ancestors could have simply left in search of a better life. Or perhaps they were involved in some political or criminal activity that got them expelled. My family's silence would suggest the latter. As far as anyone is concerned, my name is Josef John Pollen—a completely American name. My passport says this and my birthplace is San Francisco. No one could possibly figure out that my grandfather came from Moldova from that information. They could have stolen cattle, robbed banks, or were mass murderers. Whatever they did, good or bad, happened long ago and really has nothing to do with me. I won't go around looking for long lost relatives. I've lived my life without too many relatives around and I am quite happy."

"Still, promise me you will be careful."

"I will be careful. I'm not one who goes around looking for trouble. I have been in places in my own country that are at least as dangerous as this place. I will be aware and cautious. I promise. I want to be back with you just as much as you want me back. I won't do anything to jeopardize that."

"Good, that's all I ask. Wherever you go, know that I am thinking about you."

They spent the day walking around the city. Ekaterina took him to some interesting churches, art galleries, parks, and coffee shops. A few people on the streets recognized him from the concerts.

They had dinner at a nice restaurant where the same two Gypsies that had previously come to the hotel came in and played. They played two numbers at Dizzy and Ekaterina's table, bringing them both to tears. Ekaterina had asked them to play something romantic and they really poured it on. Dizzy, who was still new to this music, was totally enthralled. He gave then a generous tip. They thanked Dizzy profusely and made their way on to the next place.

Dizzy and Ekaterina arrived home late and they made love until exhaustion put an end to it all and pushed them into a deep sleep.

In the morning, he Dizzy got up first and made the coffee, bringing it to Ekaterina in bed. They languished for a while, going over some of the details for his trip. He tried to reassure her that all would be okay, but she was still worried about him wandering around a place that she had little knowledge of except for stories and rumours—none of them very nice. Dizzy had checked out of his hotel and was ready to leave from Ekaterina's place. She gave him about forty dollars' worth of tattered Moldavian currency, which would last for several days until he could exchange some on his own.

Dizzy had some misgivings about his trip into the unknown, but at the same time, he realized that if he didn't go, he would spend the rest of his life wondering about it, no doubt regretting it. In the end, it was an exciting prospect and his enthusiasm easily overcame whatever doubts he had. It was around noon when he fired up the toy car, kissed Ekaterina goodbye, and drove down the street to where he would make the one turn to put him on the road to his destination.

CHAPTER 7

This was it: he was on his way at last. The open road was before him, though did not seem like the open road in America. It was a winding, narrow road with barely enough room to fit two cars side by side, let alone a truck. He was driving at about sixty kilometers per hour at most, and down to thirty on the rough spots. The scenery was pastoral with hills, dips, and tight curves. There were plenty of horse drawn wagons, a few old cars, and a bicycle here and there. The occasional herd of cows ruminated lazily in pastures. There were rivers with one-lane bridges looking like they wouldn't hold a wheelbarrow, much less his tiny car.

His map proved only marginally useful. All the villages and small towns had strange names. It didn't show the really small places, of which there were many. He just knew he was still heading north by the sun. He had never done anything like this before. He was well travelled in all forty-eight states where everyone spoke English, the music was in 4/4 time, and a hamburger was a hamburger no matter where you went.

He also had trouble figuring out exactly how far he had driven. He had never worked in kilometres before and with the changing speeds due to the conditions of the roads and a map full of strange names, he decided after a few hours that he was indeed lost.

With a stroke of instinct, he turned off to the right after seeing a faded sign with the name of a town that was inside the western border of Moldova. The road wasn't much more than a couple of ruts running through the fields. He looked at his gas gauge. There was just about three quarters a tank left. Enough that he needn't worry for a while. Here, he found himself feeling very alone. In a half hour drive since he made the turnoff, he only encountered one ancient truck, which looked to him as if it was the oldest truck in all of Moldova. It was carrying hay bales and was tilted over at about ten degrees with one fender missing. He had never seen so much blue smoke emitting from a single exhaust pipe in his life.

The place so far was beautiful and seemed quiet. That was Dizzy's impression, as there were few houses and a complete lack of vehicles. The serenity, though, gave him a sense of foreboding. For whatever reason, he felt alone and vulnerable. This was a first for him: taking off on a whim with no particular destination in mind in a foreign country, not knowing the first thing about the place. Would it be a good idea to let anyone know his original name? What if he couldn't find anyone who could understand him?

A half hour later, he came to the top of a hill in the middle of nowhere. Nosing over its crest and down the other side, he noticed a small structure, which on approach appeared to be a small kiosk. He had arrived at the border to the old country.

He became quite nervous when he saw the guard emerge from the kiosk.

This was not like any border crossing he had seen before. There was no concrete building with a large staff. It was what he remembered from old comic books: a small, unpainted wooden kiosk with a barrier that could be raised by hand. The barrier was painted in a yellow and black spiral pattern. Out in the middle of an idyllic pasture, an imaginary, invisible line crossed the road, marked by a small shack on which was nailed a weathered sign with one word on it: Moldova. The inhabitant of this rustic structure was a shaggy, annoyed looking border guard with a machine gun strapped over his shoulder. His uniform appeared to be the same one he wore and slept in for the last month. A cigarette dangled from his mouth with the burning end dangerously close to his outsized moustache. To complete this intimidating presence, he wore a patch over his left eye, giving him a sinister and menacing air and rendering Dizzy about as uncomfortable as he had ever felt in his life.

He knew that he would be unable to answer anything the guard would ask him, nor would he be able to explain why he just drove up to this imaginary line wanting to cross it. He just wanted in and was hoping to be able to enter despite this insurmountable language barrier. Things might have been different if he had been on a main road, with a bigger building maybe, and someone who knew at least a smattering of English.

"Passport!" the guard scowled.

Then he realized that the occupant of the car was American. He stared at the passport with a look that went from a scowl to one of puzzlement. What in Hell did this foreigner want to do here?

He muttered something that sounded vaguely threatening and Dizzy smiled like a tourist.

The guard went back to his scowl, then he threw down his cigarette, which by now had singed moustache. Dizzy caught the scent of burnt hair. The guard looked in the back window at the battered suitcase and motioned to have it opened.

Now, Dizzy thought, *this is it. He will find some excuse to turn me around.* Dizzy then remembered the Luckies that Ekaterina had him place in his suitcase. He got out of the car and pulled the suitcase out the door and put it on the ground.

The guard looked inside the suitcase. Dizzy, having never bribed anyone was unsure what to do. He saw the guard's expression change as soon as he saw the four packs sitting on top of the clothes. Dizzy gestured to the guard to take some. The guard smiled slightly and scooped them up stuffing them into one of his baggy pockets. . He went over to the kiosk with Dizzy's passport and returned a moment later with a large stamp in it.

He handed the passport back, lit up a Lucky, and pulled on the cable that lifted the barrier. It squeaked and stayed up while Dizzy started the car and drove slowly away down the rutted road, feeling a little smug at having such an easy time crossing the border. Ekaterina had been right: Lucky Strikes were indeed the best passport in this end of the world.

He drove for another hour as the road disappeared under him. It went from two well- defined ruts to hardly any ruts at all. He hadn't seen another human being since his encounter with the border guard. There were many steep hills and tight curves. The toy car needed to negotiate some of the hills in second gear. There were a few cattle grazing here and there and a very old rusted out tractor abandoned by the side of what was now passing for a road. His mind turned to other things like the gas gauge, which was telling him there was less than a quarter tank left. Besides that, where was he going to sleep tonight?

It was dusk as he approached a village. He could make out a few houses and a few slightly larger buildings. His eyes scanned the road before him, hoping to see a hotel sign or something to indicate a place where he could eat. There wasn't a streetlight to be seen. It was slowly dawning on him how completely unprepared he was for any of this journey. He didn't know where he was, didn't know how to talk to anyone, and didn't know where he would eat, sleep, or buy gas.

Still, there was a certain exhilaration to it all. The unexpected seemed adventurous for the time being. He would be at the mercy of whomever he met and so far, so good.

He was now inching his way into what seemed like the main square in the small village. There was a run-down church with the steeple leaning slightly backwards, and what looked like a store with an honest to God hitching post in front. Dizzy had never seen a hitching post except in a cowboy movie. There was a small fountain in the centre spewing a stream of water from a pipe. Two elderly women were filling buckets from it. A half dozen large trees grew near the fountain. A few park benches were strewn around in no particular order and a buggy with a team of horses stood on the other side of the square from him. They were tied up to a second hitching post. He really couldn't tell if he was even on a street anymore. It was like an old-fashioned common in the centre of an old American town.

There were a few people around and they were all looking at the toy car that had glided into their world. Dizzy pulled over to a non-existent curb, shut the engine off, and waited a few moments before getting out. He opened the door, wondering whether he should walk up and down the place looking for lodgings and leave his suitcase and horn in the car seat, but decided to carry them. A stranger wandering around looking lost with a suitcase might provoke some help in finding a room.

Dizzy decided to circumnavigate the commons, suitcase in hand. It worked. Within a few minutes, a man walked up to him and said something he couldn't understand. Dizzy replied "Hotel?"

The man smiled and motioned him to follow. They walked back past the car and Dizzy pointed to it and said, "Park okay?" The man replied, "Auto okay." A hundred feet later, they were at the door of a run-down hotel. The sign was unreadable, having little paint left on it from years of neglect. Only the H was partly visible. An elderly woman answered the door. The man said something and the woman gave Dizzy a kindly smile and beckoned him in. Dizzy thanked the man, who quietly disappeared into the rapidly approaching night.

The woman said, "Room, sleep?" Dizzy nodded and said, "Yes." He then remembered his horn in the car trunk. He put his suitcase down and said to the woman, "One minute." Returning with his horn, the woman opened the ancient registry on the desk. She handed him a pen and opened the inkwell. Dizzy signed his name with a pen and ink for the first time since high school. She asked him for his passport. Her demeanor changed slightly when she saw the country of origin. She flipped through the pages and, seeing all of the stamps from his tour, said, "Many places."

Dizzy paid the woman and was shown a small dark room on the second floor. An oil lamp by the bed provided the only light. A battered chest of drawers, a couple of coat hooks on one wall, and a worn down, stuffed chair were the only appointments. Still, he had a place to sleep. The only other problem was food. He pointed to his mouth and, remembering Washburn telling him that Romanian was related to Italian, said the word "mangiare."

The woman brought him back down stairs and into what looked like a small dining room. There were three tables, one of which was occupied by an elderly couple eating quietly. The place was dimly lit by candles and oil lamps. There were three sets of antlers and several paintings hanging on the faded, papered walls. Dizzy could hardly see anything at first but as his eyes adjusted to the dark, he began to look more closely. There were three old portraits on the wall ahead of him. At first, he didn't notice anything unusual, but halfway through his goulash, he came to realize that one of the portraits looked a little like his father. If that wasn't enough to set off his imagination, there was a small dagger stuck into the man's neck and the man had a look of horror on his face.

My God! thought Dizzy. *I wonder if that is a Polozenski.* A few minutes later, another elderly man walked into the dining room, seating himself at the third table. The hotel woman brought in another oil lamp and placed it on his table. The extra light made another portrait discernible. It was of a different person but it also bore a resemblance to Dizzy's father in a slightly different way, as if it could be portrait number one's brother. A chill went down his spine upon seeing that the second person also had a small knife stuck in his neck!

Dizzy wasn't sure and he certainly did not want to be seen staring at the portraits, but the knives seemed as if they were added later. However, it was too dark to really figure that one out. At this point, he just wanted to get to his room and not show his face anywhere until he could leave town. He wolfed his food down, paid the woman, and left the dining room. He was relieved that no one paid any attention to him.

In the presumed safety of his room, Dizzy lay on the bed trying to make sense of everything he had just seen. Were those two guys Polozenskis? Why the small daggers? Maybe Ekaterina was right and the Polozenski family got out fast because of some kind of unspeakable deeds they committed. Where did the letters fit in to all of this? He wasn't about to show them to anyone around here.

He didn't sleep well at all that night. He had a nightmare about people throwing small knives at him as he drove through villages. The knives were bouncing off the car with a hell of a noise and it woke him with a start. He saw that it was quite light outside, and his watch said 8:15. As he got ready to leave, he remembered that he needed gas. He picked up his passport from the woman at the door and pointing to his car, said, "Gas... Petrol?" She pointed in the direction that the car was headed, held up three fingers, and said "kilometer." Dizzy thought she was looking at him a little too closely, as though he reminded her of someone. Did she think she was looking at a Polozenski? He tried to fend off the emergence of paranoia in his mind. "Thank you," he said, and walked to the car.

Relieved, Dizzy started the car and drove slowly out of the common until he saw a road leading out of town. It was a real road, gravel, but better than the two fading ruts he had followed entering the town. He filled his tank about five minutes later from the strangest gas station he had ever seen. It was a small shack with a platform outside that had a dozen or so of different sized bottles of gasoline sitting on it. Most of them were corked wine bottles. The attendant was a scruffy individual who paid little attention to Dizzy but indicated that he could only sell him three bottles of gas. Dizzy had wanted to fill the tank but the man refused to sell him more than the three bottles. Dizzy suddenly had a thought...the Luckies! He reached under the seat and pulled out a pack and held it out to the man, pointing to one more bottle for the car. The man smiled and funnelled a fourth bottle into the tank.

Dizzy was on his way once more. As the sun warmed up the morning, he bounced along the road in toy car laughing to himself when he thought that he should have left his horn with Ekaterina and filled its case with Luckies. So far, they were more important than money.

However, the humour of that situation soon gave way to the image of the paintings. He couldn't shake the feeling that they were of some of his ancestors. What was the significance of the small daggers stuck in the side of their necks? Was the image symbolic or did they really die from small daggers? These dark thoughts slipped in and out of his mind until hours later, he drove through a small town and found a place to eat. He carried on until he thought to himself that he really have no idea where he was. He hadn't much cared before this. The map was under his seat. He stopped on the road but the map wasn't making much sense to him. He knew only that he was pointed east, given the sun's position. While he was stopped, he remembered all the twists and turns of the past few hours, so he decided to just drive on and ask someone whenever he stopped next. So far, he hadn't encountered more than a half dozen vehicles and one of those was a kind of buckboard wagon pulled by a couple of worn down nags.

He had driven past all kinds of turnoffs and he found that the road, much like yesterday, was beginning to get smaller again. He arrived at a "T" junction with no indication as to what road went where. He took the right turn and a half hour later, the road was identical to the one from the previous day. Two shallow ruts. It all looked distressingly familiar; however, in the distance he thought he could make out a village.

The village seemed no bigger than the first one, and it did not have the common. It was just one main street, which widened a little for about a hundred yards through the centre. The place looked a little abandoned. He drove slowly down the street, looking up the side streets for signs of habitation. All he saw were shuttered windows and closed doors. However, he did see the number 7 on more than one house. He found it odd but didn't pay too much attention to it. One side street revealed people in what looked like a square. He turned towards it. There were about a dozen people visible. A couple sat on a park bench, two ancient widows in black were emerging from a store with straw baskets. There was another hitching post and what looked like a gazebo landscaped with shrubs and a small flower garden. He also saw a very old car with a big dog sleeping next to it. A shabby looking black cab with a swaybacked, tired looking horse was stopped next to the car.

Suddenly, he heard and felt an awful clunk from under his car. The engine suddenly raced as he took his foot off the gas pedal. He had no power, even though the motor was running. Quickly steering the car to the side of the square, he stopped where he thought would be more or less out of the way and turned the engine off.

"Christ, what was that?" he said. The noise hadn't escaped the attention of the few people on the street nearby. One young man walked over to the car saying something. Dizzy got out and said back, "Sorry, I don't understand you." The man got down on his knees and looked under the car. He then got back up and, saying something, he pointed to his eye, then motioned to Dizzy to look for himself.

Dizzy got down on his knees, looked under the car, and saw one end of the driveshaft resting on the ground under the rear axle.

He knew he wasn't going anywhere. The universal joint had shattered and would have to be replaced by a mechanic. The exhilaration had now dissipated into annoyance.

He now knew where he would be staying for the next while, at least until the car got fixed. Now to find a place to sleep and eat. By now a half-dozen people were gathered around him and his car. So far, no one spoke in English. He held up his passport so they could at least see that he was American and maybe someone would be able to speak to him. Even a few rudimentary words would help break the ice.

A woman came up to the gathering and, looking at the passport, motioned for him to follow her. She started to walk away, beckoning him on. He grabbed his suitcase from the back seat and his horn from the trunk and started down the street behind her. She led him out of the square down a narrow lane. She said nothing and kept a steady pace for about five minutes, turning a corner and stopping in front of a large house on the edge of the village. It was an aging queen, early nineteenth century architecture made entirely of wood. It was somewhat dilapidated, with a few parts missing and in bad need of more than a little paint. A dim light could be seen from behind sheer curtains in a window to the left of the front door, which was massive with a leaded glass window in the shape of a complicated crucifix and flower theme. Dizzy had never seen anything quite like it, despite his travels.

The woman walked more slowly now up the front stairs. She stopped halfway, turned, and said to Dizzy while pointing to the front door, "Professor."

They walked up the large stairs together and the woman pulled a bell rope. Dizzy heard the tinkling of a small bell coming from inside. He heard the latch followed by the door opening. Standing in the doorway, a tall, bespectacled, distinguished looking gentleman faced them, at first looking a little puzzled. The woman said something to the man in the local language. Dizzy understood the word "American," but that was all.

The man smiled and said, "Welcome to my house. My name is Petroff Zablo. This young lady tells me your car broke down in the square."

"Yes, sir. My car did break down and you are the first person I have been able to speak to in English.

"My name is Dizzy Pollen. I am an American traveling around on a holiday."

"Please come in," said Zablo. "You must be tired and hungry. I'll have my servant fix you something."

"I don't want to impose."

"Please, don't worry. I haven't met anyone who speaks English in such a long time. I could use a little company and a chance to practice the language again."

Zablo turned to the woman, presumably thanking her, and sent her on her way. Dizzy was relieved to find someone who could speak English. He was trying to figure out his new host. Zablo looked about seventy or so and walked slightly stooped. He had somewhat unkempt hair, delicate features, and an obvious gentle manner.

"Thank you very much" Dizzy said to the woman. She gave him a slight smile, turned, and disappeared down the walk into the rapidly approaching night.

"You must stay here with me until your car is fixed. I have plenty of room. It's a large house and I live alone."

Dizzy looked around the room. The place looked very old, as did the furniture and just about everything else.

"Are you sure?"

"Yes, of course. My servant will show you to your room. Come back down here in twenty minutes and you can eat. I'm afraid there is no real hot water. My system broke down several years ago. It was an old complicated system and I have never had it repaired."

"Thank you very much. It is very generous of you."

The servant appeared in the room, and on Zablo's instructions took Dizzy's suitcase and horn.

"Just follow her and come back in twenty minutes."

The servant, a woman in her middle forties, started across the room and up a large curved staircase. Practically every step creaked and groaned as they ascended. He followed her down a darkened hallway with several rooms coming off it and into a room at the very end. The room had high ceilings, faded dark drapes on the windows. There was old oak furniture, a bed with a high dark wood headboard and a feeble light on the bedside table. The whole place smelled old and a little musty.

Dizzy began to feel a little creeped out. It looked exactly like some old place in a horror movie, where unspeakable things occur at night. He had never been in such an old house that looked like it could easily be haunted. He had seen Bela Lugosi as Dracula in a movie shortly before leaving the States, and while this wasn't a castle, there was a similar atmosphere. Dizzy didn't believe in ghosts, but the creaking antiquity of the place was a little unnerving. Everything he had seen so far looked frozen from a time long past.

Still, he was grateful for having found a place to stay, especially with someone with whom he could converse. Zablo spoke perfect English with quite a heavy accent, and had the air of being educated and worldly. Dizzy found his curiosity mounting about him and by the time he was supposed to return to the dining room, he had quite a few questions ready for the professor.

He opened his door into the dark musty hallway and could see light coming up the stairwell at the other end. He went to the head of the stairs and descended into the dining room just as the servant was placing a bowl of something at the table.

"Ah, you are right on time. Please sit down and enjoy your dinner." Zablo sat down at the opposite side of the table. It was a lot smaller than he imagined it should be. The room called for a large table seating sixteen people, but this one would only seat six.

"I trust you will find your room comfortable. I'm afraid everything in the place is quite antiquated."

"It is just fine, much more than I expected. I had no idea where I would sleep tonight. I wasn't even sure where I would stop until the car's driveshaft decided for me. It is dragging on the ground so I will have to find someone to fix it for me."

"We can worry about that tomorrow. Your car is perfectly safe where it is. I don't think we've ever had a car stolen in the village. By tomorrow, it will be the biggest news in town for the last six months and you will have a half dozen people offer to repair it for you."

"Mr. Zablo, you speak impeccable English. Where did you learn?"

"In Germany and London. I taught English and history in Leipzig for thirty years."

"The young woman who brought me to your house, the only word she said to me was 'professor.'"

"She is right. I was a professor and have been retired for many years."

"Were you born around here?"

"In this very house. It has been in my family since it was built in 1804. And where do you come from?"

"I was born near San Francisco in California. My family immigrated to the Unites States somewhere around 1880. In fact, my grandfather, who was the one who immigrated, came from somewhere around here. I have no idea exactly where though. None of my family ever spoke of their origins. I just know we came from the old country, which is what North American immigrants always seem to call whatever part of Europe they came from."

"Then your name isn't Dizzy Pollen?"

"No, I was born Josef John Pollen. Dizzy has been my nickname for as long as I can remember. My great grandfather, who immigrated, was named Josef Polozenski. It was a practice of the immigration people at the Ellis Island port of entry to the USA to shorten complicated European names as the average immigration officer would not know how to spell or pronounce these names."

Dizzy did not, at first, notice the expression change on Zablo's face. When he did, he asked, "You look a little taken aback."

"Do you know anything about your family here?"

"Absolutely nothing except that Josef emigrated from somewhere around here in 1880. That is really the only thing I know. I didn't even know of the existence of this country until my high school years. No one in my family ever talked about the past. Any questions I ever asked were met with evasive answers at best and silence at worst. The only reason I am here is that our band tour ended in Bucharest and I decided on a whim to visit the place."

"Interesting."

"I am a jazz musician who has played music all of my life and travelled all over the States, and this is my first trip to Europe. Since this was as close as I was ever going to get to the fabled old country, I decided to visit. Does the name Polozenski mean anything to you?"

"My dear young man, I wouldn't know where to start. Polozenski is a famous, or perhaps I should say an infamous, name around here. Are you sure you want to hear any of this? I know of an English expression, something about letting the cat out of the bag. You may not like what I tell you."

"No, that's okay. Whatever happened here a century ago can scarcely have much or anything to do with me. I am, as you know, at least three generations removed from this place."

"In your country, being a relatively new one, three or four generations may seem like a long time, but here, that is nothing. Generations are short and memories are long. The concept of time is very different here."

"As I said, I'm okay with that. I have often wondered about this place and my ancestry, but I was never going to learn much from my parents."

"All right. After your dinner, I will pour us some drinks and I will ask you to open your mind to the possibility of the impossible. I will go and warm up the study with a fire so we can be comfortable."

CHAPTER 8

As delicious as the bowl of stew was, Dizzy hardly noticed it. His mind couldn't stop wondering what stories he was about to hear from Professor Zablo. Were his ancestors highwaymen, or cattle rustlers? Maybe they were burned at the stake for something or other. Did one of them assassinate a politician? Ekaterina's words about the possibility of his family having to flee the country came back to him. Were they on the wrong side of a political struggle at the time? Depending on how the conversation went, Dizzy thought he might bring up the letters.

He found himself gulping down the goulash in anticipation of the conversation to come. Finishing the last spoonful, he got up and walked into the study. A warm fire was lit in the enormous stone fireplace. There were large bookcases on two of the walls. They were filled with old volumes of various sizes. Some looked like they contained the wisdom of ages, with ancient brown vellum jackets. More than a few had Cyrillic writing on their spines. Some had beautiful spines with writing that Dizzy had never seen. He later found out they were books written in Arabic.

A large oil painting mounted in an elaborate gilded frame hung over the fireplace. It was of a castle on the side of a hill at dusk. It was painted with some skill, as the light was perfect, giving the whole scene a sense of the foreboding. He was mesmerized by it. His thoughts flashed back to the Dracula movie while he wondered if the castle was real or a figment of the artist's imagination.

His thoughts were interrupted by Professor Zablo.

"I hope the goulash was satisfactory."

"Yes, it was delicious. Just what I needed. Thank you very much."

"Let me pour you a drink. I have some fine old brandy I keep for special occasions, and this certainly qualifies. An English speaking visitor named Polozenski in my own home!"

The professor poured the libation from a cut glass decanter into two snifters. He passed one to Dizzy and held up his own in a toast. "To your health."

"And to yours," replied Dizzy.

They both took a sip. Dizzy was impressed with its smoothness. It was obviously old and of high quality. He settled into an overstuffed chair of worn dark green velour. The professor sat opposite him, putting his glass down on a side table.

"I'm not quite sure where to start. I suppose I should tell you a little about this place. This village has been here since time immemorial. I mean that literally. You remember how I told you that the concept of time is different here? Well, no one knows how old this village is. The nearest anyone can come up with is about eighteen centuries."

"In America, some place that is three hundred years is really old. We, as you know, have nothing on that time scale. How do you know the age of the village?"

"We can only guess at it through legend, tombstone dates, a few records, and some family histories. I guess we depend heavily on legend, as there are few surviving written records about any of this.

One thing is certain: the village does go back a long way. There are about a dozen families living around here that claim a direct lineage back a thousand years.

"Is the Polozenski family one of them?"

"Yes, the Polozenskis go back probably as far back as any of them. You will be astounded to know that to the best of my knowledge, you are the first Polozenski to set foot in this village in well over fifty years. Your great grandfather was probably the last to live here, and as you tell me, he immigrated to America in 1880. You can see why I was taken aback when you told me your family name."

"Good Lord, that is astounding. If Josef Polozenski left here in 1880, how did the name trigger such a swift reaction?"

"The Polozenski family achieved a certain... how shall I say it? Notoriety, I think, is the word I am looking for."

"Were we involved in cattle rustling or bank robbery, or something like that?"

"This, I'm afraid, is going to get complicated, difficult, and intriguing—to say the least."

"I'm all ears."

"The Polozenskis go back longer than anyone can remember, but our history tells us that in the middle ages, they were a powerful family with a vast tract of land under their rule. They were feudal lords and were feared for their ruthlessness and iron fists. You didn't want to cross paths with them. They would kill someone for little reason or provocation. Life under Polozenski rule was harsh and terrifying. As time went on, their rule was challenged and there were several small wars and battles. Little by little, they lost territory here and there, and eventually their rule ended. They were run out of the castle and the land they had ruled over was re-distributed into small parcels and taken over by families who had fought against them."

"When did all of this happen?"

"The last altercations took place in the latter part of the nineteenth century. By this time, the Polozenski name was truly hated and Josef, your grandfather, fled from here for fear of his life. He was the last surviving member of the family and he slipped away one day, never to be seen again. It was always assumed that he was killed and buried in the wilderness somewhere, but no one ever found a body or a grave and so he passed into history."

"If you look above the fireplace, you are looking at the Polozenski castle. Your ancestral home."

Dizzy looked up at the painting he had noticed when he first entered the room. There was a reason that the painting was so somber and foreboding. The artist would have heard all the stories and painted his work capturing its dark history.

"I think I could use another drink."

"Of course," said the professor. He poured him another and topped up his own.

"That's a lot to take in. My family being ruthless and despotic in the Middle Ages. Here, I thought cattle rustling or bank robbing would be the worst."

"Listen, if you had never come here or just drove right through, you might have never found out about your family. But now you are learning all of this and I'm guessing that is why you came here in the first place. For you, none of this happened until this very moment. For long-time families here, it's still fresh. I told you that the passage of time in a place like this is different from in the New World. For some of these people, the hatred they feel toward the Polozenski family is alive and well and even today, can be the subject of late night drunken conversations in the taverns."

"But all of this happened long ago."

"No matter. Five hundred years is not a long time here. You see, the people around here have little or no education at all. They are good people but with no sophistication, and many of them have never travelled farther than a few kilometers from where they were born. They live with all manner of superstition, belief in the occult, ghosts—you name it. I don't think there are more than five people in the village who could read a simple newspaper column. They are good, honest, and hard working people. Your car will be fixed by someone who can't read a word but can fix some fairly complicated piece of machinery because they have no choice. They keep old farm machinery and trucks going without the benefit of a supply of spare parts. They are extremely clever with things like that."

"Then I guess it wouldn't be a good idea to let anyone know who I really am."

"You are absolutely right about that one. I know this sounds harsh and it is, but if the village finds out that you are a descendant of the Polozenski family, the great grandson of Josef, I can say with a great degree of certainly that you might be killed!"

"You can't be serious!"

"I am. Furthermore, if the village found out that I had a Polozenski as a house guest, I would probably suffer a similar fate. Now, I apologize if I have scared you, but I am telling you this out of concern for you. At the same time, given my own situation, your secret is my secret and none of this will ever leave this room. I don't hold anything against you for something that happened centuries ago. I understand the situation but the good people of the village would not."

"I guess I have to ask whether your family suffered under the Polozenski rule also."

"Yes, they did, but they fared no better or worse than anyone else. I don't have any details, but apparently a few of my ancestors did not escape the tyranny of the Polozenskis way back long before I was born. But no one really has details. After five hundred years, details are forgotten, circumstances are blurred, and nothing is left but the memory of a memory of a wronged forgotten ancestor. They remember to not forget, but they don't know what it is that they remember. I wish to assure you that I have absolutely no ill will towards you for those events."

Dizzy smiled. "That's good to know. I realize that I could have walked into the lion's den."

"That's true, except that I am educated and well travelled. I don't believe in curses and superstition, or unreasonable hatred for events that happened long before I was born. It's all in the past and will stay there, as far as I am concerned. Holding a grudge for five centuries seems a complete waste of time and soul. But the fantastic part is yet to come."

"Are you telling me there's more?"

"Yes, I'm afraid so. A lot more. But that's enough for right now. I'm sure you have much to think about and you could probably use a good's night sleep. I will take you around tomorrow and you can see for yourself where you have wound up. You should be comfortable in your room. We will have something to eat whenever you come downstairs and I'll show you the sights of our great city." He was smiling.

"Thank you again, Professor, for your generous hospitality and for the history lesson. I do indeed have much to think about. Good night."

"Until tomorrow."

Dizzy ascended the creaky living room stairway and walked slowly toward his room. It was darker now and he had forgotten to leave a light on. He was in total darkness by the time he had reached the halfway point. He tried to be quiet, not knowing whether anyone else was sleeping. There had been the servant but he hadn't been aware of her leaving the house after she served him the goulash.

He slowed down even more and put his right hand ahead of him to touch the door. He had an idea of how far away it was and at one point it felt like he should be there, but he kept walking. He was sure he should be touching his door so when his knee touched the foot of the bed, he received quite a fright. He felt down and touched the blankets and realized that he had walked through his open door. He thought back and remembered that he had closed it. He felt his way around to the night table and groped around gingerly for the light. He jumped again when he touched the frills of the shade. He had forgotten those, but found the switch and was relieved when it actually worked.

He closed the door and was happy to see that it had a small bolt to keep it locked. The low watt bulb with the red shade gave the room a ghostly glow. He undressed, crawled into the bed, and turned the light out, making the room absolutely pitch black. The darkness and silence enveloped him. There probably wasn't a car around for fifty miles. Ekaterina slipped into his thoughts briefly. He also started to ruminate about Zablo's words but fell into a deep sleep almost instantly.

At one point he awoke thinking he had heard something. He was disoriented and it took a few seconds to remember where he was. He lay perfectly still and the sound, undefinable, it came and went.

He heard something faint, as if carried on the wind. Dizzy sat up and listened with as much intensity as his musician's ear could muster. He heard it again. This time he thought he detected a sustained note as if it was a cello or viola. It wasn't a horn. It disappeared once more, only to return a minute later a little louder, but it stopped a few seconds later. Then nothing.

He awoke from a deep sleep with sunlight entering the room through a space between the curtain and the edge of the window. The slot produced only the slightest beam but it aimed directly at his eye. He lay there a few minutes and started to reminisce about the conversation with the professor.

His car had accidentally broken down in a small village only to find out that he was the personification of evil of their legends and history. He wasn't sure what would come next but the professor had promised more information. He would ask him about the painting. Dizzy's curiosity would ensure that he stayed around long enough to get to the bottom of whatever was coming next. Then he remembered the fleeting music in the darkness. What was that all about? Remembering the music really woke him up.

He got out of bed, dressed, and wandered downstairs. Professor Zablo was seated at the dining room table with an urn of coffee and a book.

"Good morning, Dizzy, I hope you slept well."

"Thank you. I did. It was very dark and very quiet. City person that I am, I almost found it too quiet."

The servant entered the room and placed a basket of what looked like scones on the table and poured Dizzy a cup of coffee.

His mind was full of questions and thoughts pertaining to the evening's conversation but he thought he would let it go for a while and see what the professor would have in store.

"Professor, I don't know if I was dreaming or not, but I could almost swear I heard a bowed instrument being played in the middle of the night. You weren't playing, were you?"

Zablo put his book down and marked his spot.

"No, but if you are asking me this, it must be because you heard something."

"I don't know what time it was but I thought I heard something like a cello playing, maybe a violin."

"You probably did. It happens periodically but my old ears can't pick it up anymore. But yes, it is there."

"Who is playing in the middle of the night?"

"No one knows. Many people have heard it but no one has ever been able to discover where it comes from. It's just there. The interesting thing is that it is part of the many legends in the village. It has been heard for generations."

"That's impossible!"

"Of course it is, yet it happens. My father heard it. I used to hear it as a younger man and my father told me his father heard it. You should know that everyone in the village has heard it at one time or another."

"Has anyone ever tried to follow it? That might not be too hard to do."

"People have tried but failed. If anyone ever discovered where it came from, I'm sure the whole village would know." He laughed. "It would be bigger news then your broken down car!

When you have finished your coffee, I will take you on a walk around the village. I think you will find it interesting."

A quarter hour later found the professor and Dizzy walking towards the broken car. Dizzy was relieved to see that it hadn't been touched. The professor, sensing his concern, assured him that the car could stay there for a year and no one would ever touch it.

The square looked almost empty. Its centre was raised about three feet higher than the road. The flattened top was landscaped with grass and flowers. A stone retaining wall held everything together. Dizzy hadn't noticed too many details the day before when he followed the woman to the professor's house. She walked fast and he just wanted to keep up. There were a few people on the street. They all respectfully acknowledged the professor when he passed and offered Dizzy a smile. Passing a small church, the professor led him up a path and made a turn onto a pathway. It came off the back corner of the church and led into a field filled with wildflowers. It was the village cemetery.

"Your ancestors are buried here. You will see the Polozenski name on quite a few of the headstones. Please do not linger over any of your ancestral graves. Pay equal attention to them all. I would hate to think someone notice you pay attention to all of the Polozenski stones and ignore the rest. You can be sure that someone, somewhere is watching us. It is just that way in the village."

They walked up and down the rows. Some markers were so old there was no discernible writing on them. Dizzy came across a half-dozen headstones from his ancestors as well as an equal number of stones bearing the name Zablo. They had this much in common, at least. Their ancestors inhabited the same cemetery.

One corner was fenced off from the rest of it. It had maybe about twenty-five visible markers.

Dizzy asked about this.

"That is the forbidden area," Zablo said. "We cannot go there. I will explain later. We should go now."

More mysteries: a cemetery with a forbidden area, faint music at night, the almost certainty that they were being watched. Things were getting stranger by the moment.

"Later we will look at the castle."

"Is it still there?"

"It lies about two kilometers from here just behind that small mountain. It is still there and is inhabited by a family who claimed it after your great grandfather left. No one really wanted to live there given its history, but this one family did and so they took it over about five years after Josef left. It has been occupied by the same family since then."

"Do you know them?"

"Yes, I do. They are called Bujak. They keep to themselves mostly. Hardly anyone ever sees them anywhere. Very occasionally, one of their servants comes to the market. The only time anyone sees the Bujak family is once every seven years at the castle. But don't ask. I will tell you tonight."

After dinner, Dizzy's mind again full of questions, they retired to the study. The same routine was followed with the fine brandy. They shared a toast to each other's health and friendship.

The professor began. "I can only guess at all the questions you may have since you arrived. Things I have told you seem impossible or at least very strange and, how do you say? Spooky. Is that the right word?"

"Yes. I can't say I haven't been spooked by some of the things I have heard. It has certainly made me curious and I suppose you are going to tell me more."

"I am. I really don't know where to start, but let's try the cemetery.

There's nothing really unusual there except for the fenced off area. Everybody buried in that section has died after attending an event at the castle. This event happens once every seven years. This is a kind of ritual that has been going on since forever. On the night of the new moon in November every seven years, a gathering is held at the castle. Again, no one knows how this started. It's just there and has been there since the time before memory. Everybody living in what used to be the tract of land held by the Polozenski family attends. There is food and wine and music. Generally speaking, it is a happy soirée—until the end of the evening. Then, a special orchestra plays one song and everyone dances. The dance ends on the stroke of midnight, and one of the participants will die before sunrise. Only one, but it never fails."

Dizzy's letters sprang to mind. This had to be what they were about. He decided to ask the Professor.

"Professor, is this called the Saltatio Mortis?"

The professor looked stunned for a brief moment before regaining his composure.

"How do you know about that? It seems you must know more than you are letting on."

"Not really, Professor. I have some old letters I found in my mother's attic. I tried to have them translated in the States, but they were partially in an antique dialect unknown to the translator. I also showed them to someone in Bucharest but ran up against the same problem except that there is mention of a Saltatio Mortis and both people called this a 'dance of death.' There were references to a ritual but no sense could be made out of most of the writings. So are we both talking about the same thing here?

"Yes, we are. I am curious about those letters. You said they were very old"

"I only know that from the brittleness of the paper. The paper and ink are faded as they had been stored for a long time." Would you like to see them?"

"Yes if you have them with you. I may be able to translate some of their content."

Dizzy retrieved the letters from his room. The professor studied them carefully for a few minutes.

You are right, they are mostly written in an almost extinct dialect that no more than a half dozen old people would know around here. And they would be illiterate. I've never seen any attempt to write in this language. But it does indeed mention the Saltatio Mortis a few times." And it looks like you may have lost a grand uncle at one of these events.

"Is this really true? How can that happen? That is really crazy. Why would anyone attend this bal macabre if that is what will happen? You are most certainly making this up, Professor!"

"No, I am not. This really does happen. This is probably the hardest part to explain about the whole bal macabre, as you call it. The attendees are compelled to go to this event, not by any exterior force or coercion, but they all attend—if not willingly, then by some irresistible urge to cheat death. It is like a giant game of Russian roulette, except that instead of one bullet in a six-chambered revolver, the odds decrease to one in about four hundred. It would be easy, I suppose, not to attend, but for whatever reason, few people ever choose to stay away. Apparently, some do if they have lost a family member or loved one recently before the event, but eventually they will return to cheat death one more time."

"That is enough to make my head spin! Tell me, Professor, do you attend?"

"I will get to that in a moment. First, let me say that everyone wears a costume and elaborate masks. Every step is taken to ensure that each attendee is so carefully costumed that no one can recognize even their best friend or brother or spouse."

"My God, that must take a great deal of preparation and planning."

"They have seven years to get ready. You are right. No effort is spared in this preparation. Now, as to whether I take part or not, the answer is yes. I have done so for most of my life, but in my capacity as a musician. For some reason, the musicians seem to be exempt from the death, so I get to be witness and be part of the ball without the risk of dying from it."

"Wouldn't everyone then want to be in the orchestra and be spared this brush with death?"

"I suppose, but then again, it is the act of surviving the event that is the attraction. To these people, it would be Russian roulette with an unloaded gun. What would be the point? You could pull the trigger all you want but nothing will ever happen."

Dizzy thought about this for a moment and could see the professor's point. You wouldn't play Russian roulette without any bullets in the gun.

"You are a musician?" asked Dizzy.

"I play the violin. I have a degree in music as well as in English and history. I have never played very much professionally, just a few recitals here and there, and sometimes in a string quartet. Mostly what you would call amateur situations. I was more interested in musical theory and history than in performance."

"Things are getting stranger by the moment, but I am glad to hear that you are a musician. That is another thing we have in common."

"Another thing?"

"We seem to have just about an equal number of ancestors buried in the cemetery."

Zablo laughed quite heartily. He wasn't expecting that one. He was beginning to like Dizzy. This newcomer had weathered all of what the professor had told him and kept calm about it. By the same token, Dizzy was beginning to like the professor. He had never met someone like him before and had certainly never heard anything like what he had heard in the last twenty-four hours. He kept thinking that things couldn't get much weirder.

◆ ◆ ◆

"Professor, I have something else I want to ask you about.

I entered the country two days ago and stopped for the night in a small village. I don't really know where it was but I stayed in an ancient inn that had no electricity. Everything was illuminated by candles or oil lamps. I ate dinner in a small dining room, if you can call it that. It only had three tables and was very dark inside. I could hardly see my food on the table in front of me. However, when my eyes became accustomed to the darkness and after the innkeeper brought another oil lamp, I noticed two portraits on the wall in front of me. Both of these portraits bore some resemblance to my late father. The distressing part is that both people in the paintings had a small dagger implanted in their necks! I couldn't tell whether the daggers were painted on after the fact or if that was how the portraits were originally painted. I quickly finished my meal, went to my room, and was relieved to get out of there in the morning."

"Did the hotel have an old sign that only had the "H" remaining?"

"Yes, that's exactly it."

"You were in Stepina. That is only forty kilometers from here."

"Forty kilometers? But I drove most of the day getting to this place."

"Aha, you must have gone in a very large circle. You didn't take any side roads and you came to a junction and took a right turn just before arriving in this village."

"That's right."

Zablo smiled. "There are next to no signs and you could have been here in about an hour.

I know where you stayed. The portraits you speak of are two of your ancestors.

They were the last known inhabitants of the castle. They were caught trying to escape and whoever killed them did so in the same way the Polozenskis killed their enemies. They would stab their victims with a small knife, in the neck being careful not to hit an artery so that death came slowly and painfully. As I have said, your ancestors were not nice people."

"Jesus! I thought the innkeeper woman was looking at me a little closely as I was leaving."

"I suppose I should tell you that the new moon of November is but three days away. I am going to put you to the final test, so to speak."

Dizzy braced himself. He had heard so many strange stories and was beginning to know that the professor probably had something really crazy up his sleeve.

"Not until I've poured myself another drink and sit down."

"Probably a good idea. You will want to be sitting for this one."

The decanter was opened one more time and the professor poured them both a stiff refill.

"Now, think about this: Would you like to join me in the orchestra? You would get to witness and take part in this."

"WHAT?"

"There are usually between fifteen and twenty people in the orchestra. They are also costumed so there is no danger of discovery. I have the music here and you could study it, and I can show you anything you need to know. The music isn't particularly difficult. We can go over it all. There is only one piece of music played by this special band all evening. It runs about twelve minutes and has to end on the stroke of midnight. The music starts at exactly 11:48 in order to end at midnight."

"How could you expect to get away with having me in the orchestra? Wouldn't someone find out? Besides, my trumpet has never been seen around here. It is a French trumpet, a rather recent one, and I'm sure there is nothing like it here. A musician could spot it easily."

"Most of the instruments are disguised by wrapping them in ribbons or fabric. Some have been painted and so forth. That wouldn't be a problem. Besides, think about it: you would be the only outsider to have ever done this. It would easily be the most interesting musical experience you could ever have—in a macabre way, of course. You would be safe with me. We just have to make sure we stay close for the evening so we don't get separated. Some people never speak, so if you were spoken to and didn't respond, it would be the norm rather than unusual.

Also, the musicians usually come in a separate entry leading directly to the stage, so you don't ever have to socialize in any way. We can go in at the last minute and just play the piece, and leave as soon as we've finished. It's nice not to be around when someone dies. This can happen at any time between the end of the dance and first light."

Incredibly, the idea appealed to Dizzy. All of this was so far-fetched and seemed impossible, yet here it was unfolding before him. Until now, his life had been normal by his standards.

Now this! It all seemed so surreal and yet it held a certain allure. He wouldn't be responsible for anyone's death. Someone would die whether he played or not. It was written in the stars. For him, it would be the most unusual gig he would ever play. It would, of course, be something he could never talk about with anyone—except the professor.

"Professor Zablo, I can scarcely believe what I'm about to say, but I will accept your proposition.

What happens now?"

"For tonight, nothing. But tomorrow I shall teach you the piece and we'll go and have a look at the castle. We should retire now. Again, you have much to think about. I do hope you have a good sleep. If you should, for whatever reason choose to not take part in this, I will certainly understand and I will not hold you to it. Nor will I have a negative response to such a decision. I think I can recognize the apparent insanity of what I have asked of you and you will need a little time to consider it."

CHAPTER 9

Dizzy lay in the black quiet of his room for quite a while before sleep overtook him, mulling over what the professor had revealed and especially the offer to join the orchestra. He wasn't sure he could believe what the professor said about someone dying because of a piece of music being played. It was contrary to everything Dizzy had ever thought about music. It brought happiness, melancholy, and all human emotions, but to have music directly kill someone was incomprehensible. How was it possible? He could understand if an individual was so sad or depressed, a really melancholic piece of music might push him or her over the edge and life might end in a suicide, but the professor did not use that word, nor did he infer it. Someone would die before sunrise. There were too many questions to answer, and Dizzy eventually drifted into an uncomfortable sleep.

He awoke at what may have been between 4:30 and 5:00 a.m. He eased gently into a sleepy consciousness and began listening intently for any music like the previous night. Amazingly enough, within a few minutes, he heard the cello again. It was a present but indistinct melody. This time he went over to the window and opened it. He tried to catch a direction. However, there was no change in the volume, nor could he tell where it was coming from. He then realized it seemed to be inside him. He thought he was hearing it internally. That wasn't completely unusual. He often had tunes running through his mind and was sometimes unable to shake them. A few minutes later, the ethereal music faded, and Dizzy returned to his bed, wondering about it all until sleep descended upon him.

"Good morning, professor." He had slept a couple more hours and after, went downstairs.

"Good morning. I trust you slept soundly."

"I did, thank you. I heard that music again but I went back to sleep. It was about the same time as I heard on the previous night."

"I haven't any better explanation for any of it than I did yesterday." Zablo smiled.

"After breakfast, we will go over the piece. I have recovered my music and we can start. I am anxious for your opinion. I have a small music room through that door."

Within a half hour, Dizzy had his horn and they went the music room. It had a high ceiling, an uncarpeted hardwood floor, several music stands, four stringed instruments hanging on one of the walls. He had never seen the likes of these instruments. One of them had more strings then he had ever seen on any one instrument. Before he had a chance to ask about them, the professor placed a large music score in front of him on one of the stands. Dizzy stared at it for a few moments. "Which part is mine for the trumpet?"

"I am not really sure. I play the violin, so let us just start playing and I'm sure you will find your part."

The professor started and Dizzy followed. The score was a little strange to him but he more or less kept up for most of the piece. It was one of the most unusual pieces of music he had ever heard. It was hauntingly beautiful, with several unusual passages. He was going to need to run this through many more times before getting comfortable with it. The professor was pleasantly surprised that Dizzy had done so well given the strangeness of the music. After the third time through, it was starting to make sense.

He asked the professor if he minded if he made a few notes on the score for reminders in some of the tricky spots.

"Of course. Whatever you need to facilitate this. I realize how strange all this is for you but when there are another fifteen players, it will sound as it should. The other musicians usually are very good and have been rehearsing this. I haven't until now, but we don't have anything else to do until we play and we'll have our parts down perfectly. The bandmaster will conduct it so we will all play as one. It really is a beautiful piece."

"Who composed it and when?"

"Legend has it that it started in the eleventh century and was re-written here and there. Again, so much is shrouded in time. Things just happen because no one remembers when they didn't happen. I guess that is an unusual concept for you coming from a modern country."

"Yes, but in the older regions of our country, there are also things lost to history. It is just the much longer time line here."

"I agree. We have done enough here for now. I will take you to see the castle."

Dizzy was anxious to see his ancestral home but also apprehensive at the same time. The painting over the fireplace in the study had made a powerful impression on him. He worried it may be dangerous to be seen there, as the professor had mentioned that someone was probably watching them in the cemetery the day before.

"As long as no one discovers that you are a Polozenski, we are all right. It is not against any law for me to have a visitor. Mind you, it has been a long time and people are curious. Besides, I have an old car. If it will start, then we will drive around the place. There is a road around the castle and we can view it from a couple of hundred meters away. It will give you an idea of its size. It's not quite as big as it looks in the painting, but looks are deceiving and its placement in the landscape gives it the foreboding atmosphere. Sometimes, I think it was built to look frightening to intimidate anyone who wandered too near, but as castles go in this part of the world, it is just another among many, and they all have dark histories. None of them would have been great places to live in. The inhabitants of these places are afforded a little more protection than that of the average peasant, but it is not a healthy life. The ever-present chill and dampness make everyone susceptible to illnesses and arthritis. You won't be able to see because of the costumes, but the inhabitants all look unhealthy and half dead."

"Delightful," said Dizzy. "I can't believe the world I have wandered into."

The professor laughed. "I must say you are taking it quite well. It must be a shock to you."

"Yes it is, but you only live once and in my travels around my own country, I have seen and heard of all kinds of unspeakable things that have been equally shocking. It is just that I have only peripherally witnessed them. Here, I feel I am wandering into the middle of something I have no comprehension of but I strangely feel quite safe—a lot safer than I felt traveling in the deep south of my own country."

The car started all right. The professor sat at the wheel, manipulating the spark advance and throttle. Dizzy turned the motor with a large crank and the aging beast sputtered into life one more time. It was a boat-tailed Citroen from about 1925, an open car well-worn from many miles of driving over bad roads. Dizzy was quite surprised that it started at all. They drove slowly out of the village and onto what amounted to no more than two ruts as a road. Heading for the small mountain a few kilometers away, he found the land-scape an unusual colour with trees and shrubbery he had never seen before. A few minutes later, he noticed where the road split in the distance.

"That's the road doubling back on itself. The castle is directly behind the mountain."

The professor took the right fork. The road steepened and the car struggled with the hill, even when geared down to second gear. When the car leveled out, the road turned to the right through a small wooded area with the tree branches forming a tunnel for about fifty meters. They emerged from the tunnel with the castle not two hundred meters away.

"Jesus!" said Dizzy.

It was right out of the painting. The artist had made nothing up. It was exactly as portrayed in oils in the professor's wall. The artist was even more skilled than Dizzy had thought. He imagined what the place would look like at dusk, which would be much more foreboding than on a sunny day like they were enjoying.

They didn't stop. That, explained the professor, would be unwise. They kept driving and Dizzy never took his eyes off the place for the full five minutes that it was in view.

He laughed nervously. "We are going to play a gig in there?"

"That's right," said Zablo. "It will be the gig of your life." He was smiling.

"Somehow, I feel you consider this less serious than I do," said Dizzy.

"Probably. It has been going on for so long and the outcome of a participant dying before sunrise is not new to anyone around here. It is just what happens every seven years. Whether you and I take part in it or not, the outcome will not change. No one will die because you and I are going to play the piece. An unfortunate person will die because the piece was played at the exact time and place. We are not responsible for anyone's demise. Some inexplicable curse or something is responsible. We just play the music, and even if some lightning bolt of rationality struck everyone and this ritual was cancelled, the cultural repercussions would be too great. People live and prepare for this event throughout all of their lives. Every seven years, they spin the chamber and wait for the bullet to strike.

If it doesn't strike, then the survivors experience a renewal in their hard lives and drudgery. Their appreciation of life approaches the euphoric for a while and after a while when it subsides, preparations are begun for the next *bal macabre* a few years down the road.

It would inflict a great psychological depression on these people if they did no go through this event. It is like a cleansing for them."

Dizzy sat in silence but he could see the professor had a point. Who was this American jazz musician to pass judgement on anything like this when at the same time coloured people were forbidden just about all of the freedoms and amenities that his own country had to offer to him, simply because his skin was white. These people were much freer than millions in his country and if they chose to engage in this ritual, then so be it.

"We should practice the piece some more. I want to get it right. I don't want to give myself away by blowing a wrong note somewhere."

"You won't. As a jazz musician, you will figure out any tricky situation that pops up. Some people make mistakes but I doubt that any of them can think their way through the music like you can. It's what you have done for a living, after all."

"That's right, and I have been good at that stuff forever. I was blessed with a great ear. I did nothing to acquire it, it was always there, but I still want to do more work on it."

"Of course."

After dinner, they ran through the piece another three times. Dizzy felt comfortable with it and was on the verge of having much of it committed to memory. The professor was amazed at Dizzy's ability to learn something so fast. Though a good musician, Zablo had never considered improvisation as an option in music. It just never existed for him.

Meanwhile, Dizzy was becoming intrigued with the piece and set about memorizing his part. He took the score to bed that night and just stared at it for a half hour before falling asleep. It is how he learned music sometimes; he just read it over and over, playing it in his mind. It was like memorizing a poem or a passage from the Bible.

He didn't hear the music in the middle of the night this time. He was thankful for that, as he did not want any distraction. Upon awakening, he played the piece in his mind and to his surprise, there were only two small parts missing from his memory.

He corrected that after breakfast and soon the piece was fully committed to memory. At least his part. He hadn't really paid a great deal of attention to the other parts, as he didn't want to clutter his brain with stuff he wouldn't play. However, he still didn't know what any of this would sound like with other musicians in the mix. At this point, he felt confident knowing his part and would deal with any unusual musical situations if and when they arose.

"How are we going to get there?"

"I'm afraid we will have to walk. It only will take thirty minutes. My car would be recognized.

We will leave the house at about 11 o'clock. We will see people on the road, but there will be no communication. Everyone we see will look as bizarre as us. It's really quite a sight when you will see everyone in the one room."

"I can imagine," said Dizzy. "Well actually, I can't."

He had stepped into such a strange world causing him to lose all track of time. Working backward, he concluded he had been on Moldavian soil for four days. He had completely forgotten he had a broken down car in the village. On the morning of the new moon of November, the professor's doorbell sounded.

"Go into the study," said the professor. "Just close the door and I'll see who this is and what they want."

Dizzy became a little apprehensive but obeyed. He closed the door behind him and waited quietly. He heard the professor talking to someone with a male voice. Was it a nosy neighbour or the police?

There was a short burst of laughter and the door closed. Dizzy could hear the professor walking back towards the study. The door opened and the professor said, "That was someone who will fix your car for you. He will try to do it tomorrow. He says he can get the part you need and he will install it. He will do it right there where it is stopped. He says he can jack it up and fix it that way.

"I didn't quite expect that," said Dizzy.

"Actually, I did," said the professor. "I just didn't know it would happen on the day after the ball at the castle."

They both took it easy that day. At Dizzy's request, they ran the piece two more times. The second time, he turned away from the music stand and played it all from memory without a single note missing. All twelve minutes of it. The professor was astounded. "You mean that whole piece is in your head?"

"That's right. I can't wait to hear it in its entirety with everyone playing together. But don't worry, I will keep the score in front of me. I might be a little nervous and my memory slips a little sometimes. I won't take any kind of a chance. I'll follow the score."

After dinner, the professor packed the score in his briefcase. Dizzy was a little apprehensive for what was about to come. Noticing this, the professor assured him everything would be okay. They didn't have anything to worry about. However, that was like someone telling you not to be nervous before playing Carnegie Hall. There is no use in that; nerves always play their part. Dizzy was okay with the music, but his apprehension stemmed from the cultural aspect of it all, especially the fact that someone would die after they played the piece. This just wasn't in his cultural sphere. It all landed on his head so fast, and he hadn't had the time to digest it.

Still, he thought, *if I back out now, I will disappoint the professor and regret not experiencing it.* He resolved to go ahead with it and that any death would not be his fault. It was an acceptable rationale. Besides, he was so curious about all of this. What would the castle and the ball look like? How would this unusual piece sound with a full orchestra?

At about 10:30 the professor said, "Time to get dressed. Let's see how we look." He did not seem at all apprehensive about this. In fact, Dizzy got the impression that he was really looking forward to playing this gig, as if it was a wedding. He was in a good mood, that's for sure.

He couldn't help himself. "Professor, you seem to be in a very good mood for attending such a somber event."

"Nonsense, this event, despite the outcome for one unfortunate individual, is quite a happy occasion for all of the attendees. I told you it was a cleansing and a rejuvenation of their lives. You will hear much laughter and mirth. The musicians have all practiced the piece and it is a great matter of pride that they play it perfectly. The costumes will be out of this world and visually it will be something you couldn't have ever dreamt up.

I am also extremely happy that you are here sharing this with me, especially since we will play music together. In my own small way, I feel that I will have struck a blow against the forces of darkness that still hover over this land."

"I don't understand."

"One day, this ritual will come to an end. There will be no more bal macabre. One day in the future, people won't think any of this is a good idea. They will stop when whatever passes for civilization gradually comes over this land. People will move into the new century. It's inevitable but it will take its time. For some unknown reason, my bringing a Polozenski descendant to play in the orchestra seems to me to be undermining this ritual in some small way. I don't know why exactly, it's just something I feel. I can never tell anyone, but if the forces of superstition who rule this land are upset by this, then I will be happy. I don't even believe in any of this, but I must face the fact that someone will die before sunrise and I have never been able to explain that.

"Now, let us go up to the attic. The family never threw anything out, no matter how old or ragged it had become. There are trunks and closets with three generations of old clothes hidden in them. We might wear something that is a hundred years old."

They went into the attic using a ladder that swung down from a trap door in the ceiling. The room was filled with all kinds of paraphernalia, including some old furniture, trunks, and armoires full of clothes on racks. It had just about anything you could use as a disguise. They spent a half hour looking through cloaks, waistcoats, hats, masks, and any manner of things you could use to hide yourself from recognition. Everything was musty and ancient. Their nostrils became clogged and Dizzy had a sneezing spell. When they were finished, he looked like some macabre clown-cowboy. The professor looked like a Victorian scoundrel with a floor-length cloak. It was really quite a sight. Dizzy tried to imagine an entire orchestra dressed like this but wasn't having much luck. He was glad he wouldn't be socializing, as his costume was in bad need of a good cleaning. They both smelled as musty as their surroundings.

Dizzy found a couple of old sashes, which he used to disguise his trumpet. He shook them out well as he didn't want to have a sneezing fit in the middle of the piece.

"We should be going now. I have a small lantern to light the way but it doesn't throw much light so we will have to be careful not to trip in these costumes."

They left the house and went to the corner of the square and hadn't seen anyone else around. They would arrive at the event long after it all started, so the square and roads were deserted. There being no moon or any electric lights for miles, billions of stars were visible. It was uncommonly black to Dizzy. He couldn't see well at all but was mesmerized by the heavens. As a city slicker, he wasn't used to seeing so many stars like this. The only thing he could hear was his breathing and the sound of his feet on the soft pathway. He walked closely behind the professor, who used his torch only sporadically so as not to be seen. Dizzy thought Zablo must have a much better night vision than himself. He couldn't imagine moving more than a few feet without needing the light.

The surreal nature of this whole adventure had momentarily crowded Ekaterina from his thoughts. What on Earth would she have thought if she could suddenly see them skulking down this path late at night dressed like buffoons headed towards a castle just on the other side of the mountain to play a song where someone would die after hearing it? None of this was making any sense to Dizzy, even finding himself in the middle of it all.

"Stay cool," he muttered to himself. "It will all be over soon and I am going to get through this unscathed. I just have to stick like glue to Zablo and I'll be okay."

They walked along for the most part in silence. The air was chilly but the costumes kept them warm. They came to the fork in the road took the right branch this time.

It was so dark that Dizzy could not see the castle, but a large area in front of him was devoid of stars. The small mountain and castle had blocked them out so he knew he was close. It was the eeriest thing he had ever seen. It was bigger than he had thought. Either that or he was really close. A minute later, he saw the actual wall they were walking towards.

"My God, it's huge!" he said.

It rose up before them and Dizzy thought that the painter should have seen this at night. It was a lot more foreboding in darkness. The professor's lantern was extinguished as soon as they saw the small wooden door in an arched recession in the wall. They approached it and the professor knocked once. In about a half minute, the door slowly creaked open. There was no one on the inside! The professor entered first, followed by Dizzy. The door closed behind them. The professor turned to Dizzy, whispering, "We cannot talk together anymore until I deem it safe to do so. Put your hand on my shoulder like a blind man and I'll guide you."

"I am blind," Dizzy whispered back.

"Shh!"

They slowly walked down a narrow damp corridor. A minute later, they reached another door. The professor opened it slowly. They emerged into a room at back of the stage. It was lit by a few candles and that was it. There were a few instruments on the floor. No one else was there. The professor turned to Dizzy.

"We can speak quietly here while no one is around. You can look down at the event from that small window over there. Go now, as you may not have the chance later until we enter the stage." Dizzy looked down through the window and was completely taken aback by what he saw.

The window was about thirty feet above the main floor. From there, he saw everyone in their collection of colourful surrealistic costumes, including human, semi-human, devil, monster, animals, and others that could not fit any category. There must have been three or four hundred people. Mardi Gras was a kindergarten compared to this. It was like nothing he could have ever imagined. He returned to the professor. "Now I've seen everything. It's a good thing you swore me to silence because I could have never described this in any believable way."

The door opened again and five musicians entered the room. Now Dizzy would not be able to speak until after the piece was played and they were on their way home. Dizzy counted the instruments on the floor and the musicians present. That made eleven in all. It was now 11:40. There was eight minutes until downbeat. Then another ten or so musicians came in. Dizzy stayed close to the professor's side.

A door opened to the stage area. The professor nudged Dizzy and they went to their seats. They sat in the back row together. The stage filled up. Everyone put their score on music stands in front of them. A bear with a cello sat down beside Dizzy and a skeleton with a drum sat beside the professor. There were horns, violins, and even an ophicleide, which is an early keyed bugle.

A hush came over the main hall and the conductor appeared out of nowhere with a baton. This man looked quite normal in a tuxedo, except he was wearing a horse's head. It looked like an honest to God head from a real horse. It was an orchestra from the interplanetary zoo with a horse to conduct them. The surrealism of the situation was increasing by the moment. By now Dizzy had completely blocked everything from his mind but the music that was about to be played by this band of creatures.

The conductor raised his baton and said something. Everyone started to tune. Thirty seconds later, the orchestra was ready.

Horsehead raised his arms and they started to play. Dizzy listened intently with one ear to the professor and to the bear on his left with his other ear. Thirty seconds into the piece and the orchestra was working remarkably together. Dizzy began to relax and concentrate on the music. He listened to how the band sounded in its entirety. The piece was more complex than he had imagined and the musicianship was of high quality. The most unusual part of it all was that even though it was harmonically strange to Dizzy, it all made perfect sense. He even thought there was an underlying element of an Argentine tango in some parts. He was happy he had memorized it. He could play through some of the parts by rote and concentrate on listening to whatever was going on around him. He had never heard an ophicleide before and there was some kind of primitive looking three stringed cello that was being used as a rhythm instrument. It wasn't bowed but the strings were being tapped with a wooden stick.

About halfway through the piece, Dizzy saw something fall on the floor next to him. He saw it flip past his eye and when he glanced down, it was someone's mask. He knew it wasn't the professor's mask so he assumed it belonged to the second violinist standing on the far side of the professor. He didn't pay anymore attention to it preferring to concentrate on the music. It wasn't till closer to the end of the piece that as he looked over at the professor he saw that the violinist was no longer there. He thought the violinist had run out because he had lost his mask. Then, the finale and it was all over. Dizzy would hve given anything to be able to play the piece again, but that would have to wait. Everyone started packing their instruments and as Dizzy was putting his trumpet in its case which was on the floor, a figure in a Middle Eastern outfit stood staring at him from a few feet away. The figure wore a grotesque mask with blood dripping from its eyes. Then Dizzy saw something which froze him on the spot. The man's mask had a small dagger sticking into his neck! He felt a burst of fear come over him like never before. Was this someone who was impersonating a Polozenski staring down at him? Why him? Everyone else was as weirdly dressed as he was. Was he recognizing something that triggered off the memory of a Polosenski. His only thought was to get out as fast as was possible .He finished packing and whispered to the Professor; "Get us out of here now!"

The Professor, sensing that something wasn't right said; "Right away. Follow me." Everyone was leaving by the same door as they had come in from and Dizzy had the feeling that daggerman was right behind him. Upon reaching the door at the end of the passageway, everyone was quick to disperse and as soon as he and the Professor were alone, the Professor said;"You wanted to get out fast"

"Sorry, but there was this guy staring at me as I was packing up my trumpet and his mask had blood coming out of his eyes and he had a small dagger implanted in his.....

Dizzy was interrupted by brushing up against something in the path. His next step produced a small sharp noise which startled them both. When the professor lit his lantern they both went cold. There was a body on the ground face up with a grimace of terror on his face which froze Dizzy and the Professor on the spot.

The next thing they saw was what Dizzy had stepped on. A violin bow which was now broken in half.

The professor gasped. "He was playing beside me then he turned around before the piece ended and he left before the piece was over."

"I know. His mask fell off and landed at my feet. It was then that he turned around and left. That's all I saw. Do you think he is the victim of Saltatio Mortis?"

"I suppose, since he wasn't with the orchestra when the piece finished and that might have forfeited his immunity with being with the orchestra. I don't know but we should get home as fast as we can. We don't want to be around when someone besides us discovers this scene."

They left and walked as fast as possible. The Professor did not want to use his lantern anymore and he led the way with Dizzy staying as close as he could. He was haunted by the thought of the man in the bloody mask following him in the darkness. Several times he was sure he heard something behind him but turning around wouldn't have done any good. He could barely see the Professor two feet in front of him so if anyone was any more than five feet behind, he wouldn't be able to see him. The way back to the house seemed to be a lot longer but in his brief moments of reason, Dizzy realized that it was due to circumstances only. What terrorized them both was the sudden, tortured scream coming from behind them. They were less than ten minutes from the body. The Professor quickened his pace and Dizzy almost said "slow down" but he was happy to follow as best he could. He couldn't figure out how the Professor could navigate the path at this pace when the moonless blackness enveloped them.

As they passed the cemetary, Dizzy, who had never set foot in a church except to play music, did the sign of the cross. He was surprised by this. He decided a good stiff drink was the next thing he would need. They walked in silence until they reached the professor's house. Dizzy couldn't stop thinking about the man or woman who had died. How did something like this happen after the event? Did these people have a heart attack? Stroke? Extreme fear that death became a self-fulfilling prophesy? Again, Dizzy had many questions for Zablo.

By the time they arrived at the house, Dizzy felt cold, sweaty and exhausted. He needed one of the professor's brandy shots—maybe two or three. They removed their costumes and, leaving them where they were, retired to the study, where the professor poured the drinks. Dizzy shot it down in one gulp and presented the glass for a second.

"Thank you, Professor. I needed that."

Zablo lit a fire and they started to unwind.

"My God, that was amazing, and just about as surreal as it gets. How often have you done this?"

"I first played when I was about seventeen years old. I missed a few when I was teaching in Leipzig, but I have tried to take part whenever able. It is part of my history also. As a citizen of this little part of the world, I have also been partly shaped by the culture here. I am a lot more worldly and educated than anyone in the castle tonight but this wasn't always the case. I grew up here like everyone else. The interesting thing was that this was all quite normal to me until I went away for my education. I am living in both worlds that way. Both seemed quite normal to me, but as I became aware of the more sophisticated outside world, I realized how different and isolated this place is. I notice how ancient, unchanging, and decayed it is. I keep wondering when things will change. Not in my lifetime, I'm afraid. I am seventy-five years old and will not live to see anything of any significance."

"Professor, tell me, what kills these poor people? How do they die?"

"No one knows the medical reason. I really don't think that anyone has ever bothered to investigate. I have often wondered this myself. The unfortunate individual will be buried in the forbidden part of the cemetery. From the villager's point of view, they have been cursed by something or other and cannot be buried in the main part of the cemetery. It is a way that this society periodically cleanses itself. The fact that many of the victims have been outstanding citizens doesn't make sense. I can understand if a real ne'er-do-well dies after this bal macabre, as you call it, then people would more or less understand. Maybe they would think he or she received a just reward for a life of wrongdoing. But the fact that someone who is considered practically a saint by everyone can die afterwards lends a certain indiscrimination to it all. There really are no answers except that it will happen at the appointed time."

"Doesn't this fact depress you at all?"

"It used to, but I have let go of these things one by one and prefer my own world. I still study all kinds of subjects like science, history, and literature, and derive a great deal of pleasure in that. This is probably the last time I play the ball at the castle. If I play again, I will be eighty-two.

"That seems to be a long way off for now, but I can assure you, Dizzy, that at my age, the time moves terribly fast and this next period of seven years will pass more quickly than the last. I may make it to play in Horsehead's orchestra one more time. If I reach that time and still have the ability to play my violin, I will certainly join the orchestra. This may seem outrageous to you, but the fact that this unimaginable gig happens against all human rationality gives me a certain—what's the word?—insight and privilege in my life. I know it sounds crazy and I'm sure it is, but I am taking part in something that all of my education and academic background, which is considerable by any standards, has never given me one iota of explanation as to the nature of this event. It defies everything I have learned about life and humanity. I am no closer to solving this riddle than I was fifty years ago, and I have given it a lot of thought.

"So you can see, my dear Dizzy, that I am hopelessly fascinated by it all. It is my life's big mystery. Even more than any religion. In religion, one depends on some kind of belief in the supernatural or the existence of God. Personally, I have been an atheist all of my life. I simply don't believe. That doesn't seem too difficult. It's believe it or not, the choice is yours. But this is something I never would have believed it if I hadn't seen it personally over seven decades. I have taken part, witnessed it, lost my brother to it fourteen years ago, and have tried to come up with a rational explanation. Each time, I ended in complete failure. Every avenue of questions or thoughts winds up in, and I hate to put it this way, a dead end."

"Your brother died after one of these events?"

"Yes." He poured another large brandy. "And you cannot imagine the guilt I went through over this. I was in the orchestra at the time. I felt for a long time that I had committed fratricide. I had to call on every gram of rationality my mind could muster to assuage the guilt. I was depressed for years after that, but I worked my way through it eventually. It wasn't easy, as you can imagine. The guilt kept hitting me like a large hammer that would only temporarily stop. It still hits me sometimes, but I have compartmentalized it somewhere in my mind and can usually manage to keep it there.

"But today is difficult for me, it being the anniversary. You'd think I would have never played in the event again, but I keep thinking it is the only way I will ever come close to solving the mystery. This time around, however, your presence has made it easier, as you have been a most interesting distraction to the horror. A descendant of the Polozenski family arriving at my doorstep is astounding enough in itself, but a musician from another culture who could learn the piece in such a short time and agree to play it with me is what I would call completely unimaginable.

I cannot find the words to properly express my gratitude to you for having taken part in this. I have never talked about it with anyone, so even that brought me a great deal of pleasure."

"I'm with you on that. I could never have imagined something like this. I still feel this must be a bizarre dream from which I will awake any moment—but that isn't the case at all, is it?"

"No, I'm afraid it's all too real."

Dizzy and the professor conversed and consumed until first light. They then bid each other a good night and retired to their respective rooms.

CHAPTER 10

Dizzy didn't wake up until noon. With a well-earned headache, he staggered out of bed slowly and carefully, making his way downstairs. He hadn't bothered to take his clothes off before collapsing on the bed at dawn. The brandy had taken its toll. The servant had a cup of black coffee ready for him. The professor was reading a large book in the study.

"Good morning, Professor. You're hitting the books early."

"*The Rise and Fall of the Roman Empire*. Pretty wild stuff in its own way. I took a walk around the common earlier. Your car is being worked on. They will have it fixed in about an hour. When it's ready to go, you should be ready also. People will start being curious about your presence here. I'll deal with the questions as I see fit. I'll pay for the car so the deal will be over with quickly.

"You don't have to..."

"Nonsense. It will be the easiest way. Besides, consider it remuneration for the music. It is a small price for me to pay for the adventure we have just shared. I will remember this until my dying day.

You will probably not be back to Europe for a few years anyway. I think there will be a major war soon."

"I have picked up on that here and there The newspapers back home have had stories about the troubles in Europe. How does any of that look from here ?" Dizzy asked

"The leader of Germany, Adolf Hitler, will probably attack one or more of his neighbouring countries. That will start something that will go on for a long time, and kill an awful lot of people. I don't trust that man. I am laying low and will live out my days in this village. I am happy here and despite appearances, I live a full life with my studies. This year I intend to start to teach anyone who wishes to learn how to read. That should cause a small dent in the ignorance and darkness that has existed here for too long. Several people have approached me about this and I think it will be rewarding. I will not charge money for this. I don't need it. They couldn't afford it anyway. I'm looking forward to this. I have taught advanced courses all of my academic life, but I have never taught anyone how to read a simple sentence before."

Just then there was a knock at the door and Dizzy retreated into the study as before. He heard the voices and then the door closed. The professor came into the study.

"They have fixed your car. It's ready to go. I have paid the men and I have something here."

The professor opened a closet door and brought out a bottle of the same brandy they had been consuming all week.

"This is for you. I hope you can keep it, but you may need it to cross the border. The guards like this stuff even better than Luckies. If you manage to keep it, please have a drink for me seven years from now when, God willing, I will take my place in the orchestra one more time and play the Saltatio Mortis."

"Even if I cannot keep it, I will purchase a bottle of the finest and drink to your honour and health on that evening."

Dizzy was suddenly overcome with sadness at leaving. It had been the adventure of a lifetime but it was time to go. It had all been very emotional and a bit overwhelming and it was just starting to sink in now. They were both starting to think of the impossible circumstances that brought them together. They would remember this remarkable event in the passage of their lives and wondered how it would affect them both down the road.

Ekaterina entered his thoughts now. He would be seeing her again soon and suddenly, he couldn't wait. She was all over him and he missed her desperately. He just wanted to drive straight to her gate and pull the bell cord. He hadn't thought of what he would say when she asked about what he did in Moldova.

The fog lifted in his brandy brain quickly after the coffee. He went upstairs to pack his battered suitcase, being careful to leave the last half of the Luckies where the border guards would find them.

The professor was waiting for him when he descended the staircase and accompanied Dizzy to the door.

"I never thought I would feel sad at a Polozenski leaving town. But then again, I never thought I would meet one in person. I also can say that it has been a great honour to meet you and play music together. You have gone a long way towards cleaning up the Polozenski name in my world, which as you know, is small and private. Good luck to you, Dizzy."

The professor extended his hand and they shared a firm handshake.

"Goodbye, Professor."

"Goodbye, Dizzy."

And with that, a most unlikely friendship involving a piece of music played in circumstances beyond imagination was sealed forever.

Dizzy approached his car with a half dozen people standing around watching him place his horn in the trunk and his suitcase in the back seat. He recognized the woman who had brought him to professor Zablo's house. He smiled and said hello. She responded with a thickly accented "hello," but no more than that. Then the man who had showed him the broken driveshaft when the car stopped said something in the local language, smiled, and shook Dizzy's hand. Dizzy said, "Thank you, sir." The thought occurred to him that this was the guy that fixed his car. His shirt was a little dusty and his hands looked like they had been working with greasy tools. Dizzy pointed to under the car, then to the guy, and he nodded with a smile and pointed to himself. Dizzy thanked him again. He got into the car, started it, and realized that he was nearly out of gas.

He turned the motor off and motioned the man over to the window. Pointing to the gas gauge, he said, "No gas."

The man smiled and pointed to himself again, then pointed ahead to the road leading out the other side of the square, He walked around to the passenger side and said something that Dizzy interpreted as something like, "Can I get in?"

Dizzy unlocked the door and the man got in and held up three fingers and said "gas" and motioned Dizzy to drive. While they drove, Dizzy pointed to himself and said, "I'm Dizzy."

The man said, "Milos."

They drove in silence for a few minutes. The road was well defined, indicating how most people approached the village from this road not the road between the village and the border. In about five minutes, they reached a small building with a gas pump. Pulling up to the pump, dizzy noticed that quite a few people were hanging around the place. Several of them looked quite unsavoury and he started to become concerned as they were giving him icy stares. An old dark green Ford model "A" sat beside the building. It was the first American car he had seen in weeks. *How did that ever get here*, he thought.

A surly man approached the car, making Dizzy more concerned. Milos got out of the car and directed the man to put gas in it. They exchanged a few words, which to Dizzy sounded a little unpleasant. The man opened the cap and began filling the car with a gravity fed hose. It took about two minutes to fill the tank. Milos wrote down on a piece of crumpled paper he pulled from his shirt pocket the amount of money needed to pay for the gas. Dizzy had some currency given to him by Ekaterina. He fished what he thought was the right amount and gave it to Milos, hoping that if there was a mistake, he would be more sympathetic and sort it out with Dizzy rather than getting into a misunderstanding with the surly attendant.

It was the right amount. Milos passed the money to the annoyed attendant, and motioned to Dizzy to start the car. Right now! It was all done with gestures but Dizzy understood. The car started and Dizzy drove on as Milos motioned him to get out of there fast. Dizzy knew what was being communicated to him and he stepped on the gas. He thought it was laughable to make a getaway in a toy car that he thought would explode if they ever hit fifty miles an hour. He glanced over at Milos to try to read an expression from him. He looked back at Dizzy, and with a smile on his face gave him a thumbs up. He still wasn't making complete sense of the situation, but a couple of scenarios came to mind.

Here he was on the day after the Saltatio Mortis, a complete stranger unable to communicate with anyone besides the professor. He was riding in the car with the man who fixed it for him and had directed him to a gasoline source. He had his trumpet in the trunk and realized if someone opened the trunk and saw it, they might think that he might have played in the castle. People must know the professor played and could easily put two and two together. When he had left the car, he removed it and put it back after the car had been fixed. It could be all over the village that the stranger had a trumpet. He was getting a little paranoid.

He then thought of the sullen characters around the gas station. Maybe the person who died was a friend or relative of one of them. His thoughts were interrupted by Milos, who said something and pointing straight ahead. He was pointing to the village. They were almost there.

Dizzy stopped the car in the square and realized he had no idea how find the quickest way to the Romanian border. He said "Romania? Bucharest?" Milos pointed to the road that Dizzy had entered the village on and with hand signals told him to go straight and not to make any turns.

Milos thanked him, shook his hand, and got out of the car. Dizzy motioned him not to go. There was no one else around. He retrieved his suitcase and opened it just enough to pick out a couple of packs of Luckies. He closed the suitcase, walked around the car to where Milos was standing, and gave him the cigarettes. He looked happy and surprised. He smiled and said, "Tank you, tank you. Bye bye."

Then with a look of concern on his face, Milos said, "You go now. No stop!"

He turned and walked away across the square.

Dizzy was certainly going to heed Milos's advice without any hesitation. He fired up the car and began the journey back to Ekaterina's flat.

The ruts that passed for a road were easier to follow the farther he went from the village. He then realized that he never did ask the professor the name of the village. He had no idea. He had just gone through the adventure of his life and he didn't even know where it had taken place. He tried to piece all the parts of this adventure together as he was driving and he had trouble even recalling how many nights he spent at the professor's house. It was all a blur, with certain parts of the story standing out. The car breaking down, Zablo's house. The cemetery, the costumes. The music, the trip to the castle. So much had happened and while Dizzy took it all in stride at the time, he now felt like he was in shock.

The ruts had guided him along for about an hour. The road was anything but straight for more than a hundred and fifty yards at a time. He drove past the T-junction that had taken him to the village. The rolling hills were steep enough in parts, causing the car to have to climb them in second gear again. It was late afternoon when he approached the comical border station again. Dizzy's nervousness increased, although this was mildly tempered by the silliness of his small car nearing the comic book border post guarding the invisible line.

He stopped the car and the guard emerged from the kiosk. Another surly, grumpy individual, though at least he didn't have a gun strapped over his shoulder. His uniform was far less rumpled than that of the previous guard and he was clean shaven. He walked the ten paces over to the car and said something incomprehensible. Dizzy responded by handing his passport out the window.

The guard looked at it as though he had never seen anything like it in his life. He headed back through the door of the kiosk and was out of sight for about a minute. Dizzy, by now quite worried, started to look around him. He wasn't sure why, but he was looking to see what he could do in case everything went wrong. This guy appeared far more alert and smarter than the first guy and Dizzy would not be offering Luckies as a bribe. If the guard wanted them, so be it, but he would have to take them out of the suitcase on his own. What if he spotted the trumpet? By now, Dizzy was sure that the instrument would raise suspicions that he wouldn't be able to answer to anyone's satisfaction under the circumstances.

He returned with a sheet of paper and the passport. He handed both to Dizzy. The sheet was some kind of form with what Dizzy surmised to be questions with spaces for answers and boxes to tick off—all in a language he didn't know, of course. He wondered if the guard even knew how to read. Wondering what to do next didn't take long. He caught sight of a car approaching in the distance out of his rear view mirror. It was still some distance away but approaching fast. Christ, it was the green Model A Ford from the gas place. Dizzy didn't need another carload of discontented people surrounding him. What was that car doing here?

The guard had started to walk over to his kiosk when he looked up and saw the other car. Dizzy decided to use the distraction to make a getaway.

He started his and took off. This momentary distraction allowed him to make what was a risky, stupid move to extricate himself from this situation. He swerved the car to the left and zipped between the kiosk and the pillar anchoring the gate. There were scarcely six inches on either side when he went through.

Hopping back into the ruts again, he gunned the car to get him up the steep hill ahead. When he dared look in the rear view mirror, he couldn't see the guard. The next time he looked, the guard was standing near the gate with his gun raised pointing at the car. Dizzy heard the shot, then another. Nothing happened. He was struggling to get the car over the crest of the hill and out of sight. A third shot rang out and Dizzy heard an incredibly loud noise near the back of his head. A bullet had just grazed the roof of the car. Then he heard an explosion behind him. He was fifty feet from the top of the hill. Looking in the mirror, he saw lots of smoke, the guard down on the ground, and the car that had been behind him approaching the gate was tipped over on its side. It was off on the right side of the gate opposite to where Dizzy had gone.

Dizzy was now over crest of the hill. Driven by a moment of insane curiosity, he stopped the car, pulled the handbrake, and left it idling in neutral. He got out and ran back to just where he would be able to see the crossing. The guard hadn't moved and he saw no one else around, so he assumed the occupant or occupants of the car were still inside—injured or worse.

He surveyed the scene below him for about ten seconds and decided it was time to put as much distance as possible between him and the mayhem down at the crossing.

He ran back to the car and while he was driving away, he realized what had happened. The second car must have been chasing him and in going around the gate as he did, on the right side hit a land mine! Dizzy had driven around on the left side where the car fit in that small space. If there was a mine or two on that side, then he miraculously missed them. The other car wasn't so lucky. He would never make fun of the toy car again. Its small size probably saved his life.

As he sped along, he began to wonder why the other car had been chasing him. It had be that someone knew he had played at the castle and was going to get back at him for it. But how?

The trumpet had to be the giveaway. At least a half-dozen people saw him remove it from his car on that first day. According to the professor, people talked, and he warned Dizzy about being in the cemetery for too long and being careful not to stop when driving around the castle.

Then an awful fear hit him. What about the professor? They must know he played too, as he did it every time. *Maybe because I was a stranger, they thought I would report this event to the authorities*, he thought. *But what was there to report anyway?* The bal macabre was part of the culture of the region. It would have made such an implausible story anyway that anyone hearing it would quickly dismiss it as delusional at best.

Milos must have known but didn't care that Dizzy had taken part. He made sure that his car left town with a full tank of gas and warned Dizzy to go quickly on his way. The one thing that offered at least a little relief was that he was now back on Romanian soil, though still out in a lonely spot.

At no time in Dizzy's driving history had he ever spent so much time looking in the rear view mirror. He was scared out of his wits. By now, he had no doubt that this place was even crazier than Ekaterina had told him. Another hour and started to see more traffic on the road. His was no longer the only car, and somehow this felt a little safer. The road had gotten better and when he saw a sign that said "Bucharesti 68km," a great sense of relief began to push against his anxiety. He knew he had been driving in a general southerly direction but this was the first road sign he had run across. Realizing he was definitely on the road to Ekaterina's house, he began thinking of her and how within a short time, he would be with her again.

What in Hell was he going to tell her about the startling and frightening adventure he had just gone through? Secrecy with the professor had not been sworn to, but Dizzy thought it would have been implied. Would she even believe him? His story was so farfetched that he didn't even believe he could have had the imagination to make the whole thing up. Should she be told everything at once? His beautiful spy girl would interrogate him until he told all anyway.

Bucharesti 12km. Dizzy was beside himself with anxiety, desire, fatigue, and longing for Ekaterina. Time slowed as he approached her place. The toy car was speeding up and Dizzy had to watch it, not wanting to succumb to an accident or an encounter with the police.

"Keep calm and cool," he reminded himself.

The outskirts of the city began to envelop him and by some stroke of luck, he turned a corner and was suddenly in front of the forbidden gate. One last laugh coughed out of his mouth. Suitcase and horn in hand, he looked for the bell cord, then noticed the gate was unlatched. He gently pushed it open and began the climb towards Ekaterina's flat.

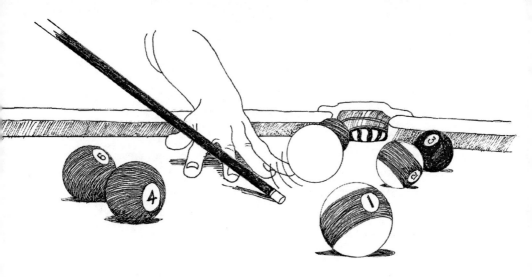

CHAPTER 11

He knocked gently at her door. "Come in, Dizzy."

It was her, his spy girl. She was home. Opening the door, nothing could have prepared him for her. Ekaterina was dressed in high waist baggy slacks, a man's white shirt and tie, and a scarf over one shoulder. He just stared for a second. She was even more beautiful then he remembered.

She melted. "Oh Dizzy!" She ran across the room literally jumped up, spread her legs, and wrapped them around his waist with her arms over his shoulders.

Dizzy was locked in her arms and legs and he let go of his suitcase and horn. Nothing else mattered. Ekaterina was holding him for dear life and he wrapped his arms around her. They were both silent.

Ekaterina had wanted this greeting to be different. She had thought of it in a slightly different scenario—soft, svelte, sexy, and romantic—but she lost all of that when Dizzy appeared before her, haggard and unshaven. Knowing right there that something untoward had happened, she could no longer contain her composure.

"Dizzy, I was so scared something would happen to you. Are you okay?" She started to weep. She was trembling and genuinely scared.

Dizzy carried her into the bedroom, where he gently lowered her onto the bed. They lay there for a few moments.

"Ekaterina, I am okay. Nothing bad happened," he lied. He didn't want to, but he would retract that statement when rationality returned to the situation. Now was not the time. It was time to let passion reconnect them.

"Don't cry. I am fine and it's so wonderful to see you again."

"Dizzy, I..."

He put his finger to her lips. "Shhh, we are back together again and for now, it's all that counts."

"I know. I didn't want to cry on your return. It's not like you have been away for a year. You have been gone only eight days—the longest eight days I have ever known."

He gently wiped her tears and kissed her softly. Ekaterina stopped trembling and Dizzy felt her grip soften. The buttons on her shirt gave way under his fingers. He could not keep his eyes from staring at his beautiful girl. He touched her breast with one hand and pressed her shoulder into the pillow with the other. Ekaterina responded by kissing him harder as she began to fumble with his jacket. Clothes flew awkwardly in all directions as they undressed themselves and each other, not wanting to let go.

Amid the strewn clothes, they found themselves skin to skin. They kissed, fondled, and wrapped each other in limbs. Dizzy slipped into her and all of the stresses and fears of the last little while began to unravel. Dizzy himself getting rough with her and Ekaterina, a little surprised by this, enjoyed it. She was rough back. It hadn't been like this before, but then there hadn't been the pent up anxiety in their previous lovemaking.

Ekaterina felt possessed as never before. She wanted to make it harder for Dizzy to possess her by resisting. She was being pressed by the shoulders into the pillow. She reached up, holding Dizzy's hair in both hands, opened her lips but not her teeth, and hissed at him like an annoyed feline. Dizzy held her even tighter as she began to feel the great miracle of the orgasm start within her. She began to feel helpless as it took her over. She held on tight as she exploded and gave out a half choked scream. One final shudder while arching her back and she knew that it was close to Dizzy's time.

When she knew that Dizzy was in the middle of his orgasm, she bit into his neck and shot her fingers down the length his of back, scratching him with her fingernails. He let out a grunt, his whole body shaking under the unexpected sensation of pain as an accompaniment to the pleasure.

They both lay still for a few moments, their bodies wet and hot. Dizzy was on top of her, propped up on his elbows. Ekaterina felt his muscles start to relax and soften one by one, the tension dissipating. She cradled his head on her shoulder just above her breast. "Dizzy... Dizzy," she whispered.

Remembering what she had done to his back, she started to apologize, but once again, he put his finger to her lips. "Don't apologize for passion. We both expressed ourselves as we needed to. Apologizing for anything that just happened would demean it."

She smiled her mysterious smile that drove Dizzy crazy. They were both back.

"What happened in Moldova? I knew something was happening. Don't ask me how, I just sensed it. Things don't normally happen to me like this"

"I got lost, I saw portraits of my ancestors with daggers in their necks in an inn, the car broke down, I stayed with a professor, played a gig with him in which somebody died as a result, got followed by a carload of nasty people while trying to leave the country, jumped the border, got shot at, and the car chasing me ran over a land mine, then I drove straight home!"

Ekaterina, still laying under him and looked a little annoyed. She slapped him on the back. "Be serious!"

"OUCH"!

"Oh Dizzy, I am sorry, I forgot what I just did to you. Now tell me what really happened."

"What I am about to tell you must never leave this room. I am sworn to secrecy, but trying to keep something from you would be futile, I think. So please swear to this. You will see why as the story unfolds. Oh yes, everything I just told you actually happened. I just compressed it into one sentence."

"My God, of course I'll swear for you. And I think I should also swear to never let you out on your own if you are going to get into that kind of trouble."

Dizzy laughed. "That will be the best idea you've had all day."

"This is going to take a while. Let's get showered, open a bottle of wine, and go back to bed, where I will tell you an amazing story. It's long and complicated and if you get bored, you can always stop me by... well, I'll leave that to your imagination."

They jammed themselves into the tiny cubicle and enjoyed a sensuous shower. They dried each other off and opened some wine.

Dizzy sat in bed collecting his thoughts and preparing for the story and its chronology. From this vantage point, being home with Ekaterina, it seemed so far away both in distance and time. He was having difficulty, especially with the chronology of events. It was a complete blur, but he figured things would straighten out once he verbalized them.

Ekaterina appeared at the bedroom door wearing only the tray carrying the bottle and two glasses.

"My my, I have never been served by a more beautiful waitress in all my life."

"Yes, and I shall expect a generous tip for my services."

She put the tray down on the table beside the bed, then climbed up and playfully straddled Dizzy, bringing her head down until her hair met his, falling over her face and making a kind of soft tunnel between them.

"Now you are going to confess all to your spy girl." She kissed him gently, climbed off to her side if the bed, poured some wine in both glasses, and handed one to Dizzy.

"Welcome home, my dear Dizzy."

"I have never felt so welcome in my life. To us."

"To us." They clinked glasses and took the first sip.

"It really did start with me getting lost."

For the next two hours, Dizzy recounted in as much detail as he could remember the events of the last eight days. Occasionally, Ekaterina would interrupt with a question or two, but for the most part, she was a rapt audience. She was amazed by the details that Dizzy was able to recount and was astounded by his description of the Saltatio Mortis.

"Dizzy, what was the name of the village?"

"Oh God, I was waiting for that one." He was looking a little sheepish.

"My God, Dizzy, you really don't know?"

"That's right. I really don't know. Isn't that the stupidest thing?"

"We can probably figure it out with a detailed map better than the one you had with you."

The aftermath of the concert in the castle and the death of one of the participants made Ekaterina's hair stand up.

"I have heard of weird goings on but no details, just gossip and stories from old people when they have had a little too much to drink. I have considered them just that—stories. All pretty garbled and confused."

"You know a true one now," he said.

"It has happened every seven years since time immemorial in that place. No one seems to know any real history and background, according to Professor Zablo. It just happens because it has always happened. As educated as he is, he has never been able to discover any rhyme or reason for it. And he keeps taking part in order to one day understand it. You see, he lost his brother one year. His brother was a participant and he was in the orchestra. His brother was the one who died. I cannot imagine what he must have gone through. It was fourteen years ago and the way he told it, I could see that it was as if it happened yesterday. He is seventy-five years old now and told me he will play again if he is still alive in seven years."

"My God! I'm astounded"

"Me too. It was unreal enough when I was there but it seems impossible now that I am telling you about it."

"Dizzy, please tell me the border incident is just something made up in order to scare me."

"My dear, it did happen and why I am alive standing here is a mystery to me.

I don't really know what saved me. I think the fact that I acted fast, and for some reason known only to God, I drove between the kiosk and gatepost. It was only wide enough to fit the toy car. A bigger car wouldn't have been able to squeeze through, so maybe there were no mines there. Maybe no one ever thought a car would have attempted to crash the border on that side of the gate. There was plenty of room on the right side, hence the land mines.

"When I gunned it making a run for the top of the hill, I realized that as charming and cute as the toy car is, she is hopeless as a getaway car. She wasn't about to roar up the hill and get me out of sight anytime soon. When I heard the first shot, I looked back, then heard the second. By this time, the car chasing me was close to the border and the third shot grazed the roof of the car. I felt sure the fourth would hit me, but the land mine blew up and that stopped everything."

"How did you know this?"

"When I heard the explosion, which was really loud, I knew something other than gunfire had happened. At that point, I was just over the crest of the hill and out of the line of fire. I stopped and got out to glance back. The guard was on the ground and the car was on its side, and there was a lot of smoke everywhere from the explosion."

Ekaterina, wide eyed with fear and concern, pleaded with Dizzy. "Please tell me you are making this part up. It's not funny."

"The car is parked just outside, go look out the window down at the roof."

Ekaterina walked over and peered down at the car. Seeing the eight-inch line of bare metal glinting in the sun, she gasped and started to tremble. She ran back to the bed and hugged Dizzy. She was crying. She held him tightly for a few moments.

"God Dizzy, you could have been killed and I would never have known what happened to you."

"After that, I only remember driving as fast as I dared and didn't stop until I reached your gate."

◆ ◆ ◆ ◆

The wine was finished. "I'm exhausted just listening to your story and you must be a thousand times more so having lived it. Just hold me and let's sleep. I want to wake up beside you."

She put her head on Dizzy's shoulder and in a few minutes, they were both asleep.

"Dizzy! Help me!" Dizzy looked around at the thick vegetation and started running in the direction the voice was coming from. He saw a bit of the white dress she was wearing through the trees. "Help!" The voice came from the opposite direction. He turned and saw the dress moving some distance away. He started to run again but as soon as he had run a dozen paces, she called out again from somewhere else.

"Dizzy! Dizzy! Wake up. You are having a nightmare. Dizzy!" She shook him gently and he sprang awake. He was stunned for a second then he pulled her on top of him holding her tight.

"You were lost and calling for help and I was unable to get to you. I thought you were being kidnapped or carried off."

"I'm right here. No one is making off with me. I'm here with you."

It was early morning. They languished in bed for a while, then Dizzy said, "Jesus Ekaterina, whatever am I going to tell Washburn about the bullet mark on his car?"

Ekaterina laughed. "I must say that's a good one. I guess there is nothing else that would make a mark like that like— maybe driving under a tree or something. I don't know. She was teasing him now. "Maybe someone jumped on the car wearing one ice skate. No, wait, you hit the horn of a giant deer. No, maybe some deranged person threw a railway spike at you from a passing train, or maybe..."

"Enough! This is serious. I have to come up with some explanation for that mark."

"Listen, we'll figure something out. I don't have to be at work for a few days so we have time to deal with it. Maybe the mechanic can fix it quickly or something. In the long run, it's a small problem. We have something much more important to deal with right now."

Dizzy knew this was coming. He was about to bring it up himself.

"What is going to happen with us? I am, as you know, very much in love with you and cannot even conceive of us not being together. I am afraid, Dizzy."

"I feel exactly the same way. I can't imagine my life without you. You, however, have a life here, and I couldn't make a living here. I am at the top of my profession in the States and I can make a good living there. I guess I will ask you this and you don't have to answer right away. This is awfully quick but will you marry me and come to the States with me?"

"Yes! Yes! Yes, I will marry you. I'm so happy you asked because I was going to become really forward and ask you."

They kissed and she trembled in his arms for a few seconds. "Dizzy, it's not going to be as complicated as it seems."

"How's that?"

"My father is most anxious to meet you. I have told him about you and although I think under normal circumstances his approval would be a little difficult to obtain, he is getting old and he has his life here. The modern world doesn't make a lot of sense to him. But he is liberal at heart and, well, you will see what he is like because we are going to dinner at his house tonight."

"So does that mean I will have to ask him for his beautiful daughter's hand in marriage?"

"It would be a good idea out of respect, but don't worry, he will not refuse. He will be wonderfully happy."

"How do you know? I am an American who makes his living playing music he probably doesn't know or would like. Musicians are not always considered stable and constant breadwinners."

"I don't want to pave the way for anything here. I want you two to meet. He will like you, and who knows, you might even like him. He really is a good, decent person with a history as long as your arm.

I am his only child and sometimes I'm still his baby girl, but he understands that I have and will have my own life. It has been difficult at times for him to watch me grow up but he made sure I had the best education and he taught me self-esteem. As I told you in the restaurant on the night of the Gypsies, my mother died when I was young and my father never remarried. But that's all I am going to say for now. We will drive to his house tonight at six."

Dizzy was nervous as he drove up a long driveway to a large house. There were four tall, white pillars supporting a roof over the circular driveway in front of the door. Two enormous sconces sat on the wall either side of the entrance. His toy car seemed a little out of its milieu in a driveway that looked like it would be home to a Rolls Royce or two.

He had his band suit on and Ekaterina had the black dress she had worn to the concert. Indeed a good looking couple. What would her father think of a jazz musician with a car sporting a bullet mark with his beautiful daughter in tow?

They sat there for a moment, and the fortress door opened. A man appeared in black and white with white gloves. He stepped up to Ekaterina's door and opened it, then went to the driver's side and opening Dizzy's door.

"Thank you, Hans," Ekaterina said.

"Good evening, Ekaterina. Good evening, Mr. Pollen."

"Good evening."

"You never told me you lived in a castle with butlers and all that," whispered Dizzy as they walked into the grand entrance.

She turned and gave Dizzy her special smile. "You never asked."

They were led into a room with all the accoutrements Dizzy thought a castle should have. A suit of armour stood guard stood by the door with a terrible looking weapon. There were antique paintings of family members, antlered stag heads, tapestries, an impossibly large chandelier, and Oriental carpets. Everything seeming to be ancient.

"I don't think I have ever been in a place like this before."

Hans the butler led the couple into a kind of sitting room. It was mostly filled with chairs and a few tables, ash trays, a liquor cabinet, and paintings of hunting scenes on each wall.

"By now you probably want a drink, so why don't you pour us a couple from that decanter. It's the good stuff. I'm sure my father will be here any minute, so let's just sit here and wait."

Dizzy didn't want to sit. Being a little nervous, he walked around the room looking at the paintings and everything that sat on the tables or on shelves. Ekaterina explained that her father was well travelled and the whole house was filled with artifacts from a few dozen countries. Dizzy knew none of it was inexpensive. It was all museum quality stuff, it seemed, but he really didn't know one way or the other. He was wondering what the old man had done for a living, when the door opened.

"Hello, Father. I want you to meet Dizzy Pollen."

He kissed his daughter on the cheek and turned to face Dizzy. He was a handsome gentleman and quite tall. With a kind but tired expression on his face, he extended his hand.

"Dizzy, I would like to introduce you to my father, Augustine Vancea."

The two shook hands. His was a firm handshake, which Dizzy liked. He always trusted a man with a firm handshake.

"An honour to meet you, sir," he said.

"Very good to meet you, Mr. Pollen. My daughter has not stopped talking about you since your concerts, one of which I attended. I don't profess to understand jazz music, but I did enjoy your concert.

Dizzy blushed. "I hope she only told you the good parts. And as far as jazz goes, it doesn't have to understand it in order to enjoy it and I am happy you did.

"Mr. Pollen, if there is a bad part, my daughter does not know it yet. because she only has very good things to say."

"Mr. Vancea, please call me Dizzy. I am more comfortable that way."

"I must say that is an interesting name."

"It's my nickname. It has been with me since early childhood. I have never been known by any other name. I was baptized as Josef, but if someone called that out, I wouldn't turn around. I have never answered to it in my life. I don't know why my parents didn't baptize me as Dizzy and get it over with."

"Welcome to my house, Dizzy. Katy, why don't you show our guest around? The dinner bell will ring in about twenty minutes."

He smiled at Dizzy, who immediately knew where Ekaterina got her smile from. He left the room without further words.

He was looking for some sign from Ekaterina that he had made a good first impression. "Did I do okay?"

"Yes, you were fine. Don't be worried. He is surrounded by all of these fancy, antique artifacts, but deep down he is a quite a humble man and not at all intimidating. Come, let me show you around."

They walked through several rooms and Ekaterina showed him her childhood room. They went up a grand staircase and past hallways, balconies, sculptures, artwork, and even a hidden passage. Dizzy was trying to absorb it all but finally, he said, "Ekaterina, if your father asks me about my origins, how much should I tell him?"

"Just what you told me before the trip. We won't mention the trip at all, but the fact your ancestors came from Moldova is okay. Don't let out your old family name. Pollen is good enough. You are a successful American bandleader. Besides, he came to hear you play. He was impressed, even though he knows nothing about jazz. He came to the afternoon concert."

"Good, so he knows what I do for a living."

"Yes, so stop worrying."

Easy for you to say, he thought. *Here I am, a visiting foreign jazz musician about to ask the lord of this castle for his daughter's hand in marriage.* He was determined to keep Ekaterina with him forever, so he was just going to stand his ground and ask. He wondered if there was an appropriate time for this subject to be broached. Would he just have to play it by ear? That was something he understood and decided that would be the best plan of attack. He had walked into another world twice now within the short space of two weeks. This couldn't be any scarier than what went on in the last few days. Would Augustine see him as a gold digger? That certainly wasn't the case, as he knew nothing of Ekaterina's family background, especially her wealth.

"Dizzy, you look preoccupied. What is the matter? Please tell me."

"I can't help thinking..." Just then, the dinner bell rang, interrupting him. The conversation could wait. Ekaterina and Dizzy made their way to the dining room. Upon entering, Dizzy almost gasped. The table must have been twenty-five feet long and could have seated forty people. There were three places set at one end, one at the head of the table and the two others either side of it along the long edge. Augustin was already there waiting for them.

"I hope you enjoyed Ekaterina's grand tour. She really does know about every piece of furniture, painting, and artifact in the house. Much more than I do."

"She is an excellent tour guide," replied Dizzy. "It is quite a collection."

"Mostly ancient artifacts from passed away ancestors. Frankly, I would like to get rid of most of it, but my dear daughter won't let me. She is more nostalgic about all of this than I am."

"It's not that I am more nostalgic, it is such odd stuff that I can scarcely think of anybody wanting it. Most of it goes back a century or more. Way more."

They were all seated now and Augustine asked Dizzy where he came from. He was cautious and told him exactly what he had asked. He did not elaborate. The conversation continued with Augustin asking most of the questions. It was all pleasant, but the questions demanded complex answers. Dizzy felt as if he was being tested. He didn't mind, as he figured the real test would come when he sprang the great question of his own.

The food was excellent, as was the wine. A couple of times, Ekaterina gave him the smile he loved. It reassured him. He knew she was right beside him in spirit, even when seated some distance away across the wide table. The dessert was served, whereupon Augustine said to Dizzy, "After this, you and I will retire to the billiard room. Do you play billiards?"

"I have played several types of games on what we in America call a pool table. May I assume that billiards is something similar?"

"It probably is."

Several minutes later, Dizzy found himself with a cue in his hand staring at a large table with only three balls. Now he was nervous. He had no idea what would transpire next, so he decided this was it. He would ask the only important question of the evening, from his standpoint.

"Mr. Vancea, forgive me if I sound a little nervous, but I am going to ask you for your daughter Ekaterina's hand in marriage. We have fallen in love and I want to marry her with your blessing and take her to America with me."

"Ekaterina has told me all about you and I know she is very much in love. As you know, she is my only child and her happiness is what I live for. But of course, I cannot keep her here forever. She, as I'm sure you are finding out, is a free spirited woman, and I have always tried to walk the fine line between leaving here to act on her own and not exert too much control. It hasn't always been easy, but we have a better relationship than a lot of families, at least among my friends.

"I have thrown a lot of questions your way this evening. It was, of course, my only way of trying to determine whether I would consent to you taking my daughter to America. Ekaterina hinted this might be coming. So in answer to your question, yes, Dizzy, I will consent to have you marry her. I have some other reasons for doing this besides her obvious happiness, and, by the way, I have never seen her this happy before. She has had a few boyfriends but she has been deliriously happy this past little while. Ever since your concerts. She has talked of nothing else but you, so I had an idea this was coming. But let us go out and find her, as I'm sure she is nervously pacing somewhere."

They didn't have to look far. She was in the next room pacing, as her father had predicted. She watched them enter, trying to gauge the expression of their faces. It didn't take long. Augustine said something in Romanian to her and she ran to him and gave him a big hug and a kiss.

"Thank you, Father. You have made me so happy."

Then she ran to Dizzy and jumped to him, much like she had done in the hallway at her house, only this time it was out of ecstatic joy. She kissed him and let herself down.

Augustine, not used to see his daughter do something like this, said, "Let us have a toast to welcome Dizzy to our little family."

They sat in luxurious chairs in one of the rooms, with Augustine breaking open a bottle of something that caught Dizzy's eye. It was the same kind of brandy as professor Zablo had given him when he left the unknown village.

The drinks were poured and Augustine raised his glass. "To Dizzy and Ekaterina, may you always be as happy as you are right now."

"Amen," said Dizzy.

"Thank you, Father."

"Now, Dizzy and Katy, there is something I want to talk about. It may seem that all of this happening so quickly is a little unreal. There is a reason for this. I am old enough to have fought in and miraculously lived through the Great War. It was terrible beyond imagination and the effects are still being felt today in so many ways. It ended just nineteen years ago and yet, it seems like yesterday. We sent Katy to live with some distant cousins in Malta and brought her back after the war.

"Looking at all of the signs, it isn't hard to imagine that another war is imminent. The ruler of Germany, Adolph Hitler, is causing all manner of consternation among the countries of Europe. He will, in all probability, invade one of his neighbours, and that will certainly draw the whole continent into another war. He is already helping Franco take over Spain and I fear that may only be practice for his army to become engaged in a much larger conflict. He also has an ally in Mussolini in Italy. None of this looks good at this time, and frankly, I do not want my wonderful daughter to be here when things start. War is no place for a woman. Enemy soldiers are not nice to women; men get shot at, but women get assaulted in a much more personal way."

"Father, are you saying you are sending me to America because of an impending war?"

"My dearest, Ekaterina, it breaks my heart beyond words to have you go away. You are all I have in the world, but if anything should happen to you when war starts, then I would have no reason to go on living. They might as well shoot me right then and there if I lose you. I won't care after that. But now, you have brought a handsome, intelligent, and creative young man home to meet me with the intention of asking for my blessing to get married and go across the ocean to America with him. I cannot believe the good fortune that has befallen all of us. You have found a good man, whom I quite like, even though I have only known him for a few hours, and he is going to take you away from a war.

"I am not sending you to America; I am letting you go with Dizzy with my complete blessing. Dizzy, I was beginning to despair that Ekaterina would not find someone to marry, period. You have made her very happy. I have never seen her like this and the fact that you will take her and keep her safe and care for her in a place away from war takes an enormous weight from my shoulders. I could not have asked for more."

Dizzy, a little taken aback, said, "Mr. Vancea, if I had known you felt this way, I would have been a lot less nervous in that billiard room. I was in such a state that I couldn't have hit one of those balls on the table if it had been the size of a grapefruit."

"And you asked with confidence. I was sure you would stumble and falter over the words, but no. You didn't show any nervousness at all. I was impressed."

"It must be my ability to handle stage fright."

"Father, there is much to do and we will talk tomorrow. It's getting late. And there are all kinds of preparations to begin to take care of in the morning. Thank you, Father. You have been wonderful and I know we shall never forget this evening." She got up and hugged Augustine, kissing him on the cheek. Dizzy shook his hand. "Thank you so much, sir. Please rest assured that I will forever take the best care of your lovely daughter. She is a remarkable woman and I cannot believe the good fortune that has befallen me. So it appears to be good fortune all around."

"Good night, Katy and Dizzy. We'll talk tomorrow."

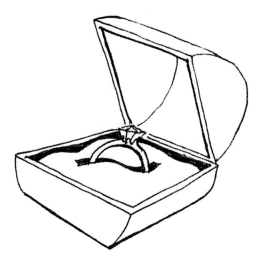

CHAPTER 12

It would be a small, simple wedding. There was not much family on Ekaterina's side and Dizzy had no one at all. Ekaterina had a few friends and among them was Washburn the consul. She had worked on and off for him for years and had become indispensable around his office at times. She knew everything about the city, like who worked where, who could be of help for official duties, and could be an efficient translator in at least three languages.

Ekaterina and Dizzy went to Washburn's office the morning after the dinner with Augustine.

"Good morning, Henry. I wanted to tell you something that will surprise you. I wanted you to be the first to know. Dizzy and I are going to get married."

Henry gasped, then broke into a smile. "Congratulations to both of you! What a surprise. I didn't quite see that one coming, but I am really happy for the both of you. I would be insanely jealous if it was any one but else. Dizzy, I'm sure you know how lucky you are. Ekaterina has become invaluable in my life and work here and I guess I'm going to have to write a letter to the States if I need advice from her."

"I'm afraid so, Henry."

Washburn was going to lose a valuable person in his life. He took it well, probably because she would be marrying Dizzy, whom he admired greatly and had grown to like a lot.

"We must celebrate. I will take you both to dinner tonight, if that's okay."

"That would be nice, Henry."

"In the meantime, can you spare me a few hours this morning?" Henry asked.

"Of course."

Ekaterina ushered Dizzy to the door and whispered, "Don't worry, I will try to figure out how to handle the car situation." She kissed him on the cheek and sent him on his way.

"So, when is all of this going to happen?" Henry asked.

"Soon, but we haven't figured that out yet. Fairly soon though. My father has given us his blessing. He likes Dizzy, and it isn't as though I haven't laid it on thick this last little while. Dizzy asked him for my hand in marriage last night at the billiard table. I think the fact that he actually had the nerve to do this even though he was scared out of his wits made a great impression on father.

He feels sure there is going to be war in Europe soon, in all probability started by Germany. What do you think, Henry?"

"I can certainly see that happening. It does not look promising, and I am privy to diplomatic information that bears that out. If your father wants to send you to America to keep you from war, then I certainly think that is noble and unselfish of him. He lived through the the Great War , and I can see his point. The fact that you are with Dizzy, that must be the answer to his prayers."

"He did make exactly that point last night."

Ekaterina put in several hours in Washburn's office but was distracted by thoughts of her wedding to be. She didn't want to make a big thing of it but what woman doesn't dream of the great white dress and all of the accoutrements? No, it would be simple and quick, and it would be at her father's house. Just a few close friends. She was glad to get home back to Dizzy.

They met Henry at the restaurant where Dizzy first heard the Gypsies play. It all seemed so long ago. Dizzy's life as a professional musician and bandleader seemed even further back. He normally practiced one hour a day when possible but hadn't picked up his horn at all except to play at the professor's place and at the Saltatio. By the same token, his life had lost all predictability and had been filled with romance and adventure. Both were quite foreign to his normal life. He had had lots of girlfriends, but nothing ever got serious for any length of time. He toured a lot and he just never met the right girl (whatever that meant). Then Ekaterina, in no time flat, showed him what the "right girl" meant. It had all become wonderfully other worldly and he was completely swept up in the moment. What would she think of the USA? If she came with him on any tour, she would see vast areas of a huge country. How would she react? What if she became homesick and a war prevented her from ever returning?

These, Dizzy thought, were not doubts, but legitimate questions that would only be answered with time.

"Dizzy, you look like you are a million kilometres away."

"I suppose I was. Sorry. Things are happening so fast that I was just swept up in thinking about everything. Forgive me. Let us order some wine and some good food. This is, after all, a celebration. I hope those Gypsies will come and play again.

After the meal was ordered, Henry asked what they would do after the wedding. "Will you be taking the train or bus back to France?"

"We haven't thought that far ahead yet."

"Here's an idea. Why don't you drive? I would like to give you the car as a wedding present."

"Are you serious?" asked Ekaterina.

"I have to dispose of the car. Orders from home, for some reason. I can easily transfer ownership to you and two birds will be killed with the one stone. There is nothing in the orders that says I have to sell it, so I can give it away, and you can drive to France."

There was elation on Ekaterina's face and relief on Dizzy's. He had had an absolute dread of having to explain the bullet mark on the car. In an instant, he knew exactly what to do about the mark. He would see that Ekaterina attach some flowers on the car over it. You can get away with that at American weddings and it would probably be the same here.

"That is very generous of you, Henry. I have actually grown quite attached to it. I call it the toy car, which is what it would look like parked beside my mammoth Plymouth."

"Yes, aren't some of these European cars tiny? Oh by the way, speaking of cars, how was your trip to Moldova?"

Dizzy was dreading this, but it wasn't hard to answer.

"It was very interesting. I just kept driving and getting lost, driving and getting lost, the whole time. The country is pretty but it seems desperately poor for the most part. Places to stay were a little difficult to find, as was gasoline. But now I have seen it and it isn't hard to see why my ancestors left the place. They probably didn't see any future for themselves or their descendants. The whole place didn't look like it had left the nineteenth century. A country that time seems to have forgotten. Anyway, I've seen it and have no desire to go back. It was a once in a lifetime chance to maybe encounter some of my ancestry, but that's all so far in the past. It's out of my mind by now."

Ekaterina smiled to herself. *Good answer, Dizzy*, she thought. The truth would only cause alarm and consternation. After all, an American citizen had been fired on and that could cause some diplomatic nastiness that they didn't want any part of. Best to make it sound like a boring trip.

The meal arrived, the wine flowed, and the Roma musicians turned up and played some amazing music. More wine flowed until the three of them were reasonably drunk. They lurched their way out of the place and Henry caught a taxi home. Dizzy and Ekaterina staggered back to her place. They barely managed the big gate and the stairway. A futile attempt was made to make love, but they both passed out half-clothed on the bed. It was not going to be a pleasant morning.

Weddings usually require an inordinate amount of planning, even a small one with limited attendance. Ekaterina made all the arrangements, as everything had to be done in her language. It would be held in one of the rooms of her family home. There was next to no family on her side, just her father, an uncle, and two cousins. Dizzy, of course, had no one. For a while, it looked like the biggest problem would be finding some clergyman versed in English, but they did find an old priest who had done some missionary work in a British colony in Africa. Neither Dizzy nor Ekaterina were members of any church, so they didn't mind who married them. Dizzy joked that he wanted to at least understand the vows.

In the process of all of this, Dizzy remembered that he would have to buy Ekaterina a ring. This was something completely outside of his experience. He would have to take her with him since he couldn't speak the language, so one day he simply said, "Let's go for a walk."

They left her flat and walked around arm in arm, finally arriving in front of a small jewellery shop.

"I wasn't sure I could do this on my own, so I needed you to come with me so I can buy you a wedding ring."

"Dizzy, that's very nice, but it is not really necessary."

"It certainly is. If I don't have a ring for you at the ceremony, what will your father think? Or anyone else for that matter? I know I asked you to marry me without much of the usual preparations like a ring on bended knee and all that jazz, but I want to do this because it really means a lot to me and to you, I'm sure."

"Nothing too much, after all, you are away from your work and haven't had access to a money source for a while."

"I'm okay for now."

Ekaterina picked out a modest ring that they both liked, and that left only one more thing from Dizzy's viewpoint.

Henry Washburn would be Dizzy's best man and Ekaterina's best friend Viorica would be her bridesmaid. Only Augustine, Henry, Dizzy, Ekaterina, and the priest Father Petru spoke English.

About twenty guests were invited and Ekaterina wanted the Roma musician Spatzo and some of his sidekicks to play some music before the wedding and at the small reception. Her father found this a little strange, but arguing with Ekaterina about things like that had longed proved futile so he just let it go. The wedding would happen on the Saturday a little over a week away. There had been no real complications so far.

Dizzy wanted to take Ekaterina to the restaurant a few times that week. She went along and they always had a great time and good food. The Gypsies always turned up and played for them. They asked them for the same piece of music each time.

The wedding day came. The Gypsies played some quiet music while the guests arrived. One didn't normally see Gypsies in the Vancea residence, but Ekaterina's friends had come to expect unusual behaviour from her, so on that level, so nobody was surprised.

The priest, Dizzy, and Henry were at one end of the room and the Gypsies played an appropriate piece and all heads turned to see Ekaterina looking even more beautiful than Dizzy could have ever imagined. She was at her father's side wearing an off white dress with a veil. Dizzy thought it might be a traditional wedding dress but he didn't have time to think of that now. In a few seconds, she was facing him. All went blank in Dizzy's head and the next thing he remembered was kissing his beautiful bride. Everyone applauded politely and then he did something that no one could have anticipated.

He gave a sign to Augustine, who, looking a little nervous, announced in Romanian to the guests that there would be a special piece of music to be played for the bride.

Dizzy turned to Ekaterina and said, "This is for you, my beautiful wife." He turned to Henry and asked for his horn.

He walked over to the two Gypsy musicians. Everyone wondered what was next—except Ekaterina. She realized what Dizzy was up to by taking her to the restaurant and asking for the same piece of music. The Gypsies started to play and eight bars later, Dizzy joined in. He played along for another sixteen bars, then began improvising over their song. It was something that no one had ever heard. Even the Gypsies were smiling and having a great time. Dizzy showed a comprehension of their music as if he had been playing it all of his life.

He wove a melody in and out of the chordal pattern and even got the Arabic sounding intonation right in the proper places. Everyone was stunned by the performance and broke into a hardy applause at the end. Even the Gypsies applauded Dizzy. They were as flabbergasted as anyone else that their music could be played by a foreigner with no prior knowledge.

Ekaterina walked over to Dizzy, her eyes streaming with tears, and put her arms around him. "Dizzy, I can't believe what I just heard. I'm sorry, I'm not supposed to cry on my wedding day but..."

"Remember, my love, we don't apologize for passion. And you look so beautiful it was truly inspiring to play that for you."

"How did you arrange all of this anyway?"

"Your father helped me a little. He organized it that the Gypsies got here early and we went over this a few times. Remember, I am not supposed to see you before the wedding, so it was easy to be out of sight. We practiced in what looks like a dungeon under here. He assured me it was soundproof."

"It is a dungeon. I'm still afraid to go down there by myself."

A wonderful meal was served at the enormous dining table. It paradoxically looked a little smaller now that there were over twenty people seated at it and not just three at one end. The guests lavished praise and numerous toasts to the bride and groom all in a language Dizzy couldn't understand, but gathered from their looks, smiles, and body language that they approved of Ekaterina's new husband.

Henry was having a good time and at one point remarked to Dizzy, "Strike one for the language of music. You cannot understand what they are saying, nor they you, but you crossed all of those barriers today with your music. It was amazing to me. God bless that black magic."

The evening wore on and a few of the guests started to leave. Ekaterina informed Dizzy that her father had reserved the best suite in the hotel he had stayed at with the band. "We have the place for three days and nights, and I can assure you, it is quite the place. I have seen a photograph of one of the rooms.

We will live like the king and queen."

And so they did. They luxuriated, lusted, ate, and drank for three days and nights. Then it was time to plan the trip to France. They looked at maps and plotted a route. Three days later, with just enough baggage to fill the toy car, they said their goodbyes. It was particularly sad for Ekaterina saying goodbye to her father with the unspoken realization that if war happened, they might not see each other for years. Neither of them said this, but it weighed heavily on them. Augustine did have the satisfaction that his beloved daughter would be safe in America and that made things a little easier, but only a little.

The car was fired up for its longest trip ever. Dizzy and Ekaterina lingered here and there to prolong the trip and they arrived in Paris about two weeks later. They spent a week exploring the city, going to hear music in clubs and bistros. They also had to procure tickets for a boat to New York. The other subject up for discussion was what to do with the car.

"We could sell it," said Dizzy, ever practical.

"That may take some time and the boat won't wait for us."

"Why don't we just give it away? It was given to us, after all."

"How do we do that? We just can't walk up to someone on the street and say, 'Would you like this car?'"

"And why not? Let's just look around for someone who looks like they could use a car and we'll give them the papers and the car and just walk away. That would be fun, don't you think?"

"Come on, Dizzy, we'll drive to Le Havre where we board ship and we'll give it to someone there."

"Craziest idea I have ever heard."

"Well my Dizzy, your spy girl is always full of them. You may have to get used to me."

They drove to Le Havre the next day and got a hotel not far from the docks. Ekaterina's French was minimal so she was going to have to do some fast talking to convince some total stranger on the street to take the car.

Once the car had been emptied of all of their stuff, they drove it to a moderately busy street with lots of shoppers and pedestrians. It was parked in a small slot on the street. Looking around, they spotted a young man with a small dog. Ekaterina approached him and began the conversation by asking if he owned a car. He stopped and asked her to repeat the question. He understood the second time.

"Non," he replied.

"My husband and I have just come from Romania and we are headed to New York tomorrow. These are our tickets." She showed him the tickets so he understood that they were indeed leaving town. He was a little puzzled. "What do you want?" he asked.

"We just drove from Romania and we have this car. We can't bring it with us so we have decided to give it away." She pointed at it parked beside her.

"Here are the papers and here is my passport. You will see that everything matches up."

"Mais ce n'est pas possible," exclaimed the young man.

"Listen Monsieur, I am going to give this car away, or if I can't, I will remove the licence plate and just walk away. That way the police will get a call or it will be towed away and with no one to take ownership of it, then it will wind up sold for parts or at a police auction."

The young man mulled this over carefully and decided that Ekaterina was legit and that he couldn't get into trouble if he accepted the car.

"Are you sure this car wasn't stolen?"

"Yes, look at the papers. Everything is in order. If it were stolen, I would just walk away from it. Instead, since it was given to my husband and me, we want to give it away. We do not have the time to sell it. Now do you want it or not?"

She was staring him down and for a few seconds, he looked a little unsure of what to do. "Oui Madame. Et je vous remercie beaucoup. Vous êtes très gentille, vous et votre mari."

With that, she gave him the papers and the keys and walked away with Dizzy at her side. The toy car was going to a new home.

"I am going to miss the little car."

"Me too," said Ekaterina. "And who knows, it may save his life like it did yours, or maybe it's just the thing he needs to run away with his mistress. I'm sure he is happy to own it. It is his lucky day."

CHAPTER 13

The ship left the next day and they said goodbye to Europe. Little did they know that it would be a decade before they would be able to return. The voyage was pleasant with no storms, and seasickness didn't strike the passengers like on Dizzy's first voyage. A few days into the trip, a dance band member recognized Dizzy and on several occasions, he sat in with the band. They were glad to have such an esteemed trumpeter play with them. For Dizzy, it was good practice time and he played Stardust for his lovely Ekaterina every time he was on stage.

Early one morning, she woke Dizzy. "There's land out there. We are here!"

Dizzy got out of bed and found himself looking at the Statue of Liberty in the distance. They both dressed quickly and hurried out on deck. "It's beautiful!" Ekaterina exclaimed.

"My ancestors saw the same thing when they arrived in the last century. I am coming home, but they were going to a strange land of which they knew next to nothing. I wonder how they felt looking at Miss Liberty out there."

"Pretty grateful that they were about to leave a stinking ship. I'm sure they didn't enjoy the great quarters and good food we had, not to mention the great music. And even though it is all new to me, I am sure I don't feel the same uncertainty they were going through. They probably didn't know English or much at all about their new home.

"You are right. They were probably in steerage below decks, and were probably not allowed above to mix with the upper class passengers. They would have been lucky to see the statue out of a porthole."

About two hours later, they were on dry land at a dock somewhere in Brooklyn. The immigration officers had processed them quickly at Ellis Island with no problems. Dizzy hailed a cab to Manhattan and they pulled up in front of the Waldorf Astoria on Park Avenue.

Mr. Washington, the doorman, greeted them. "Hello, Mr. Dizzy. Haven't seen you for a while. Welcome back."

"Thank you, Sam. This is Ekaterina, my new wife from Romania."

"Oh my. Congratulations, Mr. Dizzy. Very nice to meet you, Mrs. Dizzy."

"And you," replied Ekaterina.

During the next week, Ekaterina was lost to the wonders of the big city surrounding her. She had never seen a building taller than ten stories. There were so many cars, people, and bustle. She was completely amazed at everything. After they checked in, she just stared out of the window too excited and mesmerized to speak. Dizzy knew this would be fun for a few days, just showing her around. He took her to Macy's and let her wander around a store the likes of which she could have never imagined. They went to Central Park, the top of the Empire State Building, and then he took her to a club in Harlem, where for the first time in her life, she was in a room full of coloured people with music and dancing. She was completely amazed.

"Dizzy, look! They are throwing the girls up in the air and catching them all in rhythm to the music!"

"You have heard my band play similar music, but these boys are the real thing. They invented this music. And the dancing. You know, I am considered a master trumpet player, but when I come up to Harlem, I always feel I still have a lot to learn. It is as humbling as it is enjoyable. I studied music and would be considered an educated musician academically, but most of these players are self-taught and doing it all by ear and instinct—not unlike Spatzo and his friends." He paused.

"Speaking of music. I will have to call my agent in the morning and let him know that I haven't fallen off the edge of the Earth. When I didn't return with the rest of the band, I'm sure he wondered where I was. I will have to start thinking of a little work. The rest of the band must also be wondering where the Hell I am."

"You have been cavorting with your spy girl, but I wouldn't tell them quite that way."

"Too bad, it's a good line."

The following morning, Dizzy got on the phone.

"Dizzy? Dizzy! How da Hell are you? Where ya been?" It was Ramirez, his agent on the other end.

"I just got back, Joe. I spent a little extra time in Romania."

"What da Hell for?"

"I got married."

"No shit, Dizzy. Who is the lucky broad?" Subtlety was never among Joe's attributes.

"Her name is Ekaterina and she is no broad. She is a beautiful lady."

Dizzy had long stopped feeling slighted or insulted by Joe. He was incorrigible, but he always found Dizzy plenty of work, and he was honest. He was one of the likeable obnoxious people in the world.

He told it as it was and Dizzy always appreciated that part of it. A little too crude, perhaps, but Joe was a straight shooter. He did command respect from the bandleaders. Dizzy sometimes wondered about his lack of social skills, but realized he would never get an answer to that one.

"Listen, Joe, I need some work. See what you can do as soon as you can. I will round up the usual suspects as soon as I hear back from you. Who of my cats are in town these days?"

"The only one I know of is Spike."

"Good, let him know I'm back. I'm at the Waldorf."

"Okay, Diz, and bring the little lady down to meet me sometime."

"I certainly will. Bye, Joe."

In the meantime, Ekaterina was in a constant state of wonder over everything she saw in the big city, even all the little things that Dizzy would have never noticed or took for granted.

"My God, Dizzy, look at the size of the phone book! Ours seems like a little notebook compared to this!"

She started to look through the city phone book. She looked up her family name but found no one. However, she did find one V. Polozenski. "Hey Dizzy, there's a Polozenski in the phone book. Do you have any idea if your old name is a common one in Moldova? I have never heard it in my country."

"I have no idea. There were a number of them in the cemetery I visited, but they may have just been a local family. As you know, I know nothing about them. But listen, they were run out of town back in the nineteenth century as a despised family. Professor Zablo warned me about letting my family name out while I was with him. My ancestors were not nice people and the villagers are just as angry at them today as they were back then."

"Wouldn't it be interesting to know if you had relatives in this end of the world?"

"Interesting, yes, but interesting can mean several things, both good and bad, and I'm not for stepping into the bad. I was chased out of the place myself, remember. I was shot at and the car chasing me ran over a land mine. Now that was really interesting, if you will, but not the kind of interesting I want to pursue."

"I see your point. I'll tell you what: I'm really curious. I don't know why, but I am. Tell me where this place is."

Dizzy looked at the address in the directory. "It's fairly close to here, about ten blocks. What are you thinking?"

"I certainly don't want to phone this Polozenski character, but what if he goes to work every day? He will leave his house and I could get a look at him. What if he looks like you? He could be a relative. You know nothing of your family by your own admission. What if he equally knows nothing but shares a common heritage? Or what if he does know about your heritage?"

"Certainly an interesting thought."

"If the family Polozenski never spoke of their life in the old country, he could very well be in the same boat with a family that never told him anything."

"You know, I have looked in most of the phone books around this country while on tour. Sometimes there are long, boring evenings when you are not working. I read the phone book. It puts me to sleep pretty darn quick."

"Then you have never looked at the New York book?"

"I guess not or I would certainly have seen the name."

"I would really like to get a look at this man. I am going to walk by to see what kind of place he lives in. Maybe it's a big apartment and there are so many people living there that it would take a long time to figure out who he is. I will go tomorrow. I'm so curious about this. I hope you don't mind."

"I don't mind, but you have to be careful. Do not approach anyone. You just can't be sure about anything."

"I'll be careful, Dizzy. I promise."

Ekaterina left the hotel early the next morning, taking a taxi to the address where V. Polozenski lived. She was delighted to find a breakfast place directly across the street, so if she got a window seat, she could sit and just wait for someone she didn't know, or never saw before, come out of a building on the remotest chance that he would look enough like Dizzy. Then should would follow him to see where he might work.

It suddenly seemed absurd, but she was here and might as well carry on with this crazy idea. First, she looked at the apartment directory and did indeed see V. Polozenski's name on one of thirty apartments.

So far, so good. She walked into the Breakfast Cabin across the street. Ekaterina didn't know this yet, but this is what New Yorkers called a greasy spoon. She ordered a coffee and bagel and managed to find a place at the window directly across the front door of the apartment. She nursed the coffee for twenty minutes. With each passing moment, she felt like this was the most farfetched thing she'd ever done. She counted about seventeen people leaving the building and none the men bore any resemblance to Dizzy.

She ordered another coffee and while she was dealing with the waiter, the door to the apartment building opened and out walked a man whose appearance just about made Ekaterina do a double take. This had to be Polozenski! He dodged traffic crossing the street directly in front of the greasy spoon, walked in, sat at the counter, and ordered breakfast. The guy looked a little older than Dizzy, but there was no doubt in her mind that she was looking at a Polozenski.

Now, she was feeling a little nervous but not really sure why. She had never seen the man before and he had never seen her. She was just another customer like the dozen others in the place. She waited quietly until the man got up to leave. He walked to the cash register at the end of the counter and paid his bill, at which point the waiter said, "Thanks, Vic. Have a great day."

Vic, she thought. *So he must be Viktor Polozenski.* She hurriedly got up after he left, settled her bill, and left to follow the stranger. He walked at a leisurely speed so it was easy for Ekaterina to follow him. She stayed well behind, as there weren't many people on the street and if he looked behind, he would notice her, especially if he looked more than once.

Dizzy had affectionately nicknamed Ekaterina his spy girl right from the beginning, and as she followed this stranger through the streets of New York, she realized she was living up to her name. It made her laugh to herself. It had been less than two months since she met Dizzy backstage at the concert. Now, she was Ekaterina Pollen, walking behind someone who might be related to her new husband from God knows where in a strange country. When she looked at it from this perspective, it all looked a little unreal, though still exciting and adventurous. She thought of Dizzy and his strange trip to Moldova. How things can happen so quickly to change one's existence! She had never felt so alive in her life, though her life in Romania was good by any standards. She had a wonderful father, she had never known hardship of any sort, she was educated, socially as ease in any situation, and had the choice of any man she wanted. There were plenty of men who wanted her, but she married an American musician and suspected that most of her friends thought she was a little crazy in doing so. They had wished her well though, and in the end, they knew that Ekaterina would have jumped into something completely unexpected like this anyway.

She noticed that the stranger had stopped in front of what looked like a small storefront. He pulled a set of keys from his pocket and let himself in, closing the door behind him.

Ekaterina stopped and waited on the corner about a hundred feet away. After a minute or so, she decided to walk past the door to try to see what kind of establishment this was and carry on. She had seen enough for one day. She knew where Polozenski lived and that was her purpose today. She picked up her pace and as she approached the place, she saw that it was not a store or shop. The sign on the door read: Romania-Moldova Social Club.

What the Hell is that? she thought.

"Dizzy, you are not going to believe this." She was excited when she got back to the hotel room. "I saw him. I saw this guy who looks just like he could be your brother. A few years older but his name is Viktor and I followed him to a place called the Romania-Moldova Social Club! He..."

"Hold on" said Dizzy. "You what? Slow down and start from the beginning."

Regaining her composure, she recounted the events of the last hour in detail. Dizzy sat silent until she finished. "And that's when I decided I had seen enough for now."

"That's amazing. What do you suppose the Romania-Moldova Social Club is anyway?"

She put her arms around Dizzy, giving him the hundred volts with her smile. "I suppose there is only one way to find out. You'll have to take your spy girl out on a date."

"It's probably a private club of some kind. I have no idea."

"Tell you what, let's both go for breakfast there tomorrow morning and you can see for yourself. He may come by for coffee again and you'll know where he went. You know, he had the keys to the place, which means he is either the president or the janitor. Either one could go there in the morning. He was well dressed though, so maybe not the janitor. But I want you to see for yourself."

"Okay, spy girl. We'll go to the greasy spoon tomorrow."

"The what?"

"Greasy spoon. That is a general term for a cheap restaurant in this part of the world."

"Doesn't sound appetizing."

"On the contrary, the food can be delicious."

The next morning, they sat in the same booth as the previous day. "He came out of his building at about this time. Oh look! Here he comes." The other Polozenski dodged the traffic crossing the street and came into the shop, ordering a coffee at the counter.

"Do you see what I mean?" asked Ekaterina.

"My God, you are right. He does look like me. A few years older perhaps. I'm not going to let him see my face, as I'm sure he will come to a similar conclusion." Dizzy put his sunglasses on until the stranger left the shop. They followed him, long way behind this time, as Ekaterina knew exactly where he was headed. The stranger opened the door to the RMSC and disappeared inside. "That is it," she said.

"I don't know what to make of all this," Dizzy admitted, "but now, I am curious for sure."

"That's the point! Just for now, let us assume that the two of you are related in some way. Can you think of any possible connection? Your grandfather came to the States in the nineteenth century. Can you account for every Pollen you are related to? Did you have a great uncle who may have come here also? Are there immigration records? We also have to find out the name of the village where you were.

"Given the status of your ancestry in Moldova, we have to be careful about letting us be known for now. I know about the long memories people in my end of the world have. It's really extreme. On the other hand, if Viktor Polozenski is using his real name around this club, then perhaps no one here knows about the Polozenski reputation. You certainly didn't."

"Okay," said Dizzy. "Well call the professor. At least I have his name, and I copied down his phone number. Then we will call the immigration department."

Not knowing the village the professor lived in made for some difficulty but looking at a map, Ekaterina knew at least which district he was in, and it took about a half an hour to complete a long distance call to Moldova. Ekaterina handled the call, as she had to deal with Romanian speaking operators for most of this time. Finally, a phone rang and a male voice answered. In Romanian, Ekaterina asked for Professor Petroff Zablo. "This is he," the voice answered. Ekaterina gave the phone to Dizzy.

"Hello, Professor Zablo, this is Dizzy calling from New York."

"Dizzy, my friend, what a pleasant surprise. It is wonderful to hear your voice. I never expected this."

"I didn't also, but several things have happened to me since I last saw you. First, the good news. The female voice you answered to is my new wife. I got married to a wonderful woman in Bucharest."

"You never stop surprising me!'

"Believe me, Professor, I am equally surprised. But listen, we may not have too much time in case the line goes dead. First of all, I never did know the name of the village you live in." Dizzy went on to tell the professor the whole story about encountering a look-alike in New York.

"Do you know of any other Polozenskis besides my grandfather who emigrated from the village at any time?"

"There were rumours of another member of the family called Viktor Polozenski who vanished some years after your grandfather. Everyone was sure he died. This happened around 1910 or so."

"Thank you, Professor."

"Dizzy, what is your wife's name?"

"Her maiden name is Ekaterina Vancea."

"Oh my, do not tell me you married Augustine's only daughter!"

"Why, yes! You know the family?" Dizzy was now visibly shocked.

"Augustine and I are old friends from university!"

"Jesus! Now, who is the one with the surprises?"

Dizzy was speechless. He simply turned to Ekaterina, holding the phone, and said, "Here, say hello an old friend of your father's."

"What are you talking about?"

"Just take the phone. It's going to be a day of surprises."

There began an emotional conversation in Romanian between Ekaterina and Professor Zablo, which lasted about five minutes. When the phone was finally hung up, she was shaking and on the verge of tears.

"Dizzy, you are not going to believe this..."

He was already pouring a couple of stiff drinks. "Try me."

They both sat down and took a swig.

"I'm not sure where to start, but let's start with the professor. Now, I don't have the full story, but according to him, he and my father have known one another for fifty years or so. They were best of friends in university. Zablo is Moldavian but went to university in Bucharest with my father. They became separated during the Great War and went their separate ways after that. Zablo taught at a university in Leipzig Now that I think of it, my father used to mention an old friend from university. He referred to him as "Zabi. I know nothing about him but that has to have been Zablo's nickname. but at one point, they were both in love with the same woman, my mother. In the end, my father won her heart and I think there might have been some resentment, but from what I could ascertain from his tone of voice, all that happened long ago and there are no hard feelings. Zablo also said you were a remarkable man and he admires you very much. He wishes us a happy and long life."

"Never in a million years could I have foreseen that."

"Nor I," she replied.

"Listen, did Zablo mention anything about my presence there? That would have been quite an incident at the border with my leaving the country the way I did. The land mine knocked one car over but I don't know if anyone was hurt or even killed. That must have made the newspapers."

"No, he didn't, but sometimes strange incidents don't make the papers, especially if it is what looks like a comedy of errors like your encounter."

"Maybe I'll have to take you on a date to the Romania-Moldava Social Club after all."

"I can't wait, but we will have to be careful. We will certainly get to know what this club is all about, but let's not give your name away just yet, until we're sure of things.

This Polozenski may see you as someone who looks like him but maybe not for now. After all, I was looking for someone who resembles you. I may not have noticed him if I ran into him out of context."

They opened the door to the Romania-Moldava Social Club around 9:00 that evening. It was a small place with seating for about eighty people at tables, and there were various sofas and easy chairs scattered here and there. A small bar was against the far wall. The walls were a darkish colour decorated with a few posters and paintings. About thirty-five people were seated with a few more standing at the bar. A sombre atmosphere permeated the place as well as the stale smell of dead cigarette smoke and dried beer in the carpet. Not the classiest place they had ever visited, but they were there and might as well let things play out.

They sat at a small table in a dark corner, with Dizzy taking the place where few people would see his face. No one was speaking English in the place. A rumpled waiter looking a little greenish approached the table and Ekaterina had a short conversation with him. He returned with two glasses of the firewater they had back in the old country.

"I thought this would bring back a few memories," she said.

"My God, I can't believe they let this stuff out of the country."

They sipped the knockout drink and set about observing the people around them.

"I have to say, this certainly looks like a place that a genuine spy would frequent," Dizzy remarked.

Ekaterina put on her best mysterious accent. "What makes you think I am not the genuine spy girl you refer to?"

Before Dizzy could say anything, the door opened and in walked Viktor Polozenski.

"Somehow we have to meet this guy," Ekaterina said. "I'm not quite sure how, but I have an idea. Let's see what he does and I will try to meet him on the pretense that I am new in town and heard about this place. I will not give away your name or my maiden name. We are just new to New York, visiting maybe from California, and I will try to figure out a little of his background. Let's meet the guy. It can't hurt and if he notices that you and he resemble each other a bit, then so be it. Your name is Pollen and you are from San Francisco. No connection to any old country whatsoever. I am the Romanian here. Do you think that is a good idea?"

"I suppose," said Dizzy, knowing full well that Ekaterina was relishing every moment of the mystery and would find some way to pull this off whether he wanted to or not.

"What the Hell. I'm game. Let's find out about this could-be relative of mine. But please be careful, Ekaterina. We have absolutely no idea who this is or what his game is."

"I will. I wouldn't do or say anything that would land us in some nasty predicament."

Viktor Polozenski stood at the bar awhile before ordering a drink.

"I will go and order two more drinks and see if I can lure him to our table."

"That shouldn't be hard. I would be lured to any table you asked me to," Dizzy remarked.

Ekaterina leaned over the table and kissed him. "Dizzy, you never have anything to be afraid of."

"I know." He smiled. "Now go before the waiter returns to the bar."

Ekaterina walked over to the bar and waited for the server beside Polozenski.

She decided to lay it on right off the bat. "You bear quite a resemblance to my husband. We noticed it the minute you walked into the place. Will you join us for a drink? You can see for yourself."

She surprised herself with her forwardness but that was always the way she did things. No bullshit. Just call it like it is.

"I would be delighted to join you," Polozenski said. "What are you drinking?"

"We have been sipping Zorko."

"Zorko? Are you Romanian? Only Romanians will ever go near that stuff. The military runs army tanks on that stuff when they are short of petrol."

"And I'll bet the tanks go faster on Zorko than on petrol." Ekaterina laughed.

That did it. Soon Ekaterina and Polozenski went back to the table carrying three shots of Zorko.

Polozenski pulled up a chair and sat down. Ekaterina said, "I'm sorry, I never asked your name."

"I am Vikor Polozenski."

"I am Ekaterina Pollen and this is my husband, Dizzy Pollen."

They shook hands. "Your lovely wife invited me over to your table saying that you and I resemble each other, and I must say that she is right. We could almost be brothers."

"I have never suspected that I had any long lost brothers but we do look alike. I am an only child. Is Polozenski a Russian name?"

"Im not sure. I too am an only child. My grandfather came from Moldova. I have never been there and know very little about the place. My grandfather came to New York and I don't know a lot about my family, as they never spoke much about the old country."

Dizzy and Ekaterina were trying to keep their composure. Hardly believing what they were hearing.

"This is my place.. I own and run this little club for Romanians and Moldavians who like to get together and meet or reminisce. It's not much, but it is a home away from home for many of these people. Many are political refugees who cannot return. Some never learned English, so here they can converse in their own language. We help keep some of the traditions from the old country and I think we help people to be comfortable in what is to many a strange place. The decor is all from the old country. I have made it to resemble a typical little bar in Moldova or Romania.

Speaking of which, how did you wind up here?"

"I came from Romania as a child," Ekaterina replied. "I saw this place about a month ago and decided to come here out of curiosity. We live in San Francisco but spend time in New York."

"I am happy you discovered us. I hope you return. If you will excuse me, I have paperwork to do in my office. It was nice meeting you both. Good evening."

"Good evening," they replied.

When Polozenski was out of sight, Ekaterina said, "I have to use the ladies room, then let's get out of here."

"I'm with you."

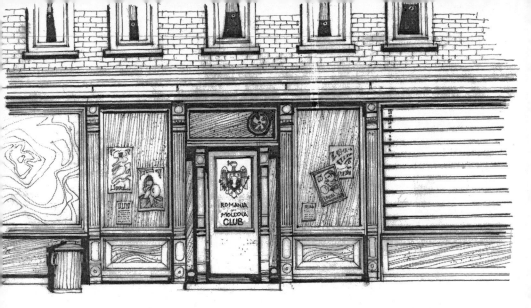

CHAPTER 14

Ekaterina went to the women's washroom down a long corridor. The walls were brown and the whole place was dimly lit by a forty-watt bare bulb on the ceiling. On the right side, there was a door halfway down the hallway that was several inches ajar with a light on inside. She paid no attention to it, as the Zorko was insistent on leaving her body. On the way out, however, driven by her cat-like curiosity, she nudged the door open a few inches and cautiously peeked in.

Back at the table, she met Dizzy. "Let's get out of here. I have just seen something bizarre."

They left the place and out on the sidewalk, the air was warm and they decided to walk home. She took Dizzy's arm. "I just looked into a room down the hallway on the way to the woman's room and you will never guess what I saw."

"I'm almost afraid to ask."

"It was a room full of musical instruments and a clothes rack full of costumes!"

"I didn't expect that."

"I suddenly got really afraid and wanted to get out of there as soon as possible."

"What made you so afraid?"

Ekaterina stopped walking and spun around. "Allow me to put it this way. When was the last time you saw a bunch of Moldavians in crazy costumes playing music?"

Dizzy's eyes went wide. "My God, what are you saying?"

"I made several observations while we were there. First of all, there were only two women in the place: a middle aged woman, who I am sure was Romanian, and myself. However, from the accents I was hearing around us, I'm pretty sure everyone or close to everyone came from Moldova.

This sounds crazy, I know, but that place is no ordinary social club for lonely old men from the old country. I don't know what it is, but I can tell you what it isn't. From here on, I am baffled. I can't figure it out at all."

They walked home in silence. He had his arm around her shoulder and she nestled her head against him. They were worried about the intriguing place they had left. They hardly said a word to each other until they reached the hotel.

Once in their room, Dizzy poured a couple of drinks and they sat down in the darkness on the sofa.

"For once, we seem to be both rendered speechless by what went on tonight," he said.

"Yes, but it is probably because we are both thinking the same thing and it is too weird to articulate without it sounding completely crazy. I'll go first." She paused.

"Dizzy, the whole thing may be innocent and completely harmless, but what if this group are actually musicians and they play the same crazy song that you played with Professor Zablo and people die as a result. It's far-fetched, of course, but what if?"

"Of course it is far-fetched, but I can tell you that it can happen—from personal experience having taken part in it myself. The thing is, is this a ritual that happens on a prescribed date like the one I took part in, or can it happen at anytime, anywhere? Is this all centered around the actual piece of music, or does it need to happen at a certain location? Does the fact that everyone is in costume make some kind of a difference?" He was getting animated.

"Now, think about this one. Could anybody do this? I haven't told you this yet, Ekaterina, but I memorized that entire musical score and have written it down. I made a real effort to do this while I was still at the professor's place. I could play my part right now without the music. My band could play that piece perfectly with about ten or twenty minutes of rehearsal. I did this because as pieces of music go, this is a real interesting one, and I wanted to play it over here. No one in this end of the world has ever heard anything remotely like it."

"Consider me amazed, my dear Dizzy, that you were able to do that. You really have that entire piece written down?"

"Every sharp, flat, and dotted note."

They went to bed and made passionate love, perhaps heightened by the events and thoughts of that evening. So far unspoken, they both knew they had to find out more. It was too weird and surreal to let go.

A few days later, Ramirez called with at least a month worth of work for Dizzy and a quintet at the Lexington hotel. The pay was good and Dizzy began trying to locate some of his usual suspects.

He got Spike and three of the others who had been to Europe, and one new guy on clarinet. All his energy went into the new band and the business of the Romania-Moldova Club became relegated to the back burner for a while. After all, Dizzy had to start making a living again.

Ekaterina wanted to find some work so she went off to the Romanian consulate. Given her qualifications, she found some temporary work as a translator right away.

Life acquired a degree of normalcy for the first time in ages and it seemed to suit them well. Dizzy wondered how Ekaterina would fare in her new life, but he needn't have worried. She was a strong, independent woman who always kept on top of things. She telephoned her father every couple of weeks, which made him very happy. She never mentioned the conversation with Professor Zablo, not wanting to tie Dizzy to the whole Saltatio Mortis affair. She couldn't help wondering if her father knew about the bizarre event and just never talked about it. She set up a bank account into which her father wired serious money every month. He figured that with war coming, the easiest way to keep any money would be to remove it out of the country. Ekaterina told Dizzy of the account but decided not to make a big deal of it.

It came to about $2500 a month. She never gave Dizzy any numbers and he never asked.

However, Ekaterina remained curious about the club. When she got to know some of her co-workers, she asked a few of them about it. She never told anyone she had been inside, and said she had only walked by the place. Petra, a Romanian girl working in the office, told her that she had been inside but it was a dingy dive filled with lonely old men mostly from Moldova, which confirmed Ekaterina's observations.

She was dying to get back into the place to try to find out more about what really went on there. Dizzy had put all of this on hold with the new band, which was due to play their first gig in a week. He gave Ekaterina a $50 bill and told her to buy something nice for the occasion. She was thrilled and shuffled out to haunt the dress shops. She had usually been frugal with money and a brand new $50 bill made her feel like a rich girl. Her bank account didn't make her feel that way. In some way, it was still her father's money.even though it was really meant for her. She had always tried to be independent not wanting to rely of her father's wealth.

Saturday night at the Lexington saw Dizzy's name in lights on the marquis. "DIZZY POLLEN and HIS HOT SWINGERS." There was a line-up of fans outside before the show.

Dizzy and the band went down early to set things up and Ekaterina would come along later with her new-found friend, Petra, from the consulate.

Down beat was at 9:00 sharp. The curtains opened and the master of ceremonies came out on stage. "Good evening, ladies and gentlemen. It is my great pleasure to announce the Lexington hotel's first engagement of Dizzy Pollen and his Hot Swingers." A second curtain opened behind the host, revealing the band ready to go. A few seconds later, Dizzy counted off and the band broke into Rosetta. Within thirty seconds, the dance floor was full.

Dizzy was looking for Ekaterina but it wasn't until the song was over that he noticed her in the wings, just like he had seen her in Romania. She wore a blue dress with sparkly rhinestones all over it and matching shoes. She looked stunning and Dizzy just about fell over when he laid eyes upon her. Flashing him that mysterious smile, she pointed upwards, waving her fingers as she drew her hand down. Dizzy caught it right away. She wanted to hear Stardust. It had been such a long time since she last heard it. Only too happy to oblige, he played it as if he had composed it himself. There was thunderous applause from the audience after that one.

It went on for hours until closing time and Dizzy was amazed at the response the band was getting. It was reminiscent of the European tour. Ekaterina stayed in the wings for a while then she sat with Petra and jitterbugged with her a few times. Petra was a real jazz fan and knew a lot about the music. She was excited when Ekaterina asked her to come along. Petra knew who Dizzy was professionally but had never figured on actually meeting him, and Ekaterina never told Petra that he was her husband until they got to the gig that night. Petra was completely taken aback when she revealed that they were married.

"Oh my God! How come you never told me before?"

"You didn't ask me anything, and besides, I'm known for my surprises."

"You pulled a good one tonight. I have every one of your husband's records. I know his music very well. How did you meet him?"

A good part of the evening was spent with Ekaterina telling Petra about meeting Dizzy. There was so much to be left out that she continually had to watch herself, but she did describe the episodes with the Gypsies and the trip across Europe with the toy car.

"That's so romantic," said Petra.

"Yes, it certainly is. He is a good man and I am very lucky to have found him." She smiled.

"And you, Petra. Do you have a boyfriend?"

"Not right now. I have just come off a divorce and I am going to give the single life a chance for a while at least. I need to recoup myself and enjoy life on my own terms for now."

"Sorry to hear that. Do you want to talk about it?"

"There's not much to tell. I simply married the wrong man. I married someone who was born here but his family came from Moldova a long time ago. He turned out to be a little weird in my books."

Ekaterina had to watch her reaction.

"The interesting thing is that my ex-husband looks an awful lot like your husband. They could almost be brothers."

By now, Ekaterina really had to fight to keep her composure, for she knew who Petra's ex was.

She decided to try to steer the conversation in a different direction for fear of giving things away.

"You don't say," she said.

She felt a little stupid for saying that because it gave an opening for Petra to carry on the conversation, much to Ekaterina's discomfort.

"Yes, we divorced about six months ago. He was nice enough I guess but I never really knew what he did for a living. He always said he had city contracts for maintenance work. I can't see that I ever really knew a lot about him so I decided to get out. I became worried he was mixed up in something not quite right. He was uncommunicative about his life and I was always afraid the cops or the mob would break into our place." She paused.

"I loved him at first, but it turned to suspicion and fear, and I simply didn't want to lead my life like that. His name is Viktor Polozenski. I haven't seen him since the divorce and am happy that way."

By now, Ekaterina was in stunned shock. Soon the gig was over and Dizzy turned up at the table.

"That went okay, didn't it?"

"It went well," said Ekaterina. "Very well indeed. Dizzy, I want you to meet my friend from work. This is Petra. Petra, this is my talented husband, Dizzy."

"It's an honour to meet you, Dizzy. I am a huge fan of yours and I would like to think that I have every recording you have ever made."

"I am very flattered. Thank you. I haven't heard some of that early stuff in years."

"I have them all, and you and Ekaterina are most welcome to come and listen to them sometime, if you would like."

Dizzy thanked her and went to pack up. Later, the boys came over to meet Ekaterina as Dizzy's wife for the first time. They had briefly seen her in the hotel room in Bucharest before she got kicked out with the Gypsy musicians. After a few minutes, everyone left the place. One of the musicians lived close to Petra and offered to drive her home. They said good night all around, and Dizzy and Ekaterina went alone in a taxi back to the Waldorf.

Once in the room, Dizzy complimented her on her dress and how beautiful she looked. They shared a passionate kiss and Dizzy just wanted to pick her up and carry her to the bedroom.

"I know what we are both thinking, and it will all happen, I promise you," she said. "You can have your way with me tonight, but I want to have a night-cap first. Pour us a couple of stiff ones, because your beautiful spy girl has discovered something quite extraordinary this evening."

Dizzy, knowing something interesting was up, went to the liquor cabinet and returned with a couple of brandies.

"First of all, you were great tonight. I was so proud of you. Everyone loved the show. I hope you are happy with the way things went."

"I certainly am. The band is working really well together and the new kid on the clarinet is great.

"Now, what is this extraordinary discovery of yours?"

"The girl I was with tonight... She's a nice girl. I like her. We chatted all evening and the conversation came around to her recent divorce. You have to imagine the difficulty I had keeping a straight face when she told me she had just divorced a man six months ago. This man was born here in the States but his family came from Moldova a long time ago, and he looked just like you!"

"My God, don't tell me..."

"Petra was married to Viktor Polozenski!"

"Jesus! Is my life with you going to be full of surprises like this?"

"I hope so!" She put her lips close to his ear. "Now you can have your way with me."

He took her in his arms, kissed her again, then swooped her off her feet and carried her onto the bed.

It was tender and rough at the same time, reflecting the unspoken tension arising from Ekaterina's discovery. As they lay in each other's arms just before sleep, they both had the feeling that this Polozenski business was far from over.

They carried on for the next few weeks, with Dizzy playing his engage-ment. Ekaterina worked at the consulate a little more than she had originally planned, but the work was there. She and Petra were becoming good friends. Ekaterina racked her brain figuring out how to find out more about Viktor Polozenski from Petra but didn't really know how to broach the subject without arousing suspicion or worse, causing her friend pain. Finally, unable to stay silent any longer, she simply asked directly one day at lunch. "Petra, I haven't asked you as it is really none of my business, but tell me about the man you divorced, Viktor. If you would rather not, then that's okay and I apologize for asking."

"Not at all. I'm okay talking about it. It seems a long way off by now anyway. He came to the consulate one day for something or other and that is where we met. He was attractive and charming and, as they say, one thing led to another. Six months later we were married. Things were fine for a while until I realized that I had no idea what he did for a living. He never talked about any work or anything like that. He left for this alleged work every day and came back in the evening, but he would never say anything about anything. I became suspicious thinking he might work for the Secret Service and couldn't talk about it, or maybe he worked for the mafia."

"I started to get paranoid after a while. My imagination kept nagging me, as I have a penchant for imagining the worst. I started to question him but he brushed it off and finally threatened me if I kept asking. Then I really got scared and decided to get out. Funny, he didn't make the fuss that I expected. He just told me if I want out of the marriage, then he wouldn't stop me. I was relieved and we came to an amicable ending. I still have no idea what he does for a living."

"Did it ever occur to you to follow him someday to find out where he works?"

"Yes, it did, but I am a bit of a coward. At any rate, I don't know where he lives now. He moved after the divorce."

"Had he ever been back to Moldova?"

"As a matter of fact, he did tell me he goes back every seven years for a week. I don't know why. He wouldn't tell me. It's strange because his ancestors came here long ago and I don't know if he has anyone back there. I heard that he went recently."

Once more, Ekaterina had to keep a straight face.

Later that day, upon returning home, Ekaterina said to her husband, "Dizzy, pour us a good one and then sit down. I don't want you to keel over this time."

By now, Dizzy knew something really interesting was going to be revealed.

Dizzy poured two doubles and handing one to her. "Okay, spy girl, what do you have for me this time?"

"Are you ready? Listen to this. Viktor Polozenski goes back to Moldova once every seven years for a week!"

Dizzy sputtered up his scotch over the floor and just about gagged on the spot.

"Jesus Christ..."

"Dizzy, this can only mean one thing: Viktor must go back to play the Saltatio Mortis!"

"If that is true, then I probably played with him!"

"Of course, we can't know for sure, but the circumstantial evidence is piling up. The instruments in the club along with all the costumes, his resemblance to you, his ancestors living in a castle, and now this. Do you remember the conversations we had back in Bucharest about fitting pieces in puzzles? Well, there are a lot of pieces of a strange puzzle growing before our eyes, snd I am having a Hell of a time trying to make any sense of any of it. It seems that every few weeks, a new piece lands on the table."

Then Ekaterina's eyes lit up. "What if you were mistaken for Viktor Polozenski over there and that is why they were chasing you? They rightly took you for a Polozenski, but maybe the wrong one. They saw the family resemblance all right and mistook you for him. After all, if someone only goes somewhere every seven years, then a person looking very much like him could easily be mistaken for him."

"I see your point. It's small consolation though. Do you suppose some people saw both of us and are wondering how we could be in two places at once?"

Ekaterina laughed. "I hope so!" She looked at him with that mischievous smile.

"Dizzy, I have to get back into that club."

CHAPTER 15

Ekaterina debated whether she should ask Petra to get a drink at the Romanian-Moldavian social club but decided against it. If Petra did not know what Viktor Polozenski did for a living, Ekaterina did and thought the better of having a scene happen. That would draw too much attention to Ekaterina, which she did not want. Besides, she had already met Polozenski.

"Dizzy, I want you to take me to the club again."

"Listen, I am getting a little apprehensive about all of this. We may be venturing close to a scene that could put us both in danger. We don't know what these people, whoever they are, might be up to. I'm inclined to think it would be no good, given my personal experience. I don't like it, not one bit."

Ekaterina could see that he was seriously concerned and she didn't want to have him alarmed in any way. However, her curiosity was killing her.

"All we are doing is going for a drink. Nobody knows what we know about all of this. And that provides us with enough security. We know the connections, which means we know enough to not say anything to anyone. I want to eavesdrop on conversations. We just can speak softly in English and I will lend an ear to the room. No one knows I know the language and can hear regional dialects."

Dizzy knew what Ekaterina really had in mind. "I know you are itching to have a look in that back room again. That's what you really want, isn't it?"

"I cannot tell a lie, but a girl has to pee sometime, doesn't she?"

"All right, but please promise me you will be careful. If you are spotted in that room, you could be arrested—or worse."

"I know, which is why I will not do anything reckless. I promise, Dizzy."

On Dizzy's night off from the gig, they went to the club. They decided not to dress fancily, as no one in their previous visit was dressed beyond ordinary clothes. Ekaterina did not want to draw attention to herself. Dizzy said, "The day you are in a room full of old men and not be noticed is not going to happen anytime soon."

They reached the club around 10:00. There were about the same number of people as the last time. Sitting at the same table, Ekaterina decided to order scotch and not the infamous Zorko because that would be more noticeable. The disinterested waiter took their order and soon they were sipping bad scotch and she was listening to conversations going around them.

"Those three men over there are from the northern part of Moldova, as are the man and woman over there. The husband and wife are having a quiet spat. But three men are talking about something. Wait, I heard the word 'castle' and 'seven years' and oh my God, I just heard the words Saltatio Mortis! Isn't that what you called it?"

"Yes, but…"

"Shhhh!"

A minute later, the three men got up and left the club.

"Dizzy, at least one of those men played at the bal macabre when you did!"

"Jesus, that makes two people from Horsehead's band!"

"I'm going to the lady's room, then we can go," Ekaterina said. "I've heard enough for one night."

"Me too."

Ekaterina opened the door to the hallway leading to the lady's room. It was quite dark and she went straight to the lavatory. On the way out, she would sneak a peek in the room halfway down the hallway where the instruments and the costumes were stored. She was nervous beyond belief and the adrena-line was causing her to tremble. She got up and tried to calm herself while washing her hands. Looking in the mirror, she told the frightened face, "You can do this."

She opened the door and walked the ten feet to the door off the hallway. She stopped and put her hand on the knob and turned it. It was locked!

Looking down, she saw the corner of a piece of paper sticking out from under the door about one inch or so. She wet her index finger with her tongue, reached down, and pulled it out. She picked it up, quickly folded it, and stuffed it into her bra. She almost reached the door leading back to the bar when it opened and she came face to face with Viktor Polozenski.

"Mr. Polozenski! I didn't expect you. Good evening." She was sure that the panic was written all over her face despite her smile.

"Good evening, Mrs. Pollen. Nice to see you exploring my little club again."

"My husband and I were walking by and decided to pop in for a drink. We were just on our way out."

"Well, nice to see you, and say hello to your husband. Come again some-time. Goodnight."

"Goodnight."

Ekaterina was shaking when she got back to her table. "Dizzy, we have to go right now," she whispered.

He went up to the bar and settled up, then walked Ekaterina out of the place.

A few feet out the door, she turned to him. "Just hold me a minute."

"What happened? You're trembling."

She held on for a while and Dizzy felt her relax a little.

"Dizzy, hail a cab please."

He flagged down a Yellow Cab and once inside, repeated, "What happened?"

"I'm not sure yet. We'll talk about it when were home. Just hold me."

Once inside their room, Ekaterina relaxed. "Please pour us a scotch," she said. "Then I want you to do something." She was smiling now.

Dizzy returned with the usual prelude libation for one of Ekaterina's discoveries.

"Now, take my blouse off please."

Used to her unusual behaviour, he was completely taken aback by this one.

"I'm always happy to undress you, but this is completely unexpected."

He unbuttoned her blouse to reveal her lacy bra. This was getting a little distracting.

"Now, look in the left cup of my bra."

"What?"

"Go ahead, look."

Dizzy reached into her bra and felt something strange.

"Go ahead, pull it out."

Dizzy removed the folded sheet of paper. It was a hand written sheet music.

"Tell me what you think this is. Is it what I think it is?"

Dizzy looked it over and his eyes got wide. "Jesus Christ, where did you get this?"

"A small corner of the page was sticking out under the door to that room where they keep those musical instruments and costumes. I picked it up, and seeing that it was a piece of sheet music, I quickly folded it and stuffed it into my bra. Seconds later, Viktor Polozenski came into the hallway just as I was about to open the door to leave. Talk about a fearful surprise. I just about fainted when I saw him face to face. That's why I was shaking when I got back to the table and had to leave. I was so scared."

"This is part of the score to the Saltatio Mortis. I recognized it right away. I told you I memorized it and wrote it down. This is exactly it!"

"Then there is a group of people who, in this end of the world, play that music. We know at least two of them played it with you a few months ago. I am utterly confused as to the meaning of it all. From what you described, this takes place every seven years at this one castle and someone dies as a result. Now, since you told me all of this, it stands to reason, and I use the term loosely here, that since this has been going on for so long, that it is expected that someone will die after listening to this piece. But back there, it is an old tradition by and for people who are filled with superstition and believe in witchcraft or whatever, and the belief if so strong that that is what makes it happen. That is how I see it. But we are in a modern country where this is not supposed to exist. What are they doing there?"

Ekaterina downed the last of her drink. "My dear Dizzy, I think you should take the rest of my clothes off. Then we can go to bed."

For the next few weeks, Dizzy occupied himself with the band and there wasn't a lot of discussion about the Polozenski affair, as they called it. They hadn't found a place to live yet so they decided to stay at the Waldorf. They were happy there and it was convenient for both of them.

One day, Ekaterina decided to call Professor Zablo and discuss what she and Dizzy knew about Polozenski and the possibility of playing at the last Saltatio Mortis. She and Dizzy began the process of calling the professor but by now, she knew the town and number and it only took a few minutes.

"Dizzy, my friend, what a pleasant surprise to hear your voice again."

"That is not the only surprise I have for you. You remember, we told you about the fellow Viktor Polozenski who looks like me?"

"Yes."

"It's going to take a while to explain this but, we met him face to face and a club for Moldavians living here." He went on to explain the information they had gathered so far. Finally, he said,

"And so, Professor, those are my surprises for the week."

"My God, Dizzy. What does this all mean? Do they play that music there? To what end?" The professor was full of questions but Dizzy only had one for him.

"Professor, could they use that piece of music to kill people?"

"I don't know. But I suppose it could work. The fact that it works here every seven years despite all reason suggests perhaps it could work elsewhere."

The remainder of the conversation was between Ekaterina and Zablo in Romanian.

"Professor Zablo seems like a very nice, thoughtful man. I'm sorry I never got to meet him. He thinks that while it makes no sense at all, the circumstances in rural, backward Moldova are much different from those here, but maybe it is the music itself. Or maybe it is produced by people from the village. It may be that a number of people from here go back every seven years to perform in that orchrstra, but that's an expensive journey and from the look of some of the denizens of Viktor's club, I can't imagine they can afford it. You were all in disguise and we are already pretty damn sure that Viktor was among them. We don't know any more than that."

Again, they decided to leave it all alone for a while. They had learned enough and Dizzy did not want the whole affair to become an obsession.

Ekaterina was still curious and she wasn't ready to let it go completely, but did agree with Dizzy to put it on the back burner for now. In the meantime, he figured he could use a car. They decided to go to a used car place on a Saturday afternoon. He already had an old Plymouth in San Francisco, but he didn't think it would make it across the country, so he would just put it up for sale.

They walked onto a used car lot. Dizzy was open-minded about what to get. He really didn't have any preferences, he just wanted something that was maybe a few years old at best, with low mileage—the usual. Of course, for Ekaterina this was far more exciting. She had never bought a car in her life.

"Oh look, Dizzy, there's a beautiful car. What kind is it?" Her eyes were wide with excitement.

"I'm not sure." They walked over for a closer look. "It's a DeSoto Airstream." It sat majestically among its automotive sisters. "Can we buy that one? It's the only one I like."

Dizzy thought it was rather special and went to find the salesman. Ekaterina walked around it, looking at its streamlined shape with all its heavy chrome and coat of dark green paint When Dizzy came back, he had the keys and the papers in hand. Ekaterina was delighted. She sat in the front seat beside Dizzy and he drove them back to the hotel. On the way, she whispered into his ear, "You must drive out to the country and find a deserted road somewhere and park. Your spy girl will seduce you in the back seat."

When they arrived back at the hotel, she said she would name the Airstream "Stardust." Within a week, she got up enough nerve to get behind the wheel herself, and while it was so much bigger than the toy car, she soon got used to the feel of it and the sense of modernity and power it had.

Dizzy had landed a six month contract at the Lexington. The pay was good. He was playing to full houses every night. Ekaterina had about three days' work every week and they had several days of the week to spend together. They were having a good time. Once a week, they went up to Harlem somewhere with Spike for dinner. He and Dizzy had become close and Ekaterina was fond of him and found him to be irresistibly funny.

One evening, they were driving Stardust down the street where the Romanian Moldavian Social Club was. Much to their surprise, there were three large expensive cars parked in front of the place. "They must have a better clientele than when we went there a few months ago."

"That can't be," he said. "That place is a dive, whichever way you look at it. Strictly old country peasants and working class. But you are right, what are those cars doing there?"

"Now my curiosity is back again," said Ekaterina.

"Oh no."

"I can't help it. We share such an incredible secret that I keep wanting to get to the bottom of it all. I think I will—how do you Americans say?—stake out the place for a while."

"Now you are going to start worrying me. I know that it is going to be futile to ask you to leave it, but you must promise me that you won't do anything stupid or dangerous. We have only the vaguest inkling of what really goes on in that place."

"Yes, now that there are snazzy black cars parked there, that is certainly interesting."

For the next little while, Ekaterina drove Dizzy to his gigs and would then spend an hour or so parked down the street about a half block away to keep an eye on the club. She was a safe distance away and could see down the sidewalk if she sat on the passenger side. Nothing really happened for about ten days, and she was beginning to lose patience with it all. Then on the eleventh evening, two big black cars moved in and parked in front of the club ahead of her. One man got out of the first car and looked around in all directions. Then all doors to the second car opened and four people got out.

They walked to the passenger side and hustled a fifth person out of the back door of the car. It looked like he had great difficulty walking and he was quickly ushered inside. Five minutes later, the four men came out, jumped in the cars, and took off, leaving the fifth man behind in the club.

Ekaterina drove to the Lexington and listened to Dizzy and the band for the last set.

"I saw something really interesting tonight," she said as they were driving home. She recounted her evening.

"It really looked like this guy was half dead, or he had been drugged up. He couldn't walk under his own power, and the first man made sure no one was around before they took him inside.

Do you want to hear my theory?"

"I'm all ears."

"To me, even at that distance, all those men looked like gangsters. So these gangsters have captured someone from a rival gang or maybe someone who owes them money and can't pay his debts. Maybe a gambler or something. They take him to the club, tie him up to a chair, and give him a little concert after hours. And guess what tune they play?"

"My dear, have you lost it completely?"

"Think about it. It could be a body disposal service for the gangs. They don't have to kill anyone. The denizens of the club put on the costumes, play the Saltatio Mortis, and the man dies. They then have to dispose of the body, but that is another matter. Let's assume they can kill someone with the song, then it is a completely safe way to do it. No one commits a violent act, no gunplay. They just tie him up and play the song. This guy looked half dead anyway. He was probably unconscious when they brought him in. Either beaten up or drugged."

"As crazy as it seems, I suppose that is a possibility. But it is so far-fetched as to be nearly impossible."

"Impossible? Dizzy, you took part in that whole scenario in Moldova. It is not impossible. You know that. Unlikely? Well, yes, but only because we aren't sure that it works here."

"There are a lot of questions besides the obvious ones," she said. "Why don't any members of the orchestra die? Is it because they are in full costumes? If the full band is playing and one person is tied up and forced to listen to the piece, is it a guarantee that he will die?

There may be a completely different explanation for all of this and if you can think of one, then it's my turn to be all ears."

"Not this kid. I'm stumped. You may be right about this and since it is so completely crazy and unlikely, then you couldn't exactly go to the police with a story like that. They would laugh you out of the precinct."

"Like I said, it's a completely safe way to kill someone. There's only the matter of disposing of the body. Even if we knew for sure, what could we do? Get branded as a couple of hysterics at the police station? We hold a secret so strange as to make it safe from discovery because of its supposed impossibility. Isn't that amazing in itself?"

"Yes it is. Now, let's go to bed. I will be lucky to get to sleep tonight with what you've come up with."

"I have any number of ways to make you fall asleep. Guaranteed."

Dizzy and Ekaterina decided to give it a rest for a while. As exciting as it all was, they agreed that there was a certain dangerous aspect to it, and neither of them wanted to risk getting into trouble with a bunch of unsavory characters. The men in limousines looked like tough guys who meant business, whatever that business could be.

Of course, that lasted for all of ten days, especially after Ekaterina spotted her friend Petra with Viktor Polozenski in Macy's Department Store After all the talk about her divorce and not seeing her ex-husband, Petra was there shopping with him.

"Dizzy, what is it with these weird people? First, Petra tells me she hasn't seen her husband since the divorce, then they look like they are having a perfectly good time shopping together."

"I have no idea. I have become aware of so many weird people since I went to Moldova, I don't know what to think anymore. I am just a simple jazz musician playing music to make people happy and have them dancing. The thought of an orchestra made up of people in disguise playing music that will kill someone is a concept I cannot understand or get used to. It is so far beyond my reality, I cannot make any sense of it, and yet I was seduced into taking part in just such an event. Which, I suppose, makes me as weird as any of them. I am beginning to think that we are all capable of engaging in behavior that is completely unlike what we think our nature is. Who knows, maybe they realized that their divorce was too hasty and want to resume their lives together. I do find it a little strange."

"Are you feeling guilty about having played in that orchestra?"

"I sometimes think of that poor violin player and I haven't told you this, but I occasionally have a bad dream about playing music with Horsehead. It's never pleasant, but to answer your question, no, I don't think I have much guilt for the simple reason that whoever died after my gig with Zablo would have died anyway. I just happened to walk into this situation. And Zablo, I think, knew that I wouldn't be able to resist. He was right. I would never do it again. However, it is one thing to have this crazy tradition in a forgotten out of the way village in the outback of Moldova, and another to think that this ritual could be used by the mafia or the government to rid themselves of their enemies in such an unusual way."

"The government?"

"Why not? Governments always have enemies, except they are supposed to act in accordance with the law. I can imagine any government has as many enemies as the mob. Quietly making someone disappear might suit their purpose for the same reason it suits the mob. Remember, the mob in itself is an enemy of the government."

"Of course, but it is still speculation on our part. We are sure of nothing here. We have concocted a scenario based on little real evidence, just a mountain of circumstantial evidence. The only real situation is that we are pretty sure this is happening because you saw it happen, but no authority would ever believe it in a million years. Even if they were caught in the act, all anyone would see would a bunch of costumed people playing funny music."

Ekaterina's curiosity kept nagging at her and yet she was frightened about the whole affair. Rationally, she thought that whatever was happening would go on indefinitely, and maybe it had been going on for many years. And so what? She was sure it was wrong, but who was she to get involved in trying to stop it? It was dangerous and she promised to be careful to Dizzy. She did not want to break that promise. She decided she would do nothing but observe the situation from afar and leave it at that.

She would drive Stardust down and park it where she could observe the entrance to the club from the farthest point possible. Sometimes she spent several hours reading a book and watching. Eventually, a pattern became clear.

"I've has been watching the club off and on at different times of the day, and guess what? Nobody goes into or out of the club all day. The only person I have ever seen going into the place is Polozenski. Yet, both times we've been there, there have been at least thirty people. What does that mean?"

"Maybe there's another entrance and the front one is for visitors only."

"You mean an entrance off the alley?"

"If they really are doing something clandestine, then maybe no one wants to be seen coming or going.

Let's go and see for ourselves. But we shouldn't use the car, it is a noticeable one, as you well know by now. We can walk up and down the street for an hour and check if lots of foot traffic goes in and out of the alley."

They went walking up and down the street the next day. In the course of an hour and a half, they spotted at least two dozen people go up to the back door of the club through the alley.

It was now apparent that whatever mystery was ongoing at the club, it was done through the back door. Absolutely no one went in or out of the front door.

"But wouldn't the big black cars that apparently deliver the victims go into the alley?" asked Dizzy.

"Good question. Maybe it looks suspicious to have large snazzy cars in the alley. It is more normal to park on the street. Which brings me to another question: Why wouldn't they use a delivery truck? It's completely normal to have one of those in an alley."

"Maybe they do and we just haven't seen one yet."

A few days later, they spotted a food delivery truck in the alley and watched the people quickly usher someone into the place, much the same way as happened in the front with the black cars.

"Now, we haven't seen any bodies removed, just deliveries. What do you suppose they do with them?" asked Ekaterina.

"I'm not sure I want to know."

One more time, they decided to let things go. Realizing that they both wanted to live a normal life without all this spying going on, they started to plan a holiday to be taken when Dizzy's engagement at the Lexington was over. Ekaterina wanted to see the country and, not having ever been to the States, she didn't mind where they went, as it would all be new for her. For the most part, she left things up to Dizzy. His contract came to an end a few weeks later, and they were ready to embark on a road trip. By the time they left, she was excited and told Dizzy not to say where they were headed. She wanted to be surprised.

And she was surprised when Dizzy steered Stardust in a northwesterly direction. She had always thought they would head south. About a day later, she said, "We are headed to Chicago, aren't we?"

"Yes, for a few days, then it's off in another direction, but I won't say where yet."

Once in Chicago, they found a nice small hotel downtown and spent the next three or four days walking around and listening to music at night. They heard Duke Ellington on one of the nights and on another, they heard some Negro musicians in a small club playing blues. Ekaterina was now beginning to see what Dizzy had said about Negro musicians and their music. She was discovering what the word 'swing' felt like. Dizzy explained the concept of blue notes, playing on or ahead of the beat, syncopation, and a number of the other subtleties of jazz music. They put the craziness of the Romania-Moldova Social Club behind them as they walked around the Windy City. Dizzy took Ekaterina to see a performance of Of Thee I sing." She had not really known what Dizzy meant when he told her that one of the songs they heard along the way came from a musical. He figured the best way to explain it was to take her to one. She was completely amazed by the whole thing. They were slowly walking back to the hotel after the play when Ekaterina stopped dead in her tracks.

"Oh my God, Dizzy! Look at that!"

She pointed to a door that said, "Romania-Moldova Social Club."

"Jesus Christ. Don't tell me there's a chain of them!"

Dizzy had a sinking feeling about what was coming next.

"We have to go in and have a drink."

"Listen, my darling spy girl. Don't you ever get enough of this?"

"Listen, my darling husband. No. Not when there is another genie to be let out of another bottle."

She was standing in front of him. She put her arms around him and whispered, "And besides, you haven't taken me for a drink today. I'm thirsty and desire a shot of Zorko."

With her devilish smile, Dizzy resigned himself to walking into the club.

He opened the door and found the place a little swankier than the one in New York. Definitely a cut above Polozenski's place. The clientele looked similar though—working class for sure. They picked a corner table where Ekaterina could survey the room and try to pick up on what she could hear.

"I'll walk over to the bar and get our drinks so I can survey things a little," said Ekaterina.

As a well dressed and beautiful woman, Ekaterina garnered plenty of stares from the mostly male patrons. Dizzy could tell the bartender was a little surprised when she ordered a couple of shots of Zorko. Upon returning to her seat, she told Dizzy that she thought she recognized someone in there from the place in New York.

"I'm going to need that drink."

"From what I can tell, there are mostly Moldavians in here. Besides me, there are only three women."

They were there for about fifteen minutes or so when Ekaterina said, "I have to use the ladies room, but don't worry, I won't snoop. That's too scary for me."

"Promise?"

She had just disappeared behind the door when someone came towards where Dizzy was sitting.

"Viktor! How've you been? It's been years. I haven't seen you since the Saltatio Mortis fourteen years ago."

The stranger extended his hand and Dizzy, who realized that he was being mistaken for Victor Polozenski, did the only thing he could think of at the time. He shook the stranger's hand. "I'm sorry, you seem to have the wrong person. My name is not Viktor."

"Ha! Always the joker, eh? It's me, Santo. Don't tell me you've forgotten already."

"Sir, there is nothing to forget. Like I said, my name is not Viktor and I have no idea who you are."

"Viktor, c'mon friend, we go back thirty years."

"Actually, Mr. Santo, I really don't know you. I have never been here in my life and..." Just then, Ekaterina re-appeared with two more Zorkos in hand.

"This gentleman has mistaken me for someone called Viktor, and I have assured him that we are indeed complete strangers." He knew she would catch on.

"Sir, this is my husband and I can say with some degree of confidence that his name is not Viktor."

"My apologies. You look very much like my old friend Viktor Polozenski. Enjoy your drinks."

The stranger returned to his seat. He was sitting with friends and no doubt was about to recount his story about meeting someone who looked like Viktor Polozenski. They noticed all four people at the table look over at them within thirty seconds.

"I didn't count on something like that happening. How strange," said Ekaterina.

"Not only that, but he says we last saw each other at the Soltatio Mortis fourteen years ago!"

"Oh for God's sake. Really?"

Dizzy downed his drink in one shot and was rewarded with a violent body shudder and a gasp.

"I know I promised, Dizzy, but is it snooping if I walk by an open door and don't stop, but just turn my head sideways?"

"What now?"

"Instruments. Lots of them!"

Back at their hotel, the conversation didn't leave subject of the new branch of the club.

"Can it be that there's a whole chain of these places and they are contracted out to the various mobs and organized crime with the object of getting rid of one's enemies?" asked Ekaterina.

"I suppose so, but probably only in major cities. That's where the big crime happens with gangs and such. And I understand that Chicago has more than its share of these people."

"You know, when we get back, we could write an anonymous letter to the police telling them that there is some suspicious business going on at the club. We don't have to fill them in on the real evidence, especially the part about the Saltatio Mortis. If we say just enough to make them curious, they may bite and then the problem becomes theirs. If they start watching the place, they will surely see one of those deliveries. It's only a matter of time then. After all, we have witnessed three of them already."

"A great idea," said Ekaterina. "But let me bring something up just for argument's sake. What if these people are doing a service to society? What if they are ridding the world of crooks and mobsters? There could be any number of so-called bad guys off the streets and they are keeping the criminal population down. We might be throwing a monkey wrench into a functioning social system we know nothing about. Did I use that phrase right?"

"Yes, you did," replied Dizzy. "But that kind of moral judgement is not ours to make. Mind you, any kind of killing is wrong, period, and we can't say that killing a criminal is right, and it looks like someone is being contracted to do exactly that. We have no idea who these people are. Maybe they are ordi-nary people who were in the wrong place at the wrong time and witnessed something they shouldn't have. Maybe it's some unfortunate individual who had a gambling debt to the mob and they want to make an example of him. Or someone from a rival family trying to muscle into another territory selling drugs or moonshine. And here's the kicker: maybe the police already know and they choose to turn a blind eye because in the end, their job is a little easier. Fewer murders to investigate, or something like that. A variation of wild west vigilante justice right here in modern day New York and Chicago."

The rest of the vacation was spent without any talk of the Polozenski affair. They drove south through Illinois into Missouri, then through Tennessee, North Carolina, the Virginias, and back to New York. All the while, Dizzy told Ekaterina of the history as far as he knew about the places. She was shocked at the overt racism in places that had Whites only places and Negro only places. They drove through hillbilly country, where Ekaterina could hardly understand a word and wondered if they were really speaking English at all.

"My God, this place is big," she remarked.

"Yes it is, and we haven't seen a quarter of it yet. That will be for another day. We will see it all eventually. I may have to tour again sometime, but there is so much uncertainty around now that was has started in Europe. I have no idea how it will affect things here. Who knows, the States may even get directly involved someday. I hope not."

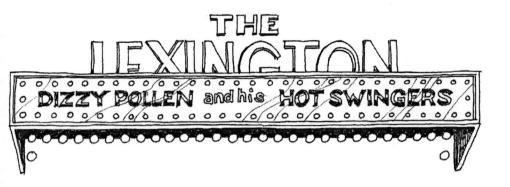

CHAPTER 16

Back at the Waldorf, Dizzy immediately called Joe, his agent.

"Hi ya, Dizzy. Where ya been? I've got work for you."

"Hello, Joe. I have been on vacation with my wife for the last three weeks."

"Never mind that. I have a six-month contract back at the Lex again for you and your usual boys. They really like you there."

"Good. I'll head over there right away and let them know I'm back and ready to go again. Thanks a million, Joe."

"Okay, and stop by with the little lady and say hello sometime. I'd like to meet your missus."

"Will do. See you later."

The following week, Dizzy started at the Lexington with a big opening show that included several guests joining him for the occasion. The place was packed and Dizzy, more popular than ever, was off on his six month engagement with a bang. He was looking forward to the stint, which, thanks in part to Joe Ramirez, was going to bring in some good money for half a year anyway.

Ekaterina got called in by the Romanian consulate for a job for two days a week. This was good news to her, She expected that the consulate would eventually close due to the war putting her out of her job. Since she was still obsessed with the whole Polozenski affair, this would keep her in contact with Petra, whom she had not seen since having spotted her with Viktor Polozenski at Macy's.

Dizzy, on the other hand, was content to put the whole affair behind him. He felt that the situation was fraught with some kind of unknown danger. He knew this first hand from his experience in Moldova and was not anxious to probe the matter too deeply. He was genuinely worried for Ekaterina's safety and was certainly concerned regarding her ongoing curiosity about the whole affair.

Ekaterina, however, had a burning desire to get to the bottom of all of this. She was not foolish or careless, however, and she had promised Dizzy that above all, she would be careful and not do anything reckless or crazy. She would keep that promise, but she just couldn't let it all go. Sometimes she would lie awake in the small hours cogitating the matter.

She reconnected with Petra and their friendship resumed. They were very comfortable with each other and it seemed that it wouldn't be too long before Petra might be open to her questions, if they were framed appropriately and didn't seem too probing. She had to be careful about this, as she was normally forward and knew this trait could get in the way of getting straight answers. She didn't want to scare Petra off, but knew her friend knew a helluva lot more than she was letting on.

On the Tuesdays and Thursdays that she was at the consulate, she and Petra would go for a drink after work. Sometimes, they went out to the Lexington to hear Dizzy. Saturday nights, Ekaterina always went and sat backstage. She liked to watch the band play from that vantage point where she could see the audience and the dancing. On Sunday, they would take Stardust and drive out to some place they hadn't been before and sometimes stay overnight in a hotel.

They were a happy couple living a good life together. Dizzy was becoming a household name in NYC and it looked like his contract might be extended for another six months.

One Tuesday afternoon after work, Ekaterina and Petra were enjoying their afternoon libation when Petra announced that she was in the process of reconciling with Viktor.

"No kidding," exclaimed Ekaterina. "How did that come about? The last time you mentioned him, that certainly did not seem the case."

"No, you're right, and it wasn't. But we met some time ago and we started talking. It would seem that we still really like one another and may be ready to patch up our differences. He seems to be more relaxed and easy going than before."

"I'm happy for you, Petra. I hope it all works out for the best. Now tell me all about it, as much as you feel comfortable with, that is." She laughed. She wanted it to sound like small talk among girls and not give it the seriousness that was really going on inside her. The feeling of curiosity and foreboding that had become familiar to her in the last months was coming to the forefront again. Petra was opening up a little.

"We are still living apart but sort of dating, if you will. I want to be sure everything is completely okay before moving back. I have become attached to my independence and am leery of giving it up unless I am dead sure of everything."

"Did you ever find out where he works or what he does for a living?"

"He runs a little club called the Romania-Moldova Social Club."

Ekaterina was a little stumped as to what she was going to say next, since she had been there with Dizzy and met Viktor. She decided on the truth for now.

"Oh, you don't say. Dizzy and I visited the place once and we must have met your husband. We met the owner, which as you know by now bears a striking resemblance to Dizzy."

"Let's make it a double date and we can all go to the club one evening. It's not the greatest place, but it's a little homey. Viktor usually has to be there in the evenings."

Ekaterina was unsure whether Dizzy would want to get that close, but she told her that she would talk to him. He had only Monday nights off and did not always want to go out. She would stall things until she spoke to Dizzy. Petra seemed okay with that.

She asked him about it when they got home that night.

"Listen, I'm just a little uncomfortable going to that place and meeting those people. It's like walking into the lion's den," he said.

"Dizzy," she replied, "you have nothing to worry about. You are still Dizzy Pollen. You were born in San Francisco, and you have no connection with anyone in that place whatsoever. You have never been to Moldova; you are a jazz musician who met me in Bucharest and that is as far as you got. No one need ever know anything else about you. No one would possibly ever guess about what happened in Moldova. I am the one who is Romanian and being in that place would be more fitting than you. I really don't see the harm. Besides, Petra has all of your records. She is a devoted fan. Who knows, maybe Viktor is a big fan too."

"Well, you do have a logical way to put it. Maybe I'm just being paranoid because of what I know.

So, let's play it this way. If I get uncomfortable, then I will signal you and we are out of there."

"Fair enough. I don't want to make you uncomfortable in any way, but you know I'm still curious about the big picture."

"I know only too well. Just remember you have promised to be careful."

"And I will always keep that promise."

A few weeks later on a Monday night, Dizzy and Ekaterina went to the club. They took a table in a corner so Ekaterina could observe the room. Dizzy sat next to her. Petra and Viktor hadn't arrived yet. Ekaterina was already listening for snippets of conversation. There weren't a lot of people there yet. They both ordered a beer, which would soon be chased with a shot of Zorko. Ekaterina informed Dizzy that most of the patrons were from Moldova from their accents. Then she asked Dizzy what signal he would use to leave.

"I'll place my hand on your thigh under the table."

"I should hope you would do that anyway. You have to do better than that."

"I'll tap it out in Morse code. Three short taps followed by three long taps followed by three short taps."

"What does that mean?"

"S.O.S. It's the only thing I know in Morse code."

The door opened and Petra and Viktor entered. Ekaterina waved them over. Dizzy muttered under his breath, "Here goes nothing."

Viktor and Petra sat down and ordered drinks, and they began a round of polite chit-chat. This went on for about twenty minutes or so and Dizzy saw that Ekaterina was getting bored and was about to make the conversation a little more serious if she could.

"Viktor," she asked, "you say your ancestors came from Romania. Have you ever been back there to see if you still have relatives?"

He was a little taken aback by the question. "Actually, I have a few times. I have never really met anyone who is related to the family. I think they all disappeared. I have seen a few gravestones with the family name but nothing with a date in this century. I made a few discreet inquiries here and there and it would seem that the Polozenski family weren't about to win any popularity contests in their day. People still mention the name with revulsion. They seemed to be a bunch of nasty people and you didn't want to cross their path. They had some kind of a fiefdom and ruled it with an iron hand."

"Where is this place?" she asked.

"Some one horse town called Andinca off in the middle of nowhere. The Polozenski castle is still there. A frightening looking place. There are Polozenzki gravestones in the local cemetery. It looks like the place never left the eighteenth century, let alone the nineteenth."

"How on Earth did you find it?" asked Dizzy.

"I looked up some church records here and there until I came across the name. From there it was simple detective work, except that I quickly found out that it wasn't a good idea to mention the Polozenski name in any context. They gave me the third degree at the border and it took a little while to figure out that it was the name that did it. They must have been some pretty mean bastards."

To change the subject, Viktor said; "I almost feel embarrassed that I didn't recognize you when we first met. I never connected it to the recordings that Petra plays at home. She is a big fan of your music." Viktor asked Dizzy about his musical life. This subject went on for a few minutes, then took a startling turn when Viktor said they had a little orchestra that met at the club once a week.

"We play mostly old Moldavian folk music. It is really obscure stuff and has not ever really been heard much outside of rural Moldova. These people like it. It is the music they heard back then and it reminds them of home. They don't understand the music in America. Especially jazz. No offense."

"None taken, Viktor. A lot of Americans feel the same way. I'll bet the music you play would be strange to our ears. I am curious about it and wouldn't mind hearing some of it one day. Do you play?"

"I play the violin. Not particularly well, but good enough for this music."

"What other instruments do you have in your orchestra?"

"We have a couple of cellos, two clarinets, an ophiclide, another violin, a coronet, a zither, a cymbalom, a couple of domras, a bass balalaika, and a gardon cello. Other people show up sometimes with different instruments. It's really quite a sound all in all."

"I have no idea what some of those instruments are," said Dizzy.

"The domra and balalaika are Russian stringed instruments, the ophiclide is a horn, and the craziest one of them all is the gardon cello. It looks like a cello made from old barn door wood and the strings are tapped with a stick rather than bowed."

"That combination must produce an interesting sound. I can hardly imagine."

"Then you should come and hear us play sometime. I can assure you, you have never heard anything like it in your life. Consider this an official invitation. Bring your trumpet. Everything is scored and you should have no trouble reading it. Besides, having a real professional play with us would help. We are all self-taught amateurs. A lot of our songs are in different time signatures like nine-eight or seven-four.

I must confess that I have never encountered those rhythms. They don't exist in American music. I would love to come and try this out. It would be a musical adventure for sure."

Now it was Ekaterina who was becoming really uncomfortable. She put her hand on Dizzy's thigh under the table and began tapping S.O.S.

Dizzy changed the subject and Ekaterina stopped tapping. The evening carried on. They all had several drinks and the evening drew to an amicable conclusion. Dizzy and Ekaterina left the club and as soon as they were some distance from the door, she spun around in front of him. "Have you lost your marbles? Are you going to play with them? That could be really dangerous. Please tell me you are not going to do this!"

"My dear, you are the one who hasn't let this go and now that I have a legitimate way into the place, aren't you more curious than ever? I am. We are now going to find out a lot more about the place and its denizens."

"Maybe more than we want to know. You have made me promise to be careful and now I feel I must extract the same promise from you. I don't want to be scared. Rest assured that I will not let you out of my sight if you go and play music with those people."

"Of course. I promise to be really careful. I don't want you to worry."

That night, Dizzy was struck with a bout of insomnia. He awoke thinking about what he had gotten himself into. This was becoming unreal. He had now considered playing music with the stateside version of Horsehead's orchestra and had no way of knowing what would happen. Of course, he was curious about the music. He had heard enough music in Eastern Europe to make him want to explore more of it and the thought of being presented with some scores was in itself exciting. As long as he didn't play *the* piece, things should be okay. He would get to play some interesting stuff in a band that used a variety of musical instruments that he had never heard of, so he would be presented with some completely new sounds. Who knows what ideas and inspirations would come of it.

Did they wear the costumes every time they played? Did any of the other pieces they knew have the same effect on some unfortunate listener? These questions bothered him until he finally fell into a rocky sleep. He awoke feeling hungover, even though he hardly drank anything the previous evening.

Ekaterina was worried about Dizzy. "What are you going to do if Viktor actually calls you to play with him and his crazy band?"

"I'm going to accept his invitation, of course. I am intensely curious about the music from a musician's viewpoint. It's really interesting stuff. And furthermore..."

Ekaterina cut him off. "Dizzy, what if they want to play the piece you played with Zablo? What are you going to do about that?"

"Honestly, I haven't thought that one out yet," he admitted.

"You should think about it. It they start playing that song, they may have someone tied up in the next room listening to it. Then... well..."

"Yes, I know. I really haven't come to grips with that yet. I could always duck out if that piece comes up. I will recognize it right away and make some excuse that I have to be somewhere, having not paid attention to the time— or something like that."

"Sounds pretty flimsy to me, Dizzy."

"I suppose you are right."

"I am not trying to dissuade you from doing something you want to do. I understand completely your fascination with all of this. I am on your side. We are in this together. I just don't want anything to go wrong, so I am trying to... cover the bases. Did I use that expression right?"

"Yes, and you have never even been to a baseball game."

"I suppose you are going to tell me that you will play this situation by ear."

"Playing things by ear means that I have to be flexible to anticipate the unexpected. In a case like this where I have no idea what the outcome is, it is hard to have a plan. An escape plan, maybe, but my knowledge of the situation gives me some protection. No one has the remotest idea that I played the Saltatio Mortis in Moldova or even know about its existence. I will just be an outsider invited to play with an oddball band. On the surface, it's all pretty harmless. It's what we know that makes it scary. Even if I had never played the gig in Moldova, I would jump at the chance to play with this band."

"All right, my dearest Dizzy. Just keep your promise that you will not put yourself in danger."

"I will keep that promise."

Dizzy's phone rang about a week later. Viktor asked if he could join his orchestra on the following Saturday at noon. Dizzy accepted and promised to be there. After conferring with Ekaterina about whether she should come along or not, she told him that he should go by himself for now and see if maybe it would be okay to bring her along sometime.

He was a little relieved to know that Ekaterina didn't want to come along.

Saturday, he fired up Stardust and drove to the club. He parked in front found the front door locked. He thought better of going around back, which was the entrance he suspected everyone used. He knocked and a few moments later, Viktor answered.

"Hi Dizzy, and welcome. C'mon in and I'll introduce you to the orchestra. Mind you, not all of them speak any English, so if someone is silent, they aren't snubbing you."

"No problem," said Dizzy. "We will all be speaking the language of music in no time."

Viktor laughed. "Speaking of time, some of the time signatures in this music are a little... well, unusual. Very little of the music is in 4/4 time."

"That's good. I could use the challenge."

They walked into the club, which had been re-arranged for the occasion. All the tables were stacked in the corner and the chairs were in a semi-circle around a tiny podium. There was a music stand in front of each chair with sheet music already on it. Dizzy was impressed with the organization. Viktor said something in Romanian to the assembled group. He heard his name mentioned but understood nothing else. When Viktor finished, the musicians all broke into an enthusiastic applause.

"What did you say?" asked Dizzy.

"Not a lot beyond the fact that you are a famous band leader who has exhibited an interest in our music and has come to play with us today."

"That rather large individual over there is the conductor. His name is Nosso."

Dizzy looked over at Nosso and couldn't help imagining him with a horse's head and his baton, just like in Moldova. He then wondered how many of these people ever went to Moldova to play the Saltatio Mortis, as he knew Viktor had done. This may be an important ritual for many of these people, much like the professor. He knew the professor's motivation in all of this, or at least he thought he did. Zablo, he felt, did it out of an immense curiosity about it all. Dizzy started to realize that he himself possessed that too. He was well aware that Ekaterina was also intensely fascinated by it.

Here he was in a room full of Moldavian musicians who may have all played the Saltatio Mortis at some point in their lives. What made it especially weird to Dizzy is that he had been there and none of them could have known this. For some reason, he felt that this fact would offer some protection, but against what? He didn't know. It just felt safer to him that he had been there and none of these people knew.

"Where would you like me to sit?"

"Over there beside the opheclide player."

Nosso tapped his baton against a chair and everyone meandered to their seats. Dizzy sat down and looked over the first piece of music on his music stand. It was in a 7/4 time signature. He had never played anything in his life in 7/4 but he could read anything. The feel of the music would be very different to him, as he knew from encountering Latino musicians who were very good on their instruments and had an incredible sense of rhythm and yet initially struggled with the seemingly simple 4/4 stuff that American jazz musicians thought was easy.

All this was going through Dizzy's mind when Nosso stepped up on the little podium, holding up his baton. Everyone was quiet. Nosso brought the baton down and the music started with a bang. It was quite a bit faster than Dizzy had anticipated but he managed to keep up with it all. He was fascinated by the sound of the band with all of the strange instruments. It was like nothing he had ever heard with the possible exception of the Saltatio Mortis, but this was a bigger group with a fuller sound. Dizzy was amazed at their proficiency and musicianship. The scales and chords were definitely strange to his ears, although he did recognize some of it from hearing music in Romania.

The time went by quickly as piece after piece was played. Dizzy only faltered a few times in the whole time they played, but he was mentally and rhythmically exhausted halfway through the session. The odd time signatures and phrasing were completely unfamiliar to him, but he found a lot of it really cool. He had momentarily forgotten all about the Saltatio Mortis when, as he picked up the last piece of music of the stand, he just about had a heart attack. It was the piece from the castle in Moldova! He recognized it at first glance.

Now what? he thought. He was torn. Should he play it or not? He decided in the end to go along and just play the piece. He figured no harm would come of it. There was no one else besides the musicians in the room and according to the professor, the musicians never died as a result, just someone among the attendees. Dizzy rationalized that if no one was there to listen, it would be okay. Besides, he did like the piece the professor taught him. It had all made sense to him when he played it in Horsehead's orchestra. In fact, he wanted to play it again sometime. Why not now?

Nosso brought his baton down and the piece was underway. It was still vaguely familiar to Dizzy, as he had memorized it enough to write it down. He followed the music and was gratified that he was playing it easily. It unfolded exactly as he remembered it. When it reached the final coda, he was gripped by mixed emotions about having played the piece. It ended and the musicians gave themselves some mild applause. They all had fun, obviously, including Dizzy, who had gotten into the swing of things. He was fascinated by the music with its odd time signatures, completely unusual chord progressions, and the crazy sound produced by all the strange instruments.

As he was packing up his trumpet, Viktor came over to thank him for his participation.

"You're welcome, Viktor. I really enjoyed the music. It is so unusual to me but I managed to keep up my part. The whole session is a bit of a blur, as I was so busy trying to play everything correctly that I have forgotten what I have heard today. I didn't have time to really appreciate all of the nuances and subtleness, so I would love to play these again if you don't mind."

"It would be great if you played with us again. I understand trying to play everything correctly and missing the bigger picture. You would be able appreciate it more if you didn't have to concentrate so much on playing correctly. But I must say, you did extremely well and it would be an honour to have you join us again sometime."

"Maybe it's because it was the last piece played, but I really liked that one. Can you tell me anything about it?" He was careful to observe Viktor's reaction.

Viktor seemed a little nervous, but then answered, "To be sure, we know very little about that particular piece, only that it is very old and no composer has ever been credited with it. Legend has it that it was written almost a thousand years ago but no one really knows for sure. It is traditional to a small area of Moldova near the town of Andinca, where apparently my ancestors lived."

"Fascinating."

Dizzy drove back to the hotel, where Ekaterina nervously awaited him. When he entered the room, she ran to him and jumped into his arms holding on tight.

"I was so worried. I don't know why but I just was. I'm so glad you are back."

He held her, standing perfectly still in the middle of the room until he felt her body relax and melt into him. He put her down gently and kissed her. She gave him his favourite smile and asked, "Well? What happened?"

"It's my turn to ask you to pour the drinks," Dizzy responded.

She returned with a couple of stiff ones. They clinked glasses. "We played the piece today!"

"What?! You said you wouldn't do that."

"We played for just under an hour and that was the last piece. There was no one around and besides, I wanted to hear it again. It was treated just like any of the ten or so pieces we played. But here's the kicker: I asked Viktor if he could tell me anything about it. He couldn't beyond that it was maybe a thousand years old and is traditional to the area around Andinca! He did flinch a little when I asked him and I was watching for his reaction, so he knows more than he is letting on, that's for sure. I just told him I liked it."

Dizzy downed his scotch.

"I'm not really sure what comes next. Without showing my hand, so to speak, I'm going to press Viktor to tell me more about the song and Andinca. Maybe I can get him to tell me about the Saltatio Mortis. I'm sure he knows about it, as I'm sure he played there. Maybe we could do it together. As you know, that the place is full of superstition and voodoo, so maybe we can get him to talk under the right circumstances."

"What would be the right circumstances?"

"What about an intimate dinner party with the four of us where the wine flows and maybe tongues will loosen a little? Maybe with a little Zorko."

"That's a great idea, Dizzy. I'll drum up a humdinger of a Romano-Moldavian meal. We will get him to talk. Too bad I can't use my greatest method to get him to talk, but those methods are reserved for you only." She smiled.

She kissed Dizzy and breathed softly in his ear, "Would you like to see if my methods still work properly?"

"I'm sure they do, but it wouldn't do any harm to test them out."

She pressed herself against Dizzy, nuzzling her mouth and nose on his neck. "I want you to have your way with me. It's been a long time."

"We made love two nights ago."

"We made beautiful, romantic, and erotic love, which was wonderful, but now I need you to take me and possess me. That is different, if you remember."

Ekaterina wrapped herself around Dizzy as he carried her to the bed. He turned backwards to the edge and fell over on his back, with her landing on top of him. They kissed passionately as she unbuttoned his shirt. Dizzy pulled the back of her blouse out of her pants and ran his fingers up the soft skin on her spine and in one deft flick, unhooked her bra. He then reached around and with his hand on her breast, pushed her over until she was on her back and he was on top of her. He put his other arm under her and lifted her with a sliding motion until she landed with her head on the pillow. He pressed her shoulder down into the pillow, kissing and fondling her until the inevitable interruption of having to remove each of the other's clothes. Having lost patience with the last two buttons on Dizzy's shirt, she simply ripped it off him. The buttons went flying, hitting the wall. Dizzy thought the better of ripping her blouse, knowing it was far more expensive than his shirt. Still, he did momentarily relish the thought.

Then there was nothing between them. They kissed and entwined themselves around each other, touching, stroking, and caressing each other until Dizzy's desire to enter her would not wait. Still, she made him work for it. She squirmed out of reach and struggled to get on top of him, but he kept her tightly held down, still pressing her into the pillow. His pants had not fallen off the bed and the belt buckle was just a foot away. He grabbed it and the belt slid out of the loops, and before she knew what was happening, he had it in both hands and held her down with it across her chest, just above her breasts. Her arms were by her sides and she couldn't get out of this. Ekaterina curled her lips, bared her teeth, and hissed at him. Dizzy got close to her ear and whispered, "Now, my beautiful spy girl..." and pressed himself inside her. They moved against each other, slowly at first, then more intensely as she kept struggling against the belt, but Dizzy was not about to let her go. Then she resigned as she felt herself beginning to orgasm. She let go with a hiss and a scream, arching her back against the belt, then she felt faint for a few moments. Dizzy relaxed his grip and stroked her hair and cheeks, and kissed her gently. They were both completely wet.

Ekaterina suddenly flipped Dizzy on his back without losing him out of her. She straddled him and leaned over until her face was close to his. She started to undulate her hips while propping herself on Dizzy's shoulders. She did not have to go on for long, as she knew he would soon come. She pressed into him as hard as she could and she felt herself starting to orgasm again. This time he was there with her. She started to tremble and again hissed, looking at him straight in the eyes. He knew exactly where she was and brought his hand down on her ass with one good spank in the middle of her orgasm. She let out a squeal as her whole body shuddered. She let herself fall flat on Dizzy's chest with her mouth going for his shoulder near his neck and bit him, gripping his upper arms with all her strength and pressing her fingernails into his muscle.

All was quiet. Neither of them moved. She was trembling slightly. Dizzy felt tears running down his shoulder. She was softly weeping. "Hey..."

"Shhh...I'm okay. Just hold me and let me cry."

Dizzy, held her and stroked her hair while she wept gently. Within a few minutes, she stopped and he realized she had just dozed off. He could tell from the rhythm of her breathing. He had spent countless hours watching her sleep. It was something that made his insomnia bearable. He was endlessly fascinated by watching her sleep from the first time they ever spent the night together in her flat.

He gently rolled her off of him a few minutes later and made her comfortable on the pillow. He sat up in bed and watched over her for an hour until he too succumbed to the sandman. He woke up at about four in the morning to find her sitting up in bed looking at him.

"Hi. I'm awake and I can see you are too."

"I guess I am now. How long have you been up?"

"About an hour. I have just been thinking about things and watching you as you slept. You looked so peaceful. Not at all like the man who put his wife in bondage while having his way with her in no uncertain terms."

"I hope I didn't..."

"Shhh. You know the rules. No apologizing for passion."

"What have you been thinking about?"

"Just a mixture of emotions. It's so interesting that a chunk of our lives has centred around this whole Polozenski affair. How it has crept into our consciousness and won't let us go, despite all efforts to put it out of our lives. We have made mutual agreements to let it go, but we are being drawn back into it every time. We are both so fascinated by this crazy phenomenon that we can't just let it go and get on with our lives. This is starting to feel like some kind of a curse. We are drawn to it for seemingly no good reason whatsoever. And for what? What if we find out all kinds of sinister goings on? What can we possibly do about it? Who would believe anything we had to say about it? You realize that if I had not ever bothered looking up the name Polozenski in the phone book, how different our lives would be."

"Before falling asleep, you were crying a little."

"Yes, I was flooded with emotion, but I wasn't sad. I was simply over-whelmed and I knew I would be safe with you holding me. I felt vulnerable and just wanted to cry. I was so worried while you were off with that crazy orchestra. Just like when you were wandering around Moldova. Honestly, Dizzy, I was scared stiff just like back then. Here I thought you were having a harmless trip to Moldova and that was bad enough, and then I hear about the land mines and the bullet. So when you are off playing music with these characters, it's enough to make a girl have a heart attack."

"I'm sorry. It was probably selfish for me to do that, but I felt compelled."

"I know about feeling compelled. That is the curse I'm talking about. I'm as compelled as you are about it. I am maybe a little more scared than you, but here we are plotting a dinner to get Polozenski to talk. Are we nuts? We could easily let this go, turn our backs, and walk away. But we won't, will we?"

"Now, that you put it that way."

Ekaterina slid down and put her head on Dizzy's shoulder. "I'm suddenly very tired. Sweet dreams, Dizzy."

CHAPTER 17

The table was set. Ekaterina worked several days preparing a meal of her best recipes. She found a small shop and deli specializing in Eastern European foods and bought everything she needed.

A bottle of Zorko was harder to find but she persisted and finally found some in a small shop where she was sure everything in the place was contraband.

Viktor and Petra arrived and were welcomed into the suite. Everyone was amazed at what Ekaterina was able to come up with on only a small two-burner hotplate. Dizzy had smuggled it into the suite. The meal was put to table and soon everyone was eating and complimenting Ekaterina on her cooking. Chatter was convivial and polite. The meal progressed to its conclusion and by this time, two wine bottles were empty and a third was well on its way.

They were all sitting down in the main room when Ekaterina decided to make her move. She got up and returned with a bottle of the potent tank fuel. She poured four shot glasses worth and passed them around. She held her glass high and said, "In cinstea Dumicale!

Everyone downed their glassful and as the Zorko descended into the depths of their collective esophagi, they twitched and spasmed slightly. It was that kind of a drink. She looked over at Dizzy and he suddenly knew that she was about to fire the first shot.

"Viktor, Dizzy tells me he had a great time playing music with your orchestra a few weeks ago. He said the music was all quite strange and wonderful. Very different to his ears. He told me he especially liked the last piece the band played. He couldn't remember what the title was as I suppose it was in Romanian."

Viktor was looking mildly uncomfortable but Ekaterina was probably the only one who caught it.

"It is called Dans Pentru Diavol."

"Dance for the Devil. A bit of a dark title, don't you think?" she asked.

"As you probably know, there is a lot of dark music in that end of the world."

Ekaterina went on. "When I was a little girl, my grandfather used to tell me all kinds of scary stories about what to him was the old country. His father came from rural Moldova somewhere. He used to scare the daylights out of us, my cousins and me. He told us about ghosts and all kinds of creatures that roamed the night, and I always remember a story that was particularly frightening to us about a masked ball where they played a certain piece of music that had been composed by the Devil himself. Someone who was listening to it would die on the spot. He said he had heard the piece played once in his life and it had frightened him out of his wits. He told us that children would be made to listen to the piece as punishment for doing bad things. Boy, he really knew how to scare us. My parents used to berate him for telling us those stories but as scared as we were, we kept coming back for more."

Dizzy was transfixed at how Ekaterina had made that up on the spot. He headed for the hutch where the Zorko sat and brought it over. Ekaterina took the bottle and Petra was the first to hold out her glass. She had been taken by the story, and by now Viktor was visibly nervous as he held out his glass. Ekaterina poured all around and went on.

"As you know, we Romanians live with all kinds of legends like our famous count from Transylvania, so stories like that eventually become part of our culture. I can tell you that I don't believe that some guy who sleeps in a coffin and bites people in the neck to draw their blood for nourishment exists, but you will not catch me sleeping overnight in some faraway castle under a full moon. It would be too terrifying given the stories we heard as kids. When I hear some dark Gypsy music, I am cannot help but wonder if the piece they play is the one my grandfather described. His name for the piece was Saltatio Mortis." She looked straight at Viktor. "Have you ever run across a piece of music with that title?"

Dizzy wondered how to diplomatically bring this line of conversation to an end, but he was too curious.

Petra piped up. "That name kinda rings a be..."

Viktor jumped in, cutting her off. "No, I haven't ever seen anything like that. Besides, it's just legend, much like Dracula and his coffin."

"I suppose you are right. Fascinating though. I can imagine the Devil appearing to someone and offering this great piece of music in exchange for the man's soul."

Dizzy joined in. "There was an Italian violin composer called Giuseppe Tartini. In 1713, he had a dream about meeting the Devil and the Devil did just that. He offered to show Tartini a special piece of music in exchange for his soul. The Devil played the piece for him. In the morning, Tartini jumped out of bed and wrote down what he could remember. I have heard it in concert. It is quite the amazing piece. It's called the Devil's Trill. It takes a real virtuoso to be able to play it. Have you ever heard it?"

No one had.

"Suppose you ever did run across that piece of music," Ekaterina said. "Would you dare play it in public?"

"I don't know. I'm not a superstitious person, so I might. I don't believe a piece of music could kill someone. It doesn't make any sense. This is, after all, the twentieth century.

"But do you think that in a land and culture filled with all kinds of superstition like, for instance, Romania or Moldova in the sixteenth century, before any vestiges of modern civilization had made inroads, people believed a lot of strange things. And if you had strong, unshakeable beliefs in the supernatural or the occult, no matter how strange and outlandish they seem to modern folk, don't you think it is possible that it could kill them?

I, for one, think it would be possible. But it would have to happen because it would be impossible to believe otherwise. Belief is the word here. Belief in God, in the Devil, or spirits or spells or curses.

These places remained in the Dark Ages for a long time, and had time to conjure up all manner of beliefs and superstition over the centuries. No education, no literacy, people living their entire lives within a five mile radius, conditions ripe for someone to come along and assume power. They would tell them that it is necessary to cleanse the tribe occasionally, or conduct a sacrifice, and this is accomplished by a curse or by being forced to listen to a piece of music composed by Satan himself and die because of it. Laughable for us, but not for some scared, controlled peasant back in in the 1500s."

"You certainly have a point," replied Viktor "I did get the sense that the beliefs of the people I encountered seemed to be out of the past. What you say about belief in something to be so profound that it could cause a death might be possible but even the people of Moldavia live in the same century as we do. Still, it stretches the imagination to think of some of those stories as being true". There was something is Viktor's tone of voice that wasn't ringing true to Ekaterina She felt that he was paying lip service to her previous statements. And Viktor kept wondering just how much Dizzy and Ekaterina knew about the subject but weren't letting on. There was some distrust all around. Everyone was exercising some caution.

By now, the Zorko was having its effect and Dizzy was glad. Otherwise, he would have been far more uncomfortable with the way this whole conversation was going. Ekaterina was confronting Viktor in a subtle way and making sure he believed that she and Dizzy knew nothing of the reality of the situation. They were both convinced that Viktor and his orchestra played this piece of music to kill people. Viktor's reaction and body language betrayed his rising tension and Ekaterina decided that was enough. She tried to figure a way to diffuse the conversation.

Instructing Dizzy to pour another round of the firewater gave her a few seconds to think. When the glasses were filled, she raised her glass. "Here's to the Brooklyn Dodgers!"

Dizzy broke into uncontrollable laughter, followed by Viktor and Petra. Petra was so taken by surprise she spilled her drink and Viktor could hardly put his glass to his lips. The tension breaker worked like a charm, although

Ekaterina really had little idea of who the Brooklyn Dodgers were. She had heard they were a ball team but that was about it. The conversation took a gentler turn towards music, and Petra had brought over a copy of the first record that Dizzy had ever made. They listened to both sides and Dizzy said that the trumpet player "had potential," which brought laughs all around. It was well after midnight when things broke up. It had been a fun evening.

When the door was closed, Dizzy and Ekaterina stood facing each other. "I don't know where to start," he said. "My God, you were like a trial lawyer back there. I thought Viktor was about to confess. You had him on the edge of his seat."

"I know, but I didn't want him to. I don't want him to know that we know about the Saltatio Mortis."

"Brooklyn Dodgers? How in Hell did you did you come up with that one? You don't know baseball from an oil change!"

"Actually, I changed the oil in my father's car once, just to see what it was like. I know about that. Baseball is, however, a complete mystery to me." She laughed.

She went on. "I think Petra is going to ask a few questions. Did you see how he cut her off at the mention of Saltatio Mortis?"

"Yes, I certainly caught that one."

"I am suddenly exhausted," said Dizzy.

"Me too. The Zorko has done us in. That shit is can really knock someone out."

"I've never heard you use that term before."

"I've never had three shots of Zorko in a row before. Don't worry, my sweet Dizzy, I'll talk better tomorrow." With that, they went to bed. It would be a rough morning.

A week went by. One evening, Ekaterina came home from work in distress.

"Dizzy, I am being followed. I spotted someone following me twice today. I think it's one of the characters from Viktor's club. I'm sure I've seen him before and it could only be there."

"Are you sure?" he asked.

"Yes, I'm sure, but I was careful not to let on that I was being followed. So whoever it is, he doesn't know that I spotted him. This can only mean that

Viktor is getting wise to us and suspects that we know something we are not supposed to."

"No more snooping around the club if we are being followed. I wonder how long this has been going on. They could have been following us for some time now and they could have known we were watching them."

"Yes, of course. No more snooping. That's for sure. I think, however, we should go and have a drink there. I want to see if the guy who was following me is there. I am sure I have seen him on two occasions there. He may even be one of the musicians you played with. That will make anyone think that all is normal if we just pop in for a casual drink."

"I don't like it, but you are right about making things looking normal—as if any of this could be called normal. You realize that I have played music with a number of them, so there's no anonymity for us anymore.

Why do you suppose he was following you anyway?"

"I think Viktor feels that we are on the verge of knowing something that we shouldn't, and he is desperate to keep this from us. Of course, we know the most important facet of it all. We are just not sure what he does with it. More importantly, he can have no idea that you actually know the piece and have played it, perhaps with him."

Monday, Dizzy and Ekaterina went off to the club. After sitting down at a table from which Ekaterina could survey most of the room, she told him the place was populated by the usual suspects. She didn't see the man she was sure had followed her earlier. They spent a rather boring hour and a bit until deciding that they should go home and get a good night's sleep.

Over coffee in the morning, Ekaterina told Dizzy about an idea she had in a bout of insomnia in the middle of the night.

"Why don't you ask Viktor to go out and have a drink, just the two of you without the wives along? He may seem more comfortable that way. After all, you haven't spent time alone with him and you both may get to piece some history together about the Polozenski family and who knows what you may get to talk about. We have accumulated enough evidence that we have a foolproof case. We are almost sure he was there at the same time that you were, and that you both played the Saltatio Mortis. See if you can have that conversation with him. After all, you are related and he might be thrilled to know he has a great cousin or grand nephew or whatever. You will both learn something. If you can help it though, I would keep Professor Zablo's name out of it. We don't want to cause any danger to him."

"Agreed on all counts. That's the best idea you've had all day."

"The day is young, Dizzy. I may have better ones yet." She flashed him a smile.

Dizzy called Viktor and made arrangements to have meet him for a drink on Dizzy's next night off.

Viktor didn't seem to give away any suspicion in his voice and Dizzy felt good about that. Viktor wouldn't arrive at the bar feeling defensive. He was sure that at one point, Viktor would get defensive given the conversation Dizzy planned to engage in.. They both thought about the parameters that he would adhere to, like the professor and maybe the border crossing. They felt confident the meeting would go well, if not completely smoothly.

Viktor met Dizzy in a nearby bar on the following Monday at around eight. After the usual pleasantries were exchanged, and when the second drink arrived, Dizzy took the plunge.

"Viktor, I have no idea how you are going to react to this conversation, but here goes. As you know, it's no secret that we look alike—close enough to be brothers."

"That's for sure."

"My name is and has always been Dizzy Pollen. I wasn't christened as Dizzy, but it has been my nickname forever. My family emigrated from some-place in Moldova in the late nineteenth century. They never would talk about where they came from, or anything about family history. I was born here as Josef Pollen, but my grandfather who emigrated was Josef Polozenski."

Dizzy paused a moment to let that sink in.

"Jesus."

"But there's more," said Dizzy. "The thing is, I don't know exactly what. Of this, I'm sure: we are related. I just can't make the connection. I know so little about any of my family history because of their pig-headed refusal to talk about it, so I'm going to ask you about the Polozenski history. Who was your grandfather?"

"My grandfather's name was Vadim Polozenski. I am not sure about this, but I have always believed that he had a brother close in age and that they left Moldova at different times. Josef, your grandfather, left about five or ten years before Vadim. I am the only child of Ion Polozenski. My father died when I was young. So if we can assume that our grandfathers were brothers, then we are second cousins, I think. I never knew Vadim. Family history was not a topic of conversation around our household either."

"Fair enough. Now, I am going to press a little further here, as I haven't been completely truthful so far. At the end of my concert tour in Bucharest, I got hold of a car and drove into Moldova with the same curiosity. I have been sworn to secrecy about some of this, but let me just put it to you that we were both in Moldova at the same time last November. We were both in a village called Andinca, home of the old Polozenski castle. Have I got that right?"

Viktor hesitated, looking nervous. "Yes, that's right. How did you wind up there?"

"Purely by accident. I got hopelessly lost and my car broke down in that village. I wasn't really looking for anything or anyone in particular. I just wanted to set foot in my ancestral homeland.

"I figured I'd never get that close again, so I just took the opportunity to see the place. What happened next...well, I have been sworn to secrecy, but suffice to say that I learned about the infamy of the Polozenski family, which I must say was quite the revelation.

"But where things really got dramatic is when I became aware of the Saltatio Mortis. Just to set the record straight, I was there. I played in the orchestra conducted by the guy with the horse's head."

By now, Viktor was beginning to look uncomfortable and he ordered another round.

"What I am sure of is that you were there also. My evidence is all circumstantial, of course, but I am convinced that this is true. I want to say that I am not in any way making a judgement about any of this. It was all so bizarre that I am only curious."

"So the really nice trumpet player was you! I wondered about that sound, which was usually good by those standards. Yes, I was there in that orchestra with my violin, and there were two others there also who came from here. It was my fourth time there. The two others have been twice."

"Given the fact that the Polozenski name in that part of the world seems to be poison, how did you avoid being recognized? At least my passport has the name Pollen. Since we look alike, do you think that anyone noticed that there were similar similar men in the village?"

"I bribed my way over the border and I have a friend there and stayed with him and his family. I didn't show myself in public if I could help it. He picked me up on the Romanian side of the border and drove me. There was a car in the square for a few days. Was that yours?"

"Yes, I broke down there and coasted to a stop. It was fixed by some local people a day after the Saltatio Mortis."

Then it was Viktor's turn and Dizzy knew what was coming next.

"Where did you stay, and how did you ever get mixed up in this whole affair?"

"I have to tell you that I am sworn to secrecy on that one, but I can tell you about my adventure upon leaving the country. It was hair raising to say the least."

Dizzy described his trip to that gas station, then about his incident at the border with the bullets, land mine, and the rolled over car.

"My God! You were lucky to get out of that one alive. There were rumours in town about a shooting and explosion at the border. So that was you getting out of the country."

"Now I am getting into something else here," said Dizzy. "Nobody was snooping, but Ekaterina went to the ladies room one evening in your club and walked by an open door that had instruments and costumes in it. Tell me if you will, does the playing of that song have the same effect of someone dying or does it have to be at the castle on the appointed date, exactly at midnight?"

"If the circumstances are right, it is supposed to be able to happen. It doesn't have to be at that castle in Andinca. It has to be on the night of the new moon, that is, when there is no moon to be seen at all. The costumes must be worn and the bandleader has to don the horse head. It also has to end on the stroke of midnight. It defies any logic, doesn't it? Who would ever believe it?"

"There is someone that we have seen in your club following Ekaterina. She has spotted him three times now. I am sure he doesn't know that she knows, she is being followed. We went to the club a few nights ago hoping that we would spot him there, but to no avail. He never came in."

"I do not know about this, but as you have seen, there's a few unsavoury types who hang around there. Nobody makes any trouble, but some of them, I would rather not see. But they are quiet and pay for their drinks. Why do you think she is being followed?"

"I have no idea."

Dizzy wanted to wrap this up. The real conversation could come a little later. Not wanting to spook Viktor all in one shot, he decided that the big question of why people were being escorted into the place looking drugged or half-conscious could wait. He thought that Viktor may not know everything that goes on in the place and that there could be backroom schemes that transpired unbeknownst to him and that is why Ekaterina was being followed. Viktor seemed open enough to answer the questions about the Saltatio Mortis, more so than Dizzy expected, and he felt that this, along with the realization that they were indeed related, gave them an odd sort of commonality. They had shared a part in one of the most bizarre rituals on Earth. He liked Viktor and was happy to discover a long lost relative. He hoped this could lead to a more comprehensive knowledge of the Polozenski past, of which he had become more curious than ever.

One more round and they called it a night. Viktor thanked Dizzy.

"It has been a most enlightening evening for me. I don't get to meet long lost relatives every day, especially someone who knows about the Saltatio Mortis."

Viktor left, leaving Dizzy to walk back to the hotel. Ekaterina was still awake but they decided to sleep and talk about it in the morning when things had sunk in a little. Dizzy lay on his back and his wife's head lay on his shoulder, and they both drifted off almost right away.

They decided to put all of this behind them after the evening with Viktor. They sincerely wanted to give it all a rest by promising each other not to bring the subject up again, unless some development or circumstance came up. Instead, they embarked on sort of a voyage of discovery by visiting all of the museums and galleries in New York City. They kept this up for about three months or so. They went two days a week, Tuesday and Saturday, and visited everything they could. They discussed everything they saw and were becoming regulars at a half dozen places. Life had a normalcy about it, which they both treasured.

Ekaterina was on her way from work a month later when she noticed the same person who had been following her earlier was at it again. She was surprised and scared at the same time. Keeping her cool, she didn't quicken her pace, she tried to make her walk home look as normal as possible. For whatever reason, this made her feel more secure, but only marginally.

She had never felt so glad to find Dizzy at home ready to pour her a drink. She put her purse down at the table and dropped her coat on the floor behind her. She ran into Dizzy's arms and held on tight as she started to tremble.

"That man is following me again and I'm sure he followed me home. Dizzy, I'm scared this time, really scared."

Dizzy tried to calm her down, but this time it was proving difficult. He realized how scared she was and when she did finally calm down a bit, he decided to take her out for dinner at a nice quiet place. They left through the service entrance out back in case the front door was being watched.

They walked into a small French restaurant fifteen minutes later. They hadn't spoken much since leaving the hotel. She just hung on tight to Dizzy's arm. He hadn't seen her this upset before.

The conversation began slowly.

"Listen," said Dizzy. "Things can't go on like this. It's going to be hard to figure any of this out without help."

"Help? What are you talking about? What kind of help?"

"For one thing, we have no idea what this person wants or who he is, or anything. Let's turn the tables a little and follow him. I don't mean that we will literally do this, but we should hire a private detective to follow him and learn something about him. I'm sure he won't suspect that."

They both thought this was a good idea.

"The way I see it, he is either connected with a Moldavian gang or maybe he has a crush on you and wants a date."

Ekaterina gave Dizzy a gentle kick to his shin under the table. "Be serious. He is old enough to be my father. I don't think it's a date he wants."

Dizzy laughed. "I would want a date with you no matter how old I was."

"Okay, enough. How are we going to do this?"

The following morning, Dizzy called the Shield Detective Agency and arranged to meet someone at their office that afternoon. They took a taxi, hoping that no one would be watching.

James Shield was not the person Dizzy had envisioned. His only perception of a private eye was from the movies and he expected to see a kind of Edward G. Robinson tough talking, cigar chewing, overweight person in an ill-fitting suit with a bottle of cheap gin in his desk drawer. Instead, they met a handsome, well turned out individual, fashionably dressed, sitting in an orderly office.

"So you want me to follow someone who is following you, but you don't really have a description of the guy. Is that right?"

"That's exactly right, but I can give you a vague description and we will have to work together to pinpoint him."

"I can see you have thought about this. What do you have in mind?"

"Mr. Shield, please tell me if this makes any sense to you. Now I don't want you to think that I am telling you how to do your job, but this is what I have thought of. First, you will have to follow me, which won't be too hard. I know what this guy looks like and when I spot him, I will go into a bank or store where I can leave part of the newspaper that I am carrying. In it, I will leave a note detailing his clothes and where he is, or anything that can help you spot him. You can enter the place after I have left and read my note. Maybe you can take his picture so I can positively identify him, then we can take it from there. It might take a few tries, but I think it could work."

Shield thought about it for a few seconds. "A little unusual, but it could work."

"Mr. Shield, I think you will find my wife a little unusual, but she's unbelievably clever and always full of surprises."

"Now come on, Dizzy, give this nice man a break and don't scare him with my ability to surprise."

"Not too many people are called Dizzy. You don't happen to be the great bandleader?"

"Yes, I am, Mr. Shield, and I hope I can count on your absolute discretion."

"Absolutely, Mr. Pollen. None of what is said in this office ever gets out."

"Good, and you can call me Dizzy. Everyone does."

"It's an honour to meet you and your wife."

"I'll let you and Ekaterina work out the details. I would like to start as soon as possible."

"Good, I'll come to your place tomorrow at ten and we'll take it from there."

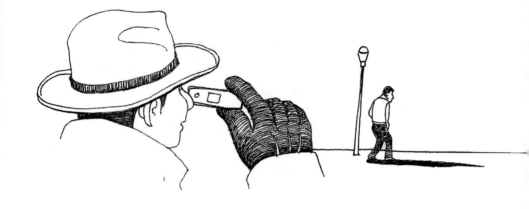

CHAPTER 18

There was a knock on the hotel room door next morning. Coffee was served and Shield and Ekaterina went to work. She gave him her work schedule and a list of places she was likely to frequent such as her bank and food shops. She would always carry a newspaper so she could leave a note.

Ekaterina was to work at noon and so Shield left before her and positioned himself to be able to spot anyone who started to follow her. This routine went on for a few days until she noticed the same man following her on her way home from work. She surreptitiously took note of everything she could, then walked into a small deli where she wrote on her notepaper: 5ft 6 in, greyish jacket, black pants, black hair, behind me, same side of street.

She put her note in the sports section and left it on the end of the counter in the crowded deli. She left carrying the remainder of the paper.

About thirty seconds later, Shield walked into the deli and retrieved the note. He then tried to spot the man fitting this description. It didn't take long. He passed the man, then waited on the next corner as if to cross the street. Shield had a tiny German Minox camera, which fit into his palm and took completely noiseless pictures on small film stock. He managed to take half a dozen shots of the man walking towards him before crossing the street. Ekaterina was a block ahead and arrived at the hotel where the doorman let her in."

She felt relieved once in the suite with Dizzy.

"I was followed again today, but this time I managed to leave a note for Shield in my paper. I haven't the faintest idea whether he retrieved it or not, or whether any of this worked."

A few hours later, the phone rang and Dizzy answered.

"Hello, this is James Shield. I think I found our man today. I snapped a few pictures and will develop them. Can I come over tomorrow at around ten?"

"Absolutely," answered Dizzy. "I'll let Ekaterina know. Good night."

"Looks like it all may have worked. Shield is coming over with pictures of the guy tomorrow. You are really beginning to live up to your nickname, spy girl."

"It would be more fun if I wasn't so terrified. I don't like this one bit."

The following morning over coffee, they looked at the pictures. "Yes, that's definitely him," Ekaterina told Shield.

"I followed him home. He lives another half-hour from where you left me the note. He didn't stop anywhere so I think he lives there. He didn't come out after he entered the place. I hung around for another hour. I will now check out his movements when he is not following you. Then I'll try to get his name from his mailbox. In a few days, I should know a lot more about him."

It was a few days before Shield phoned again and they met him in his office.

He poured three cups of coffee and put them on his desk.

"The man's name is Marius Vlado. I have followed him several times and he doesn't seem to have a job. He seems to come and go at various times of the day, with no particular purpose. He does, however, frequent a small place called the Romanian-Moldovian Social Club. Does that mean anything to you?"

"Yes, we go there sometimes. I was born in Romania and Dizzy's ancestors emigrated from Moldova in the nineteenth century."

Ekaterina began to recount all of the connections with the Polozenski name and how she discovered it in the phone book, including following Viktor to the club and discovering how he and Dizzy were related. She was careful not to mention anything related to their time in Romania and especially Dizzy's adventure in Moldova. Probably the most significant aspect of the whole story would be connected with the Saltatio Mortis, and she was determined not to let that cat out of the bag.

"That gets us no further as to why you are being followed," said Shield.

"Can you carry on for a while longer and see if you can turn up anything else? Maybe you could check on his activities at the club. Perhaps he is the one who does the following for someone else. I don't think he is connected with Viktor because we know him and I am good friends with his wife, Petra."

"Okay, I'll call you next week."

The following week, Shield called to arrange another meeting at his office.

"I'm sorry to disappoint you, but I'm afraid I don't have a hell of a lot more information about this individual. However, there are a few things of interest. First, he goes to the club just about every day. I have visited the place a few times with a friend so I wouldn't be there alone. He always meets with the same two shady characters. They mumble away in their own language and by all appearances, I would say they're up to no good. I disguised myself so he wouldn't recognize me in the outside world. So, here's what I want to do, and you tell me if you will go along with this.

"I have an assistant, Miss Chavez, who could accompany me to the club. I also own a device called a wire recorder, which can record voices through a small microphone. I had the device miniaturized so it fits in a handbag and I can record about an hour's worth of conversation with it. If we can sit within ten feet their table, I should be able to catch something of significance."

Dizzy was amazed. "You mean to say you have a wire recorder that small?"

"Yes. It cost me a few bucks to have it made, but it works really well."

"Well," said Dizzy, "that sounds like a great idea. Can you start soon? By the way, I can't wait to see your machine. I've only heard about those things."

"As soon as he goes to the club, Miss Chavez and I will be there. With a little luck, we'll all learn a more about this guy."

Three days later, Shield made the call to Chavez and she joined him a block away from the club. He had a different hair colour and fake glasses. She was dressed plainly not to attract too much attention in a place that had a mostly male clientele. She carried the wire recorder in a specially made bag carried by a strap over her shoulder. There was a decorative cloth strip around the lip of the bag and the microphone was positioned behind it, so there would be no muffling of the sound being recorded. All in all, it was an ingenious setup.

They entered the club and were lucky enough to sit within recording range of Vlado and his two comrades. Shield sat with his back to him and Chavez put the bag on the floor with the microphone pointed towards Vlado's table. She pressed the noiseless switch on the strap and the machine started recording. Shield ordered a couple of beers and they sipped them, talking in low voices so as to not interfere with the recording. In twenty minutes, they left and Shield called the hotel from a payphone.

Ekaterina answered. "I have a spool of Vlado and his two pals from the club. Is this a good time to come over?"

"Absolutely. We'll be here waiting for you."

Twenty minutes later, Shield and Chavez were at the hotel. He set up the recorder and gave Ekaterina a set of earphones. She had a pencil and note pad and began to take notes. Everyone left the room to let her concentrate. She had Shield rewind the wire so she could complete her notes. When she finished, she informed Shield that there was some useful stuff and that she would like some more information if he could repeat the exercise. He replied that he would be happy to do so and would call when he recorded again.

When Shield and Chavez were gone, Ekaterina's demeanor changed completely.

"Dizzy, you are not going to believe what was on that wire. I didn't want to say anything in front of them, but these guys think that you and I are here to expose the Saltatio Mortis to the whole world and they want to stop us!"

"What are you saying?"

"Of course, my information is incomplete, but they seem to think that we, or more to the point, I am an agent of some government bent on putting a stop to the practice, not only here, but in Moldova!"

"That's the most insane thing I have ever heard."

"It is to me also, but whatever made anyone think anything like that? What on Earth did any of us do to convey that impression?"

"Off the top of my head, I did crash the border getting out of Moldova, possibly leaving several people maybe dead in the car that hit the land mine. Somebody must be more than a little annoyed at that one. Not that that had anything to do with anything, but it remains an event."

"Do you think Viktor has anything to do with this?"

"I wouldn't think so, but I am certainly going to confront him about it. After the discussion we had last time, I felt he would not be paranoid about us. I certainly don't think he views us as any kind of threat."

"I think you are right. Besides, I had the distinct feeling he was glad to have another Polozenski in his life, however distant."

"How about you? Is anyone to the best of your knowledge a sworn enemy of your father? He's a nice enough guy, but he is an influential and powerful person and such people can collect enemies."

"As you know, my father was born into money. He never really held down a job of any sort and lives a quiet life of traveling, reading, and socializing with his peers. It's his father who built the family fortune with business and land dealings."

"Land dealings?"

I don't really know, except that now that I come to think about it, I believe he worked in both countries and maybe even in the area around where you were."

"The term 'land dealings' may mean any number of things, but it could easily entail making some enemies along the way. Think about this: your grandfather could have made some real enemies way back when and as we both know, memories are long in that end of the world. Grudges are held for generations."

"Do you think I might be the remaining living personification of that feud?"

"Could be. What if someone has found out that you are Augustine's daughter and you are being held responsible for the shenanigans of his father. I know that is far-fetched but that could be one explanation. I'm sure there are more but I am at a loss to figure anything out."

"If that's true, they'll stop at nothing to avenge their ancestors, and I could be in real trouble without any idea why I am being hunted. Can we talk to Viktor as soon as possible? Maybe he can shed some light on the matter. In the meantime, Shield will have to continue collecting info from these characters. God, Dizzy, I'm really scared."

She broke into tears and Dizzy just held her for a few minutes. She was trembling and he gently steered her towards the bedroom, where they both fell asleep almost immediately. Neither of them slept well, but in the morning, Dizzy had a few ideas.

"First of all, you are not going into work for a while. You can dream up the necessary excuses. I'm sure you'll figure it out. I'll call Viktor today and set up a meeting as soon as possible. Most importantly, I'm going to get you out of town for a few days."

"How are you going to do that?"

"I have a good friend up in Boston. She used to sing with the band. One day, she announced that she was getting married and wanted to have children. She quit singing and she and her husband live in a house with three kids. They have a big house and you can stay with them. They are both close friends of mine. I'll call them and let them know that you will be coming. They won't ask questions and you'll be safe there."

Dizzy, made arrangements to meet Viktor that day and Ekaterina would be driven to Boston by Shield, leaving in the middle of the night and arriving in the morning.

She seemed okay with this and although she really didn't want to be away from Dizzy, what with everything going on, she thought she would feel safe for a few days.

Viktor came to the hotel around noon. They were both glad to see him. Dizzy wasted no time and showed him the photo of Vlado. "Do you know who this man is?"

"I don't know him by name but he and two pretty shady-looking companions come to the club quite often. They aren't particularly sociable, they just sit and talk among themselves, pay their bill, and leave. Never any problems with them. What's this about?"

"This guy has been following Ekaterina around for some time now. She has become so scared that I put a private eye on him and that's where the photo came from. His name is Marius Vlado. Are you sure you don't know anything about him?"

"Not really, except that he and his two buddies are from western Moldova. That's by their accents. They talk just like the people living in the area where the Saltatio Mortis takes place."

"Oh God!" Ekaterina gasped.

"Again, Dizzy, what is this about?"

"Frankly, Viktor, we are not really sure, but these guys seem to think that Ekaterina is an agent of some government that wants to blow the whistle on the Saltatio Mortis in Moldova and anywhere else it happens. We have no idea how anyone would come to his conclusion, but as you can imagine, Ekaterina is terrified, as am I. The only reason I'm telling you this is because in a strange way we are family and for that reason, we trust you."

"How do you know this about this Vlado character?"

"I will leave this to your imagination, but as it stands now, none of those guys can make a move without me knowing it." Dizzy exaggerated, but felt it best if he didn't play his whole hand.

"I'll tell you one more thing. It is possible that this is part of a vendetta for something that happened back in the nineteenth century, possibly involving Ekaterina's grandfather. It's only speculation so far, but her granddad, it seems, may have been involved in land speculation or outright swindling. It might have involved our ancestors somehow."

"Dizzy and Ekaterina, I'm so sorry all if this is happening to you. Rest assured that I will poke my nose around and see what I can find out. Don't worry; I will use the utmost discretion. I'll stay in touch. Please call me if you need anything. Anything at all."

"Thank you, Viktor. I will."

It was about 3 a.m. when Shield called, telling Dizzy he would be at the service entrance in fifteen minutes. Ekaterina, who hadn't slept, was drowsy and in a bit of a snit as she really didn't want to go, but Dizzy insisted. He was determined to keep her safe from whatever danger might be ahead. None of her irresistible charms worked on him this time. She was going to Boston and that was that. He would make it all up to her when this creepy business ended.

She was in a better frame of mind when she spoke to Dizzy at around five on the following day. All was forgiven. Shield called the day after that and was busy keeping a close eye on Vlado and his pals, and was waiting for an opportunity to record them again. Within three days, he and Chavez made two recordings at the club and had another two spools for Ekaterina.

Dizzy arranged to have her hear the recordings over the phone. The whole process was interminable with Ekaterina listening to each recording twice so she could note everything down.

Ekaterina called Dizzy the following morning with everything she could decipher from the wire recordings.

"Well, my darling Dizzy, this is what I think I have figured out. It would seem that my grandfather was in a large part responsible for the Polozenski family having to leave the castle and leave the country."

"How on Earth did he do that? From the little we know, they were a powerful, mean bunch."

"It seems they were good with the gun and the sword but a little stupid when it came to understanding capitalism. My grandfather cooked up some scheme that caused the Polozenski family to lose the castle. After that, driving them from the fiefdom wasn't too hard."

"So let me get this straight. Your grandaddy swindled my grandaddy out of the family home and the Polozenski family had to get out of Dodge."

"That's about it. But what is Dodge?"

He laughed. Ekaterina became annoyed. "What is so bloody funny?"

"My dearest, first of all, the irony of the situation. We are supposed to be bitter enemies, you and I. With the length of time that grudges are held in that end of the world, we should be at each others' throats. Also, Dodge is a city in Kansas and is quite often featured in western movies. The bad guys are always getting run out of Dodge. It's just an expression denoting having to leave town quickly."

"Dizzy, can I please come home now?"

"Let's have Shield gather a little more on these guys. Maybe in a few days."

"Okay, but only a few days. I appreciate your concern but I'd rather be back with you."

"I know."

A few days after Ekaterina returned to New York, they met again with Shields. Upon listening to two more wire recordings, Ekaterina was visibly shaken. The conversations between Vlado and his comrades did not mince words. They intended to terminate Ekaterina but gave a no hint about how they would accomplish this.

Many morbid scenarios were discussed between them in the next few days. Would they try to run her down with a car or just plain shoot her on the street, or use poison somehow? The last one didn't seem plausible. Ekaterina couldn't live forever in the hotel suite as a prisoner, fearing the outside world.

After a week, she told Dizzy she had had enough and she wanted to get out. He forbade it but he knew that kind of edict would last a day, if he was lucky.

A compromise was eventually arrived at. It wasn't perfect but they both thought it would be okay. Through James Shield, they hired a bodyguard who would not let Ekaterina out of his sight, no matter what. Shield assured them that Wally was very capable and at one time worked for the Secret Service. Wally had seen Vlado's photos so he could he could keep a better eye on things. Dizzy didn't like any of this but it was better than having Ekaterina wandering around on her own. He was relieved that she was in a much better mood when she could go out.

Things returned to a loose sense of normalcy but they were both distressed about the whole affair. They thought of approaching the police but the story had become too complicated and far-fetched for the police to handle.

"Listen, Dizzy. Maybe we should lay things all out on the table for Viktor. I feel we could trust him. After all, he is a relative and the only one you have. I got the feeling that he was happy to discover you and it may be worth a shot. I would prefer to have him on our side than to have him in the dark about everything. I also have a strong feeling that he knows more than he is letting on. Maybe if you both get together and speak truthfully to each other, we can all find a way to fix this problem. We will never be able to live normally until we can make it go away."

"I think you may be right. It's worth a shot, I suppose."

The next evening found Viktor, Dizzy, and Ekaterina in the hotel room. "The reason we only asked you over was out of caution. What we are about to discuss may or may not be for Petra's ears, and we didn't want to let any cat out of the bag if this turns out to be inappropriate. We were just unsure." Ekaterina broke out the dreaded bottle of Zorko and three glasses.

"Sounds serious."

"It really is," said Dizzy. For the next forty-five minutes, they recounted everything that had gone on from the time Ekaterina noticed that she was being followed. She showed Viktor the notes from Shield's wire recorder. He was stunned and aghast.

"Now, Viktor," began Dizzy, "I need to know a few things from you. I have just told you everything and I want you to tell me anything that could be pertinent to this situation. Somehow, at the heart of all of this is the Saltatio Mortis. I know it has been performed in your place."

"How?" Viktor began.

Dizzy cut him off. "Ekaterina saw all the instruments and costumes, including the horsehead, when she walked by an open door on the way to the ladies washroom one evening. The next time she went to the washroom, that door was closed but there was a sheet of music lying on the floor outside the door and Ekaterina brought it to me. I recognized it right away as page 3 from the Saltatio Mortis. I know this because I committed the entire piece to memory back in Moldova."

Viktor knocked his Zorko back in one shot, underwent the usual shudder, and said, "My God!"

"And that's not all. I have seen people being brought into your establishment looking like they are under the influence of some drug or whatever. I have to ask point blank: Are you getting rid of people by subjecting them to the Saltatio Mortis? Before you answer that, I want you to know that I don't really care what you do. But right now, my Ekaterina is under a direct threat and I intend to get to the bottom of this before she gets hurt or worse. So please tell me the truth!"

"All I can tell you is that it is classified."

"Oh for Christ's sake. Are you saying you have a contract from Uncle Sam to make people disappear?"

"I can go to prison if I tell you more."

"This is Ekaterina's life that we are talking about here. I couldn't care less about your classified work. Does this Vlado work for you?"

"No. Honestly, I don't know where he comes from. I don't know the guy, he just comes into my club and leaves. I really don't know about him at all. He's only started to come in about three months ago."

"Does anyone else have access to your place? Do any others have a key?"

"Only Nosso, our band leader, whom you met when you played with us."

"Do you think there's any connection between Vlado and Nosso?"

"I don't know."

It was Ekaterina's turn. "Where does Nosso come from?"

"From our old region. He came from about 5 kms outside Andinca."

"So Nosso and Vlado come from the same place, more or less."

"Okay, now one more time, Viktor: Can you think of anything, anything at all, that would help us figure what is going on? All we know is that someone, presumably Vlado, wants to kill Ekaterina because her grandfather swindled our grandfather out of his land and castle back in the nineteenth century. He seems to think that Ekaterina wants to expose the Saltatio Mortis to the world."

"Jesus, it's really crazy, except for the length of time someone in that end of the world holds onto a grudge," said Viktor. "That much I can understand from our history. But why he thinks Ekaterina wants to expose the Saltatio Mortis is beyond me. I wish I had more answers, but that part of it is not making any sense at all."

Dizzy and Ekaterina rehashed the whole conversation in bed that night, and came to the same conclusion. Viktor was ridding Uncle Sam of undesirables. The war had started and it was probably an easy way to dispense with people for whom a public trial might not benefit the powers that be. It was now obvious that they were using the Saltatio Mortis to do so. The perfect crime. Absolutely no one would be able to come up with a murder weapon. The fascinating part was the apparent connection between Nosso and Vlado.

"Maybe Nosso was one of the recipients of my grandfather's shenanigans... and Vlado. But I still can't connect any of this with the Saltatio Mortis," said Ekaterina.

"It's getting late. Let's deal with it in the morning."

It was a sleep fraught with moments of fear, exhaustion, and disturbing dreams for both of them.

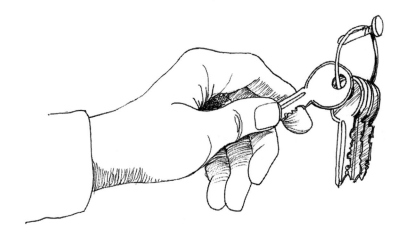

CHAPTER 19

The absurd idea came to Dizzy in the middle of the night. It was so unlike anything in his character that he dismissed it almost immediately. Then the thought had an idea of its own. It would not let Dizzy go and in a few days, he had to confess it to Ekaterina.

"Have you completely lost your mind?" he asked, shocked.

"My dear," Dizzy answered, "it does seem a little insane, but you have to admit it is quite original. I'll also admit to some desperation about all of this. Maybe I have been driven a little crazy, but I can't let anything happen to you, and you are in what I think is grave danger. You cannot deny that."

"No, I suppose not. So let me repeat this back to you as I understand it. Maybe hearing it from me might make things look a little different. By some as of yet unknown means, you want to catch or kidnap Vlado and kill him with the Saltatio Mortis. I got that, but then you will have a body on your hands. What then?"

"I haven't gotten that far, but frankly, killing that bastard would have both of us rest easier. This whole thing is so insane that I am probably not thinking clearly really can't go on living under this cloud. Sooner or later, something bad is going to happen probably to you and I just want to take matters in my own hands. We've both agreed that the police wouldn't be able to help us. We'll be carried off to Bellevue with a story like that. And the irony is that the truer the story would be, the less believable it is."

"I'm not consenting to this, but tell me how you would go about doing this?"

"The two weak links in the chain are the kidnapping and dumping the body, and that is where I reach an impasse. I have never contemplated anything like this before and I know that I don't have the wherewithal to do any of these things, but I know how to play that piece! I have it all written down and I could find some way to get my band to play it. I'd have to find out if the costumes are necessary and whether the leader has to wear the horse's head. I can find all of that out from Viktor. Hell, I might be able to get Viktor to do it. They apparently do it all the time—body disposal and all. It would appear to be no big deal to them. I'm sure Viktor wouldn't want to see you harmed in any way."

"I can scarcely believe you are entertaining such an idea. It's so unlike the gentle person that you are."

"Nobody has plotted to kill you before. I'm just as afraid as you are, and that has had quite an effect on my so called gentleness."

"Dizzy, please don't do anything stupid. I don't want to have to visit you in jail."

"Don't worry, I won't. Forgive me, I'm talking out of desperation here. But I have to have another talk with Viktor."

A few days later at the club, Dizzy met Viktor and asked to speak to him in the privacy of his office.

He asked for details about the Saltatio Mortis. Did the costumes matter? Was there a minimum number and type of instruments? Was there a certain time to play? Viktor replied yes to the costumes, emphasizing the importance of the horse's head for the conductor. There didn't seem to be a minimum number or type of instruments. The supreme importance was that the piece be played correctly, every note. The Saltatio Mortis could only happen on the night of the new moon. That is, when there is no moon at all, and it had to end on the stroke of midnight.

"Dizzy, why are you asking me about all of this?"

"As you know, we are caught up in this crazy situation involving Vlado and who knows who or what else. I'm just trying to arm myself with as much information as I can for our own protection. Frankly, I'm at my wits end with worry over Ekaterina, and I feel rather powerless right now.

Going to the police would only land us in the funny farm with such a story, so we have to think this through on our own. I don't really want to have the police conduct a raid here."

At one point in the conversation, Viktor left Dizzy in his office to fetch them a couple of drinks. Just as Viktor left the room, Dizzy spotted a ring with three keys hanging by the door. Without thinking, he grabbed them and quickly made a pencil rubbing of them with some paper that was sitting on the desk. He completed the job as quickly as he could before he lost his nerve. He finished and folded up the paper, putting it carefully in his breast pocket. He managed to put the key ring back just in time as Viktor returned with the dreaded tank fuel. Dizzy wondered if he would give himself away by shaking. This was completely out of character for him to act so impulsively. They talked a little more about the Saltatio Mortis and its history, and Dizzy asked if the people in the fenced off portion of the cemetery in Andinca were the unfortunates killed at the castle over the years.

"My, you certainly got around for the little time you spent there. The answer to that one is yes."

"From my vantage point here, I didn't get around enough. I wish I knew more about the place and its history. I did notice some Polozenskis buried there."

"How did you manage a trip to the cemetery in Andinca?"

"It's classified!" Dizzy replied with a certain sense of smugness. He was not going to involve Professor Zablo in any of this.

Viktor couldn't shed any more light on the history of the Saltatio Mortis except that it all went back so far that no one remembered anything about it this side of the Middle Ages. They wondered about the piece of music being composed so long ago. It would have been much more sophisticated than anything else in Europe at the time. Viktor suggested it may have come from the area southeast of Moldova, bringing it closer to the Middle East.

Another round and it was time for Dizzy to go to his gig. They parted company with both of them having the feeling of liking each other. Dizzy felt that Viktor was trustworthy, and Viktor was genuinely happy to have a newly discovered family member in his life.

Back at the hotel, Dizzy carefully placed his pencil rubbings flat in the page of a book. He didn't tell Ekaterina until the next morning.

"I don't know what made me do it; they were just there in front of me along with a pencil and paper. I'm going to have the keys made."

"What do you think they fit?"

"I don't know, but I had a gut feeling that I should do this. We'll see what they fit later—if anything. They were there, so they must fit something. One may even open the instrument room. We have no way of knowing until we try."

"It would all be exciting if it wasn't so scary."

Ekaterina organized the keys. She called Shield and had him do it. If questions were asked, then he would know what to say, and besides, he was a private eye and could have any number of contacts for such dubious transactions. Then the stage was set to find out what key fit where.

Dizzy and Ekaterina went down to the club on his night off. They were not prepared for what they encountered upon entering. In a darkened corner sat Vlado and his sidekick, and less than ten feet away sat Shield and his partner Miss Chavez with the bag containing the wire recorder on the floor beside them. Ekaterina spotted the bag and realized Shield and Chavez were in disguise. She wouldn't have known them if it wasn't for the bag. They sat down and Ekaterina told Dizzy to look at the people in the corner. He stole a glance. "My God, it's Vlado and his friend."

"Be very careful and look again."

"I don't see anything else special."

"Shield and Chavez are sitting near them with the wire recorder."

"You're joking! How do you know?"

Ekaterina felt relaxed for the first time in a long time, which surprised her given the fact that she was sitting in the same room with a man who was plotting to kill her. She gave Dizzy her best smile and wink, which he had missed. "Because it's your spy girl's job to spot these things."

She went to the bar, knowing that she would be seen by Vlado and Shield. She wanted Shield to spot her, as she knew that Vlado would probably start talking about her to his friend and be recorded in the process. By the time she returned with four shots of Zorko, she was sure Chavez had looked right at her walking back to the table. Viktor then entered the club and wandered over to say hello. They chatted for a while until he said he was taking the night off and would see them some other time. That was good; they didn't have to worry about him catching her trying to open some door. A half hour later, she decided to go to the ladies room.

"Keep an eye on the table. If Vlado gets up while I'm away, get behind him so I won't be alone in that hallway with him. Follow him to the men's room if necessary."

Ekaterina got up and walked through the closed door. Halfway to the washroom, she put a key into the lock for the instrument room. It didn't work. She lost her nerve and went into the washroom and locked the door. She took a half dozen deep breaths and returned to the door with another key. Click! It unlocked. She quickly locked it again and went to rejoin Dizzy.

"Okay, this key locks the instrument room. Put it in your left pocket so we remember which one it is."

She removed the key from the ring under the table and handed it to Dizzy. She asked him where the office was and he said it was down the same corridor on the right, opposite the instrument room.

"Where did you play with that crazy orchestra?"

"You see that back wall is covered with a thin curtain. All the tables and chairs were moved into that corner and we all sat more or less facing that wall.

"Of the two keys left, one is bigger than the other. I'll bet it's for an outside door. On our way out, I'll try it. When we close the door, I'll be able to figure out if it works or not."

They finished up and got up to leave. Ekaterina went out first, and as Dizzy was holding the door open, she slipped the key in the slot. It fit the slot but didn't work the lock. Outside, she said, "I'm sure it's for the back door. Let's go."

Dizzy was a little hesitant. She said, "C'mon before I completely lose my nerve."

They snuck around to the back door. It was dark with no lights, but they found the door. Ekaterina felt a satisfying click as the lock opened. There was no light inside and they didn't have the nerve to start wandering around in complete blackness, so they closed the door and went home. With access to two doors in the place, they felt successful. But for what? Dizzy's mind started to work overtime on it.

"Here's what I think. This room we played music in was strange, now that I come to think about it. Here we were, playing to a blank wall, but there was no echo coming back at us. We should have been hit with a loud echo, but we weren't."

"So..."

"It means the wall is not solid. Sound goes through it. The thin curtain must hide a second drape behind it. It must be stretched to look like a fabric covered wall but there is no actual wall. So when they play the Saltatio Mortis, someone on the other side would hear it with the usual deadly result. That's how it's done. What an elaborate setup! Now, if Viktor is paid by the government to get rid of someone, then they are put into the room, probably drugged or forcibly confined, while the orchestra plays the song, starting at exactly 11:48 to finish on the stroke of midnight."

"It has been an exciting evening, if a little scary. Let's go to bed. I promise more excitement, but without the fear."

Shield called at ten the following morning. He had one more spool of wire to listen to. Ekaterina put on the earphones and started writing everything down. It all took about an hour, in which Dizzy and Shield talked about the previous night.

"I had no idea you would be there," Dizzy said.

"Let me tell you, I just about fell over when I saw the two of you walk in," Shield answered. Dizzy said it was probably a good thing because that would steer Vlado's conversation if he saw Ekaterina.

"My thoughts exactly," said Shield.

Ekaterina entered the room looking a little shaken. "I know what they have planned for me in much more detail. They want to kidnap me and kill me sometime soon." Both men gasped.

"Do you have any more details?"

"Not really, but their intention is quite clear."

"With evidence like that on wire, we could go to the police," Shield said. "Sounds like a convincing threat for sure."

"Problem is, my name isn't said at any time on the wire. Not last night or on any other wire we have. It might prove impossible to make any kind of a case. I know Vlado is the so-called leader of the two and his sidekick doesn't seem any too bright. He doesn't seem like much of a threat on his own."

"What do we do with all of this?" asked Shield.

"For now, nothing. I will re-listen to everything and call you. You will be the first to know of any plans we make." With that, Shield departed, leaving the wire recorder with them.

As soon as he was out the door, Dizzy said, "You certainly didn't tell all, did you?"

"No. They plan to kidnap me all right, but they want to use the Saltatio Mortis to do me in. Dizzy, look at the calendar. When is the next new moon?"

"My God, it is in two days!"

"Are you sure this will only work on that night?"

"Both Professor Zablo and Viktor told me the same story. They start playing at 11:48 and end on the stroke of midnight. That part of it is for sure, and that's how it happened in Moldova. You will have to stay in here until the new moon has passed. That will give us a month to figure a way to end this madness. It sure makes me wish I had never set foot in Moldova. Who would ever have dreamed up anything like this? I'll take the next nights off so you won't be alone here."

Ekaterina listened to the sinister voices on the wire again. This time, it allowed her to concentrate on everything. It sounded to her that Vlado was indeed working alone, except for his peasant friend.

They agreed that Vlado knew the Saltatio Mortis was to be played in two days and this would allow him to sneak Ekaterina into the place and exchange her for whatever victim was present. This would be done at the last minute, just before the Saltatio Mortis began. They would free the intended victim, who would be only too happy to escape death, although he would wonder why he was in a room with an orchestra playing weird music in the next room. Dizzy figured that the victim would be tied to a chair sedated and gagged. He would be dead within minutes after the piece ended.

Dizzy and Ekaterina spent the day together holed up in their hotel suite. The got room service and listened to a baseball game on the radio. The Dodgers were playing the Yankees in the first game of the World Series and Dizzy was having fun explaining how the game worked with a pencil and paper, on which he had drawn a map of a baseball diamond and marked out all the player's positions. He was determined to get Ekaterina to understand this crazy American pastime.

By the sixth inning, she understood most of it and wanted Dizzy to take her to a real game as soon as he could, which he promised to do. They had temporarily forgotten their plight and were enjoying the time together. Around the eighth inning, there was a knock at the door. They looked at each other.

"Who could that be?" she asked.

Dizzy got up and went quietly towards the door. Looking through the peephole, he saw a man in a bellhop's uniform. As he opened the door just a crack, it flew open and two men rushed inside. One of them thrust a cloth with chloroform on it into Dizzy's face. He fell to the floor. The other man ran towards Ekaterina, who was paralyzed in shock and only managed to let out a small scream before she suffered the same fate as Dizzy. They were both out cold.

CHAPTER 20

It was several hours before Dizzy awoke. It took some time for him to regain enough consciousness and sense to realize what had happened. Ekaterina was missing and he knew she had been kidnapped.

He was blaming himself for opening the door, but that was in the past. He called Shield.

"James, Ekaterina has been kidnapped from right under my nose. Can you get over here right away?"

"Jesus! What happened?"

"It's too long to explain over the phone, but I have a pretty good idea of what is happening. And by the way, do you own a gun?"

"Yes. I do, but..."

"I'm pretty sure you won't have to use it, but you should have it just in case."

"All right, I'll be right over."

A half hour later, Dizzy tried to explain to Shield where Ekaterina would be at a few minutes before midnight, but was having little luck getting him to understand the Saltatio Mortis.

"Are you trying to tell me that she will be killed in a back room in that club? Are they going to shoot her?"

This was, of course, where things got dicey. Dizzy said, "No. That would be too noisy. They will strangle her or knife her quietly, or something like that."

"And what is this about it being midnight? How do you know this?"

Dizzy had to give one of the great ad-libs of his life. He was a master on the trumpet, but now he had make up a plausible story on the spot to save his beloved.

"Back where Ekaterina comes from, ritual murders are always committed just before midnight. It's some kind of tradition that has its roots in antiquity and probably no one knows why. It's just the way they do things. Ekaterina's grandfather in the late nineteenth century did something nasty to Vlado's family and it's payback time."

"Dizzy, that sounds a little far-fetched, don't you think? I mean, that was a long time ago. Another place, another time."

"To you and I, that would seem to be the case, but over there, family feuds never really end. They carry on for generations. Seems a little senseless to the likes of you and me, but remember our own classic American feud between the Hatfields and McCoys. It's similar."

"Shouldn't we be at the police station right now telling them about all of this?"

"If they encounter police, they might not wait and kill her on the spot. I know it seems like I am taking a hell of a chance here with my wife's life, but I really do know what is going to happen and we can stop it if we play things right."

"I am going to call one more person to assist us, my horn player, Spike. He is a good human being but he grew up on the south side of Chicago and while he is a gentle person, if a fight should occur, we'll need his strength!"

An hour later Spike, Dizzy, and Shield were in a cafe where Dizzy explained his plan. They had four hours to go before midnight. He explained that he had the keys to the back door and one other key, which he figured would open the door to the room where Ekaterina would be brought.

"I want to do this quietly, but in the event that the inner door is locked, then Spike will have to shoulder it." He gave another performance to explain the orchestra's final piece.

"There is an orchestra that practices there on the other side of the room we will be in. It will cover any noise we make. Now we get to the tricky part. There may be someone already in the room, but he may be unconscious in a chair. We will get him out and replace him with Vlado, who will be bringing Ekaterina into the room."

Dizzy showed Spike a photo of Vlado. He explained that he may or may not be alone. "Shield, you may have to draw your gun to keep everyone still. We may have to play a lot of this by ear. The whole idea will be to get Ekaterina out of there before midnight. We take whoever is in the chair and replace him with Vlado. That's the important thing. Ekaterina out and Vlado stays. We'll deal with the other guy afterwards."

Spike and Shield were a little puzzled about all of this, but Dizzy seemed quite sure about his plan.

At eleven o'clock, they pulled up in Dizzy's car to the side street and parked near the lane that ran behind the club. They looked around, exited the car, and walked down the lane quickly. Dizzy led the way and upon reaching the door, put his ear to it.

"I hear nothing," he whispered.

He carefully put the key in the lock and opened the door. It was pitch dark inside. Doubt began to really hit at him. He whispered for Shield to shine his flashlight, partially covering it with his hand, and look for another door. Shield scanned the room and a saw door in the wall quite close to them. By this time, he was trembling and scared stiff. He put the remaining key into the door and turned it gingerly. A soft click went off and the door opened slowly. Again, there was total darkness.

"Shield, let's see what's here."

Shield turned his light on. In front of them, a man was tied up to a chair, slumped over with his head bowed. He was asleep, unconscious, or dead.

Shield put the back of his hand on the man's neck and said, "He's alive. I can smell chloroform. He has been drugged."

"Okay, let's untie him and put him somewhere." Shield looked around. "There's an old sofa at the end of the room."

"Quick, untie him and put him on the sofa but save the rope. And be quiet." They did so.

Dizzy took Shield's light and went back to lock the doors. Now everything would look normal.

"What now, boss?" asked Spike.

"We wait. If my gamble is correct, within a few minutes, Vlado will come in here with Ekaterina. She is probably drugged but able to walk if held up. We will get her and he will have to be neutralized and tied to the chair. Then we have to get out as soon as we can. If there are two people, they both have to be knocked out. Vlado has to be tied to the chair. The other one, his sidekick, will have to be dragged outside, as well as our unconscious friend. I'll explain later. Whatever happens, we have to act fast and get out."

"I'll knock them bastards out, jus' watch," said Spike.

Dizzy knew he could handle that part without any problem.

They waited in silence. It was pitch black and everyone was nervous and sweaty. Seconds stretched into minutes and time lost its meaning. It was just the three of them waiting for God knows what in total black silence.

Then they heard a faint click. The outer door was being opened. Dizzy and Shield were on the hinge side of the inner door so when it opened, they could be behind whoever was entering. A key was inserted into the lock to the inner door. It opened normally and in walked three figures. Shield flashed his light in their eyes long enough to recognize Vlado and a blindfolded woman. In a flash, Spike took out the third man with an incredible punch to the jaw, and with an amazing lunge, caught the man before he hit the ground with a thud, lowering him gently. Before Vlado had any chance to act, he was hit with an uppercut. The noise of a cracking jaw said it all. Vlado was out cold. Dizzy rushed to get to Ekaterina before she fell down, as she was still drugged. He let her down, took off the blindfold, and put his hand over her mouth so she wouldn't make any noise.

Shield and Spike started to tie Vlado to the chair when this strange music started to come in through the wall.

"What the hell is that?" asked Spike.

"It's the crazy band, and it means we have five minutes to get out of here. No fucking around. Finish quickly." Dizzy knew they actually had twelve minutes, but the quicker they got out of there, the better.

THE CURSE OF THE MOLDAVIAN TANGO

"I'll need help to get Ekaterina out of here. We have to carry her to the car. Now, there may be a car in the lane with a driver, or maybe not. Spike, if there is, can you deal with him?"

"I'll add him to the list of the evening's Kos."

With Vlado securely gagged and tied to the chair, Dizzy and Shield walked Ekaterina towards the door. A third man came towards them in the darkness. Spike cracked another jaw and laid him out on the floor. They quickly dragged him into the room with the two others. Now there were four people laid out in the room.

"We have got to get the three others out of here quickly."

Dizzy sat Ekaterina down in a corner, and the three men pulled the three flattened individuals out to the car. The trunk where Ekaterina had been kept was still open. Two of them were stuffed in the trunk and the other was plopped on the floor behind the front seats. Dizzy turned off the engine, taking the car keys with him.

He gave the door keys to Spike, instructing him to lock them back up.

They started up the lane when Spike said, "Let me carry Ekaterina. You guys run ahead and make sure that nobody sees us. Get the car door open. I'd hate to see anything go wrong now. This wouldn't be easy to explain, especially to the cops."

Dizzy and Shield scooted ahead and gave Spike the all clear sign when they reached the street.

Dizzy got in back and Spike put Ekaterina in the seat next to him. Shield got behind the wheel with Spike beside him.

"We'll go to my office and unwind there," said Shield. "Then you need to give us some kind of explanation for all of these shenanigans."

Ekaterina started to regain consciousness. Eyes slowly opening, she looked over and saw Dizzy beside her.

She put her arms around him and started to cry. "How..."

"Shhh. You're okay now, my love. We are on our way to Shield's place. We'll be there in twenty minutes. I'll tell you all about it."

They drove in silence, not knowing how to make any sense out of the evening's events, except that Ekaterina was safe and Dizzy's harebrained plan actually worked. Shield and Spike had no idea how or why.

Arriving at Shield's office, Ekaterina had two cups of black coffee and toast, and was back in the land of the living. They had hardly spoken since arriving at Shield's apartment. Dizzy wanted to wait until Ekaterina had recovered from her scary adventure. Shield poured a stiff scotch for everyone, and they told how she was rescued. It had been a close call, but Shield and Spike had no idea how close.

"What about that back room with Vlado tied to a chair?" Shield asked.

Dizzy looked at his watch. "He died about a half hour ago."

"How do you now that?"

Knowing what was coming next, Ekaterina said, "James, do you have a couch I could lie on for a while? It's been a long day."

They toasted Ekaterina, and Dizzy escorted her into another room, giving her a pillow and blanket. He lovingly tucked her in. They spent a few minutes together until she fell asleep. He returned to the office.

They toasted Dizzy and his seemingly bizarre rescue plan, which went off without a hitch, and Dizzy toasted Spike and Shield.

"There are no words to adequately express my gratitude to you. Without you, Ekaterina would have been dead by now. I know you both have questions, which I feel I must answer, but I have one request. Will you, James Shield, and Spike Washington swear that what I am about to tell you will never leave this room? You will know why when I am finished."

"I swear," said Shields.

"I swear too," said Spike.

"Pour us a stiff one, James. It's going to be a long night. Let me tell you about the curse of the Moldavian Tango."

The End

About the Illustrator

Edward R. Turner is a Vancouver graphic artist who has illustrated books and magazines of all sorts. He is best known for his book on building Japanese style lamps and lanterns as well as for the illustrations for a book on building kayaks. He has specialized in pen and ink drawings but has also done full-colour cover art as well.

Work as an illustrator, however, is seldom steady and he has had to turn his hand to many other trades. He has brought his talent to virtually every job he has been hired to do, from boat building to architecture. For many years, to supplement his income, he was a craftsman woodworker building musical instruments, custom furniture and even Canadian canoes. Now in retirement, he lives in the Caribbean.

CPSIA information can be obtained
at www.ICGtesting.com
Printed in the USA
LVOW10s0313160518
577317LV00001B/3/P